The Man with Two Left Feet and Other Stories

P. G. Wodehouse

KALPAZ

ISBN: 978-93-5128-520-5

First Published in 1917
Indian Reprint in 2017

Published by

Kalpaz Publications
C-30, Satyawati Nagar,
Delhi – 110052
E-mail: kalpaz@hotmail.com
Website: kalpazpublications.com
Ph.: +91-9212142040

Cataloging in Publication Data—DK
Courtesy: D.K. Agencies (P) Ltd. <docinfo@dkagencies.com>

Wodehouse, P. G. (Pelham Grenville), 1881-1975, author.
The man with two left feet and other stories / P.G. Wodehouse.
pages cm
"First published in 1917"—Title page verso.
ISBN 9789351285205

1. Humorous stories, English. I. Title.

PR6045.O53M36 2017 DDC 823.912 23

CONTENTS

BILL THE BLOODHOUND

THERE'S a divinity that shapes our ends. Consider the case of Henry Pifield Rice, detective. I must explain Henry early, to avoid disappointment. If I simply said he was a detective, and let it go at that, I should be obtaining the reader's interest under false pretences. He was really only a sort of detective, a species of sleuth. At Stafford's International Investigation Bureau, in the Strand, where he was employed, they did not require him to solve mysteries which had baffled the police. He had never measured a footprint in his life, and what he did not know about bloodstains would have filled a library. The sort of job they gave Henry was to stand outside a restaurant in the rain, and note what time some one inside left it. In short, it is not "Pifield Rice, Investigator. No. 1.—The Adventure of the Maharajah's Ruby," that I submit to your notice, but the unsensational doings of a quite commonplace young man, variously known to his comrades at the Bureau as "Fathead," "That blighter what's-his-name," and "Here, you!"

Henry lived in a boarding-house in Guildford Street. One day a new girl came to the boarding-house, and sat next to Henry at meals. Her name was Alice Weston. She was small and quiet, and rather pretty. They got on splendidly. Their conversation, at first confined to the weather and the moving-pictures, rapidly became more intimate. Henry was surprised to find that she was on the stage, in the chorus. Previous chorus-girls at the boarding-house had been of a more pronounced type—good girls, but noisy, and apt to wear beauty-spots. Alice Weston was different.

"I'm rehearsing at present," she said. "I'm going

out on tour next month in 'The Girl From Brighton.' What do you do, Mr. Rice ?"

Henry paused for a moment before replying. He knew how sensational he was going to be.

"I'm a detective."

Usually, when he told girls his profession, squeaks of amazed admiration greeted him. Now he was chagrined to perceive in the brown eyes that met his distinct disapproval.

"What's the matter ?" he said, a little anxiously, for even at this early stage in their acquaintance he was conscious of a strong desire to win her approval. "Don't you like detectives ?"

"I don't know. Somehow I shouldn't have thought you were one."

This restored Henry's equanimity somewhat. Naturally a detective does not want to look like a detective, and give the whole thing away right at the start.

"I think—you won't be offended ?"

"Go on."

"I've always looked on it as rather a *sneaky* job."

"Sneaky !" moaned Henry.

"Well, creeping about, spying on people."

Henry was appalled. She had defined his own trade to a nicety. There might be detectives whose work was above this reproach, but he was a confirmed creeper, and he knew it. It wasn't his fault. The boss told him to creep, and he crept. If he declined to creep, he would be sacked instanter. It was hard, and yet he felt the sting of her words, and in his bosom the first seeds of dissatisfaction with his occupation took root.

You might have thought that this frankness on the girl's part would have kept Henry from falling in love with her. Certainly the dignified thing would have been to change his seat at table, and take his meals next to some one who appreciated the romance of detective work a little more. But no, he remained where he was, and presently Cupid, who never shoots with a surer aim than through the steam of boarding-house hash, sniped him where he sat.

He proposed to Alice Weston. She refused him.

"It's not because I'm not fond of you. I think you're the nicest man I ever met." A good deal of assiduous attention had enabled Henry to win this place in her affections. He had worked patiently and well before actually putting his fortune to the test. "I'd marry you to-morrow if things were different. But I'm on the stage, and I mean to stick there. Most of the girls want to get off it, but not me. And one thing I'll never do is marry some one who isn't in the profession. My sister Genevieve did, and look what happened to her. She married a commercial traveller, and take it from me he travelled. She never saw him for more than five minutes in the year, except when he was selling gent's hosiery in the same town where she was doing her refined speciality, and then he'd just wave his hand and whiz by, and start travelling again. My husband has got to be close by, where I can see him. I'm sorry, Henry, but I know I'm right."

It seemed final, but Henry did not wholly despair. He was a resolute young man. You have to be to wait outside restaurants in the rain for any length of time.

He had an inspiration. He sought out a dramatic agent.

"I want to go on the stage, in musical comedy."

"Let's see you dance."

"I can't dance."

"Sing," said the agent. "Stop singing," added the agent, hastily.

"You go away and have a nice cup of hot tea," said the agent, soothingly, "and you'll be as right as anything in the morning."

Henry went away.

A few days later, at the Bureau, his fellow-detective Simmonds hailed him.

"Here, you! The boss wants you. Buck up!"

Mr. Stafford was talking into the telephone. He replaced the receiver as Henry entered.

"Oh, Rice, here's a woman wants her husband shadowed while he's on the road. He's an actor. I'm sending you. Go to this address, and get photographs and all particulars. You'll have to catch the eleven o'clock train on Friday."

"Yes, sir."

"He's in 'The Girl From Brighton' company. They open at Bristol."

It sometimes seemed to Henry as if Fate did it on purpose. If the commission had had to do with any other company, it would have been well enough, for, professionally speaking, it was the most important with which he had ever been entrusted. If he had never met Alice Weston, and heard her views upon detective work, he would have been pleased and flattered. Things being as they were, it was Henry's considered opinion that Fate had slipped one over on him.

In the first place, what torture to be always near her, unable to reveal himself; to watch her while she disported herself in the company of other men. He would be disguised, and she would not recognize him; but he would recognize her, and his sufferings would be dreadful.

In the second place, to have to do his creeping about and spying practically in her presence——

Still, business was business.

At five minutes to eleven on the morning named he was at the station, a false beard and spectacles shielding his identity from the public eye. If you had asked him, he would have said that he was a Scotch business man. As a matter of fact, he looked far more like a motor-car coming through a haystack.

The platform was crowded. Friends of the company had come to see the company off. Henry looked on discreetly from behind a stout porter, whose bulk formed a capital screen. In spite of himself, he was impressed. The stage at close quarters always thrilled him. He recognized celebrities. The fat man in the brown suit was Walter Jelliffe, the comedian and star of the company. He stared keenly at him through the spectacles. Others of the famous were scattered about. He saw Alice. She was talking to a man with a face like a hatchet, and smiling, too, as if she enjoyed it. Behind the matted foliage which he had inflicted on his face, Henry's teeth came together with a snap.

In the weeks that followed, as he dogged "The Girl From Brighton" company from town to town, it would be difficult to say whether Henry was happy or unhappy. On the one hand, to realize that Alice was so near and yet so inaccessible was a constant source of misery; yet, on the other, he could not but admit that he was having the very dickens of a time, loafing round the country like this.

He was made for this sort of life, he considered. Fate had placed him in a London office, but what he really enjoyed was this unfettered travel. Some gipsy strain in him rendered even the obvious discomforts of theatrical touring agreeable. He liked catching trains; he liked invading strange hotels; above all, he revelled in the artistic pleasure of watching unsuspected fellow-men as if they were so many ants.

That was really the best part of the whole thing. It was all very well for Alice to talk about creeping and spying, but, if you considered it without bias, there was nothing degrading about it at all. It was an art. It took brains and a genius for disguise to make a man a successful creeper and spyer. You couldn't simply say to yourself, "I will creep." If you attempted to do it in your own person, you would be detected instantly. You had to be an adept at masking your personality. You had to be one man at Bristol and another quite different man at Hull—especially if, like Henry, you were of a gregarious disposition, and liked the society of actors.

The stage had always fascinated Henry. To meet even minor members of the profession off the boards gave him a thrill. There was a resting juvenile, of fit-up calibre, at his boarding-house who could always get a shilling out of him simply by talking about how he had jumped in and saved the show at the hamlets which he had visited in the course of his wanderings. And on this "Girl From Brighton" tour he was in constant touch with men who really amounted to something. Walter Jelliffe had been a celebrity when Henry was going to school; and Sidney Crane, the baritone, and others of the lengthy cast, were all players not unknown in London. Henry courted them assiduously.

It had not been hard to scrape acquaintance with them. The principals of the company always put up at the best hotel, and—his expenses being paid by his employer—so did Henry. It was the easiest thing possible to bridge with a well-timed whisky-and-soda the gulf between non-acquaintance and warm friendship. Walter Jelliffe, in particular, was peculiarly accessible. Every time Henry accosted him—as a different individual, of course—and renewed in a fresh disguise the friendship which he had enjoyed at the last town, Walter Jelliffe met him more than half-way.

It was in the sixth week of the tour that the comedian, promoting him from mere casual acquaintanceship, invited him to come up to his room and smoke a cigar.

Henry was pleased and flattered. Jelliffe was a personage, always surrounded by admirers, and the compliment was consequently of a high order.

He lit his cigar. Among his friends at the Green-Room Club it was unanimously held that Walter Jelliffe's cigars brought him within the scope of the law forbidding the carrying of concealed weapons; but Henry would have smoked the gift of such a man if it had been a cabbage-leaf. He puffed away contentedly. He was made up as an old Indian colonel that week, and he complimented his host on the aroma with a fine old-world courtesy.

Walter Jelliffe seemed gratified.

"Quite comfortable?" he asked.

"Quite, I thank you," said Henry, fondling his silver moustache.

"That's right. And now tell me, old man, which of us is it you're trailing?"

Henry nearly swallowed his cigar.

"What do you mean?"

"Oh, come," protested Jelliffe; "there's no need to keep it up with me. I know you're a detective. The question is, Who's the man you're after? That's what we've all been wondering all this time."

All! They had all been wondering! It was worse than Henry could have imagined. Till now he had pictured his position with regard to "The Girl From Brighton" company rather as that of some scientist who, seeing but unseen, keeps a watchful eye on the denizens of a drop of water under his microscope. And they had all detected him—every one of them.

It was a stunning blow. If there was one thing on which Henry prided himself it was the impenetrability of his disguises. He might be slow; he might be on the stupid side; but he could disguise himself. He had a variety of disguises, each designed to befog the public more hopelessly than the last.

Going down the street, you would meet a typical commercial traveller, dapper and alert. Anon, you encountered a heavily bearded Australian. Later, maybe, it was a courteous old retired colonel who stopped you and inquired the way to Trafalgar Square. Still later, a rather flashy individual of the sporting type asked you for a match for his cigar. Would you have suspected for one instant that each of these widely differing personalities was in reality one man?

Certainly you would.

Henry did not know it, but he had achieved in the eyes of the small servant who answered the front-door bell at his boarding-house a well-established reputation as a humorist of the more practical kind. It was his habit to try his disguises on her. He would ring the bell, inquire for the landlady, and when Bella had gone, leap up the stairs to his room. Here he would remove the disguise, resume his normal appearance, and come downstairs again, humming a careless air. Bella, meanwhile, in the kitchen, would be confiding to her ally the cook that "Mr. Rice had jest come in, lookin' sort o' funny again."

He sat and gaped at Walter Jelliffe. The comedian regarded him curiously.

"You look at least a hundred years old," he said. "What are you made up as? A piece of Gorgonzola?"

Henry glanced hastily at the mirror. Yes, he did look rather old. He must have overdone some of the lines on his forehead. He looked something between a youngish centenarian and a nonagenarian who had seen a good deal of trouble.

"If you knew how you were demoralizing the company," Jelliffe went on, "you would drop it. As steady and quiet a lot of boys as ever you met till you came along. Now they do nothing but bet on what disguise you're going to choose for the next town. I don't see why you need to change so often. You were all right as the Scotchman at Bristol. We were all saying how nice you looked. You should have stuck to that. But what do you do at Hull but roll in in a scrubby moustache and a tweed suit, looking rotten. However, all that is beside the point. It's a free country. If you like to spoil your beauty, I suppose there's no law against it. What I want to know is, who's the man? Whose track are you sniffing on, Bill? You'll pardon my calling you Bill. You're known as Bill the Bloodhound in the company. Who's the man?"

"Never mind," said Henry.

He was aware, as he made it, that it was not a very able retort, but he was feeling too limp for satisfactory repartee. Criticisms in the Bureau, dealing with his alleged solidity of skull, he did not resent. He attributed them to man's natural desire to chaff his fellow-man. But to be unmasked by the general public in this way was another matter. It struck at the root of all things.

"But I do mind," objected Jelliffe. "It's most important. A lot of money hangs on it. We've got a sweepstake on in the company, the holder of the winning name to take the entire receipts. Come on. Who is he?"

Henry rose and made for the door. His feelings were too deep for words. Even a minor detective has his professional pride; and the knowledge that his espionage is being made the basis of sweepstakes by his quarry cuts this to the quick.

"Here, don't go! Where are you going?"

"Back to London," said Henry, bitterly. "It's a lot of good my staying here now, isn't it?"

"I should say it was—to me. Don't be in a hurry. You're thinking that, now we know all about you, your utility as a sleuth has waned to some extent. Is that it?"

"Well?"

"Well, why worry? What does it matter to you? You don't get paid by results, do you? Your boss said 'Trail along.' Well, do it, then. I should hate to lose you. I don't suppose you know it, but you've been the best mascot this tour that I've ever come across. Right from the start we've been playing to enormous business. I'd rather kill a black cat than lose you. Drop the disguises, and stay with us. Come behind all you want, and be sociable."

A detective is only human. The less of a detective, the more human he is. Henry was not much of a detective, and his human traits were consequently highly developed. From a boy, he had never been able to resist curiosity. If a crowd collected in the street he always added himself to it, and he would have stopped to gape at a window with "Watch this window" written on it, if he had been running for his life from wild bulls. He was, and always had been, intensely desirous of some day penetrating behind the scenes of a theatre.

And there was another thing. At last, if he accepted this invitation, he would be able to see and speak to Alice Weston, and interfere with the manœuvres of the hatchet-faced man, on whom he had brooded with suspicion and jealousy since that first morning at the station. To see Alice! Perhaps, with eloquence, to talk her out of that ridiculous resolve of hers!

"Why, there's something in that," he said.

"Rather! Well, that's settled. And now, touching that sweep, who *is* it?"

"I can't tell you that. You see, so far as that goes, I'm just where I was before. I can still watch—whoever it is I'm watching."

"Dash it, so you can. I didn't think of that," said Jelliffe, who possessed a sensitive conscience. "Purely between ourselves, it isn't *me*, is it?"

Henry eyed him inscrutably. He could look inscrutable at times.

"Ah!" he said, and left quickly, with the feeling that, however poorly he had shown up during the actual interview, his exit had been good. He might have been a failure in the matter of disguise, but nobody could have put more quiet sinisterness into that "Ah!" It did much to soothe him and ensure a peaceful night's rest.

On the following night, for the first time in his life, Henry found himself behind the scenes of a theatre, and instantly began to experience all the complex emotions which come to the layman in that situation. That is to say, he felt like a cat which has strayed into a strange hostile back-yard. He was in a new world, inhabited by weird creatures, who flitted about in an eerie semi-darkness, like brightly coloured animals in a cavern.

"The Girl From Brighton" was one of those exotic productions specially designed for the Tired Business Man. It relied for a large measure of its success on the size and appearance of its chorus, and on their constant change of costume. Henry, as a consequence, was the centre of a kaleidoscopic whirl of feminine loveliness, dressed to represent such varying flora and fauna as rabbits, Parisian students, colleens, Dutch peasants, and daffodils. Musical comedy is the Irish stew of the drama. Anything may be put into it, with the certainty that it will improve the general effect.

He scanned the throng for a sight of Alice. Often as he had seen the piece in the course of its six weeks' wandering in the wilderness he had never succeeded in recognizing her from the front of the house. Quite possibly, he thought, she might be on the stage already, hidden in a rose-tree or some other shrub, ready at the signal to burst forth upon the audience in short skirts; for in "The Girl From Brighton" almost anything could turn suddenly into a chorus-girl.

Then he saw her, among the daffodils. She was not a particularly convincing daffodil, but she looked good to Henry. With wabbling knees he butted his way through the crowd and seized her hand enthusiastically.

"Why, Henry! Where did you come from?"

"I *am* glad to see you!"

"How did you get here?"

"I *am* glad to see you!"

At this point the stage-manager, bellowing from the prompt-box, urged Henry to desist. It is one of the mysteries of behind-the-scenes acoustics that a whisper from any minor member of the company can be heard all over the house, while the stage-manager can burst himself without annoying the audience.

Henry, awed by authority, relapsed into silence. From the unseen stage came the sound of some one singing a song about the moon. June was also mentioned. He recognized the song as one that had always bored him. He disliked the woman who was singing it—a Miss Clarice Weaver, who played the heroine of the piece to Sidney Crane's hero.

In his opinion he was not alone. Miss Weaver was not popular in the company. She had secured the rôle rather as a testimony of personal esteem from the management than because of any innate ability. She sang badly, acted indifferently, and was uncertain what to do with her hands. All these things might have been forgiven her, but she supplemented them by the crime known in stage circles as "throwing her weight about." That is to say, she was hard to please, and, when not pleased, apt to say so in no uncertain voice. To his personal friends Walter Jelliffe had frequently confided that, though not a rich man, he was in the market with a substantial reward for anyone who was man enough to drop a ton of iron on Miss Weaver.

To-night the song annoyed Henry more than usual, for he knew that very soon the daffodils were due on the stage to clinch the verisimilitude of the scene by dancing the tango with the rabbits. He endeavoured to make the most of the time at his disposal.

"I *am* glad to see you!" he said.

"Sh—h!" said the stage-manager.

Henry was discouraged. Romeo could not have made

love under these conditions. And then, just when he was pulling himself together to begin again, she was torn from him by the exigencies of the play.

He wandered moodily off into the dusty semi-darkness. He avoided the prompt-box, whence he could have caught a glimpse of her, being loath to meet the stage-manager just at present.

Walter Jelliffe came up to him, as he sat on a box and brooded on life.

"A little less of the double forte, old man," he said. "Miss Weaver has been kicking about the noise on the side. She wanted you thrown out, but I said you were my mascot, and I would die sooner than part with you. But I should go easy on the chest-notes, I think, all the same.'

Henry nodded moodily. He was depressed. He had the feeling, which comes so easily to the intruder behind the scenes, that nobody loved him.

The piece proceeded. From the front of the house roars of laughter indicated the presence on the stage of Walter Jelliffe, while now and then a lethargic silence suggested that Miss Clarice Weaver was in action. From time to time the empty space about him filled with girls dressed in accordance with the exuberant fancy of the producer of the piece. When this happened, Henry would leap from his seat and endeavour to locate Alice; but always, just as he thought he had done so, the hidden orchestra would burst into melody and the chorus would be called to the front.

It was not till late in the second act that he found an opportunity for further speech.

The plot of "The Girl From Brighton" had by then reached a critical stage. The situation was as follows: The hero, having been disinherited by his wealthy and titled father for falling in love with the heroine, a poor shop-girl, has disguised himself (by wearing a different coloured necktie) and has come in pursuit of her to a well-known seaside resort, where, having disguised herself by changing her dress, she is serving as a waitress in the Rotunda, on the Esplanade. The family butler, disguised as a Bath-chair man, has followed the hero, and the wealthy and titled father, disguised as an Italian opera-singer, has come to the place for a reason which, though extremely sound, for the moment eludes the memory. Anyhow, he is there, and they all meet on the Esplanade. Each recognizes the other, but thinks he himself is unrecognized. *Exeunt* all, hurriedly, leaving the heroine alone on the stage.

It is a crisis in the heroine's life. She meets it bravely. She sings a song entitled "My Honolulu Queen," with chorus of Japanese girls and Bulgarian officers.

Alice was one of the Japanese girls.

She was standing a little apart from the other Japanese girls. Henry was on her with a bound. Now was his time. He felt keyed up, full of persuasive words. In the interval which had elapsed since their last conversation yeasty emotions had been playing the dickens with his self-control. It is practically impossible for a novice, suddenly introduced behind the scenes of a musical comedy, not to fall in love with somebody; and, if he is already in love, his fervour is increased to a dangerous point.

Henry felt that it was now or never. He forgot that it was perfectly possible—indeed, the reasonable course—to wait till the performance was over, and renew his appeal to Alice to marry him on the way back to her hotel. He had the feeling that he had got just about a quarter of a minute. Quick action! That was Henry's slogan.

He seized her hand.

"Alice!"

"Sh—h!" hissed the stage-manager.

"Listen! I love you. I'm crazy about you. What does it matter whether I'm on the stage or not? I love you."

"Stop that row there!"

"Won't you marry me?"

She looked at him. It seemed to him that she hesitated.

"Cut it out!" bellowed the stage-manager, and Henry cut it out.

And at this moment, when his whole fate hung in

the balance, there came from the stage that devastating high note which is the sign that the solo is over and that the chorus are now about to mobilize. As if drawn by some magnetic power, she suddenly receded from him, and went on to the stage.

A man in Henry's position and frame of mind is not responsible for his actions. He saw nothing but her; he was blind to the fact that important manœuvres were in progress. All he understood was that she was going from him, and that he must stop her and get this thing settled.

He clutched at her. She was out of range, and getting farther away every instant.

He sprang forward.

The advice that should be given to every young man starting life is—if you happen to be behind the scenes at a theatre, never spring forward. The whole architecture of the place is designed to undo those who so spring. Hours before, the stage-carpenters have laid their traps, and in the semi-darkness you cannot but fall into them.

The trap into which Henry fell was a raised board. It was not a very highly-raised board. It was not so deep as a well, nor so wide as a church-door, but 'twas enough—it served. Stubbing it squarely with his toe, Henry shot forward, all arms and legs.

It is the instinct of Man, in such a situation, to grab at the nearest support. Henry grabbed at the Hotel Superba, the pride of the Esplanade. It was a thin wooden edifice, and it supported him for perhaps a tenth of a second. Then he staggered with it into the limelight, tripped over a Bulgarian officer who was inflating himself for a deep note, and finally fell in a complicated heap as exactly in the centre of the stage as if he had been a star of years' standing.

It went well; there was no question of that. Previous audiences had always been rather cold towards this particular song, but this one got on its feet and yelled for more. From all over the house came rapturous demands that Henry should go back and do it again.

But Henry was giving no encores. He rose to his

feet, a little stunned, and automatically began to dust his clothes. The orchestra, unnerved by this unrehearsed infusion of new business, had stopped playing. Bulgarian officers and Japanese girls alike seemed unequal to the situation. They stood about, waiting for the next thing to break loose. From somewhere far away came faintly the voice of the stage-manager inventing new words, new combinations of words, and new throat noises.

And then Henry, massaging a stricken elbow, was aware of Miss Weaver at his side. Looking up, he caught Miss Weaver's eye.

A familiar stage-direction of melodrama reads, "Exit cautious through gap in hedge." It was Henry's first appearance on any stage, but he did it like a veteran.

"My dear fellow," said Walter Jelliffe. The hour was midnight, and he was sitting in Henry's bedroom at the hotel. Leaving the theatre, Henry had gone to bed almost instinctively. Bed seemed the only haven for him. "My dear fellow, don't apologize. You have put me under lasting obligations. In the first place, with your unerring sense of the stage, you saw just the spot where the piece needed livening up, and you livened it up. That was good; but far better was it that you also sent our Miss Weaver into violent hysterics, from which she emerged to hand in her notice. She leaves us to-morrow."

Henry was appalled at the extent of the disaster for which he was responsible.

"What will you do?"

"Do! Why, it's what we have all been praying for—a miracle which should eject Miss Weaver. It needed a genius like you to come to bring it off. Sidney Crane's wife can play the part without rehearsal. She understudied it all last season in London. Crane has just been speaking to her on the 'phone, and she is catching the night express."

Henry sat up in bed.

"What!"

"What's the trouble now?"

"Sidney Crane's wife?"

"What about her?"

A bleakness fell upon Henry's soul.

"She was the woman who was employing me. Now I shall be taken off the job, and have to go back to London."

"You don't mean that it was really Crane's wife?"

Jelliffe was regarding him with a kind of awe.

"Laddie," he said, in a hushed voice, "you almost scare me. There seems to be no limit to your powers as a mascot. You fill the house every night, you get rid of the Weaver woman, and now you tell me this. I drew Crane in the sweep, and I would have taken twopence for my chance of winning it."

"I shall get a telegram from my boss to-morrow recalling me."

"Don't go. Stick with me. Join the troupe."

Henry stared.

"What do you mean? I can't sing or act."

Jelliffe's voice thrilled with earnestness.

"My boy, I can go down the Strand and pick up a hundred fellows who can sing and act. I don't want them. I turn them away. But a seventh son of a seventh son like you, a human horseshoe like you, a king of mascots like you—they don't make them nowadays. They've lost the pattern. If you like to come with me I'll give you a contract for any number of years you suggest. I need you in my business." He rose. "Think it over, laddie, and let me know to-morrow. Look here upon this picture, and on that. As a sleuth you are poor. You couldn't detect a bass-drum in a telephone-booth. You have no future. You are merely among those present. But as a mascot—my boy, you're the only thing in sight. You can't help succeeding on the stage. You don't have to know how to act. Look at the dozens of good actors who are out of jobs. Why? Unlucky. No other reason. With your luck and a little experience you'll be a star before you know you've begun. Think it over, and let me know in the morning."

Before Henry's eyes there rose a sudden vision of Alice: Alice no longer unattainable; Alice walking on his arm down the aisle; Alice mending his socks; Alice with her heavenly hands fingering his salary envelope.

"Don't go," he said. "Don't go. I'll let you know now."

The scene is the Strand, hard by Bedford Street; the time, that restful hour of the afternoon when they of the gnarled faces and the bright clothing gather together in groups to tell each other how good they are.

Hark! A voice.

"Rather! Courtneidge and the Guv'nor keep on trying to get me, but I turn them down every time. 'No,' I said to Malone only yesterday, 'not for me! I'm going with old Wally Jelliffe, the same as usual, and there isn't the money in the Mint that'll get me away.' Malone got all worked up. He——"

It is the voice of Pifield Rice, actor.

EXTRICATING YOUNG GUSSIE

SHE sprang it on me before breakfast. There in seven words you have a complete character sketch of my Aunt Agatha. I could go on indefinitely about brutality and lack of consideration. I merely say that she routed me out of bed to listen to her painful story somewhere in the small hours. It can't have been half-past eleven when Jeeves, my man, woke me out of the dreamless and broke the news :

" Mrs. Gregson to see you, sir."

I thought she must be walking in her sleep, but I crawled out of bed and got into a dressing-gown. I knew Aunt Agatha well enough to know that, if she had come to see me, she was going to see me. That's the sort of woman she is.

She was sitting bolt upright in a chair, staring into space. When I came in she looked at me in that darn critical way that always makes me feel as if I had gelatine where my spine ought to be. Aunt Agatha is one of those strong-minded women. I should think Queen Elizabeth must have been something like her. She bosses her husband, Spencer Gregson, a battered little chappie on the Stock Exchange. She bosses my cousin, Gussie Mannering-Phipps. She bosses her sister-in-law, Gussie's mother. And, worst of all, she bosses me. She has an eye like a man-eating fish, and she has got moral suasion down to a fine point.

I dare say there are fellows in the world—men of blood and iron, don't you know, and all that sort of thing—whom she couldn't intimidate ; but if you're a chappie like me, fond of a quiet life, you simply curl into a ball when you see her coming, and hope for the best. My experience is that when Aunt Agatha wants you to do a thing you do it, or else you find yourself wondering why those fellows in the olden days made such a fuss when they had trouble with the Spanish Inquisition.

"Halloa, Aunt Agatha!" I said.

"Bertie," she said, "you look a sight. You look perfectly dissipated."

I was feeling like a badly wrapped brown-paper parcel. I'm never at my best in the early morning. I said so.

"Early morning! I had breakfast three hours ago, and have been walking in the park ever since, trying to compose my thoughts."

If I ever breakfasted at half-past eight I should walk on the Embankment, trying to end it all in a watery grave.

"I am extremely worried, Bertie. That is why I have come to you."

And then I saw she was going to start something, and I bleated weakly to Jeeves to bring me tea. But she had begun before I could get it.

"What are your immediate plans, Bertie?"

"Well, I rather thought of tottering out for a bite of lunch later on, and then possibly staggering round to the club, and after that, if I felt strong enough, I might trickle off to Walton Heath for a round of golf."

"I am not interested in your totterings and tricklings. I mean, have you any important engagements in the next week or so?"

I scented danger.

"Rather," I said. "Heaps! Millions! Booked solid!"

"What are they?"

"I—er—well, I don't quite know."

"I thought as much. You have no engagements. Very well, then, I want you to start immediately for America."

"America!"

Do not lose sight of the fact that all this was taking place on an empty stomach, shortly after the rising of the lark.

"Yes, America. I suppose even you have heard of America?"

"But why America?"

"Because that is where your Cousin Gussie is. He is in New York, and I can't get at him."

"What's Gussie been doing?"

"Gussie is making a perfect idiot of himself."

To one who knew young Gussie as well as I did, the words opened up a wide field for speculation.

"In what way?"

"He has lost his head over a creature."

On past performances this rang true. Ever since he arrived at man's estate Gussie had been losing his head over creatures. He's that sort of chap. But, as the creatures never seemed to lose their heads over him, it had never amounted to much.

"I imagine you know perfectly well why Gussie went to America, Bertie. You know how wickedly extravagant your Uncle Cuthbert was."

She alluded to Gussie's governor, the late head of the family, and I am bound to say she spoke the truth. Nobody was fonder of old Uncle Cuthbert than I was, but everybody knows that, where money was concerned, he was the most complete chump in the annals of the nation. He had an expensive thirst. He never backed a horse that didn't get housemaid's knee in the middle of the race. He had a system of beating the bank at Monte Carlo which used to make the administration hang out the bunting and ring the joy-bells when he was sighted in the offing. Take him for all in all, dear old Uncle Cuthbert was as willing a spender as ever called the family lawyer a bloodsucking vampire because he wouldn't let Uncle Cuthbert cut down the timber to raise another thousand.

"He left your Aunt Julia very little money for a woman in her position. Beechwood requires a great deal of keeping up, and poor dear Spencer, though he does his best to help, has not unlimited resources. It was clearly understood why Gussie went to America. He is not clever, but he is very good-looking, and, though he has no title, the Mannering-Phippses are one of the best and oldest families in England. He had some excellent letters of introduction, and when he wrote home to say that he had met the most charming and beautiful girl in the world I felt quite happy. He continued to rave about her for several mails, and then this morning a letter has come from him in which he says, quite casually as a sort of afterthought, that he knows we are broadminded enough not to think any the worse of her because she is on the vaudeville stage."

"Oh, I say!"

"It was like a thunderbolt. The girl's name, it seems, is Ray Denison, and according to Gussie she does something which he describes as a single on the big time. What this degraded performance may be I have not the least notion. As a further recommendation he states that she lifted them out of their seats at Mosenstein's last week. Who she may be, and how or why, and who or what Mr. Mosenstein may be, I cannot tell you."

"By Jove," I said, "it's like a sort of thingummybob, isn't it? A sort of fate, what?"

"I fail to understand you."

"Well, Aunt Julia, you know, don't you know? Heredity, and so forth. What's bred in the bone will come out in the wash, and all that kind of thing, you know."

"Don't be absurd, Bertie."

That was all very well, but it was a coincidence for all that. Nobody ever mentions it, and the family have been trying to forget it for twenty-five years, but it's a known fact that my Aunt Julia, Gussie's mother, was a vaudeville artist once, and a very good one, too, I'm told. She was playing in pantomime at Drury Lane when Uncle Cuthbert saw her first. It was before my time, of course, and long before I was old enough to take notice the family had made the best of it, and Aunt Agatha had pulled up her socks and put in a lot of educative work, and with a microscope you couldn't tell Aunt Julia from a genuine dyed-in-the-wool aristocrat. Women adapt themselves so quickly!

I have a pal who married Daisy Trimble of the Gaiety, and when I meet her now I feel like walking out of her presence backwards. But there the thing was, and you couldn't get away from it. Gussie had vaudeville blood in him, and it looked as if he were reverting to type, or whatever they call it.

"By Jove," I said, for I am interested in this heredity stuff, "perhaps the thing is going to be a regular family tradition, like you read about in books—a sort of Curse of the Mannering-Phippses, as it were. Perhaps each head of the family's going to marry into vaudeville for ever and ever. Unto the what-d'you-call-it generation, don't you know?"

"Please do not be quite idiotic, Bertie. There is one head of the family who is certainly not going to do it, and that is Gussie. And you are going to America to stop him."

"Yes, but why me?"

"Why you? You are too vexing, Bertie. Have you no sort of feeling for the family? You are too lazy to try to be a credit to yourself, but at least you can exert yourself to prevent Gussie's disgracing us. You are going to America because you are Gussie's cousin, because you have always been his closest friend, because you are the only one of the family who has absolutely nothing to occupy his time except golf and night clubs."

"I play a lot of auction."

"And, as you say, idiotic gambling in low dens. If you require another reason, you are going because I ask you as a personal favour."

What she meant was that, if I refused, she would exert the full bent of her natural genius to make life a Hades for me. She held me with her glittering eye. I have never met anyone who can give a better imitation of the Ancient Mariner.

"So you will start at once, won't you, Bertie?"

I didn't hesitate.

"Rather!" I said. "Of course I will."

Jeeves came in with the tea.

"Jeeves," I said, "we start for America on Saturday."

"Very good, sir," he said; "which suit will you wear?"

New York is a large city conveniently situated on the edge of America, so that you step off the liner right on to it without an effort. You can't lose your way. You go out of a barn and down some stairs, and there you are, right in among it. The only possible objection any reasonable chappie could find to the place is that they loose you into it from the boat at such an ungodly hour.

I left Jeeves to get my baggage safely past an aggregation of suspicious-minded pirates who were digging for buried treasures among my new shirts, and drove to Gussie's hotel, where I requested the squad of gentlemanly clerks behind the desk to produce him.

That's where I got my first shock. He wasn't there. I pleaded with them to think again, and they thought again, but it was no good. No Augustus Mannering-Phipps on the premises.

I admit I was hard it. There I was alone in a strange city and no signs of Gussie. What was the next step? I am never one of the master minds in the early morning; the old bean doesn't somehow seem to get into its stride till pretty late in the p.m.'s, and I couldn't think what to do. However, some instinct took me through a door at the back of the lobby, and I found myself in a large room with an enormous picture stretching across the whole of one wall, and under the picture a counter, and behind the counter divers chappies in white, serving drinks. They have barmen, don't you know, in New York, not barmaids. Rum idea!

I put myself unreservedly into the hands of one of the white chappies. He was a friendly soul, and I told him the whole state of affairs. I asked him what he thought would meet the case.

He said that in a situation of that sort he usually prescribed a "lightning whizzer," an invention of his own. He said this was what rabbits trained on when they were matched against grizzly bears, and there was only one instance on record of the bear having lasted three rounds. So I tried a couple, and, by Jove! the man was perfectly right. As I drained the second a great load seemed to fall from my heart, and I went out in quite a braced way to have a look at the city.

I was surprised to find the streets quite full. People were bustling along as if it were some reasonable hour and not the grey dawn. In the tramcars they were absolutely standing on each other's necks. Going to business or something, I take it. Wonderful johnnies!

The odd part of it was that after the first shock of seeing all this frightful energy the thing didn't seem so strange. I've spoken to fellows since who have been to New York, and they tell me they found it just the same. Apparently there's something in the air, either the ozone or the phosphates or something, which makes you sit up and take notice. A kind of zip, as it were. A sort of bally freedom, if you know what I mean, that gets into your blood and bucks you up, and makes you feel that—

> God's in His Heaven:
> All's right with the world,

and you don't care if you've got odd socks on. I can't express it better than by saying that the thought uppermost in my mind, as I walked about the place they call Times Square, was that there were three thousand miles of deep water between me and my Aunt Agatha.

It's a funny thing about looking for things. If you hunt for a needle in a haystack you don't find it. If you don't give a darn whether you ever see the needle or not it runs into you the first time you lean against the stack. By the time I had strolled up and down once or twice, seeing the sights and letting the white chappie's corrective permeate my system, I was feeling that I wouldn't care if Gussie and I never met again, and I'm dashed if I didn't suddenly catch sight of the old lad, as large as life, just turning in at a doorway down the street.

I called after him, but he didn't hear me, so I legged it in pursuit and caught him going into an office on the first floor. The name on the door was Abe Riesbitter, Vaudeville Agent, and from the other side of the door came the sound of many voices.

He turned and stared at me.

"Bertie! What on earth are you doing? Where have you sprung from? When did you arrive?"

"Landed this morning. I went round to your hotel, but they said you weren't there. They had never heard of you."

"I've changed my name. I call myself George Wilson."

"Why on earth?"

"Well, you try calling yourself Augustus Mannering-Phipps over here, and see how it strikes you. You feel a perfect ass. I don't know what it is about America, but the broad fact is that it's not a place where you can call yourself Augustus Mannering-Phipps. And there's another reason. I'll tell you later. Bertie, I've fallen in love with the dearest girl in the world."

The poor old nut looked at me in such a deuced cat-like way, standing with his mouth open, waiting to be congratulated, that I simply hadn't the heart to tell him that I knew all about that already, and had come over to the country for the express purpose of laying him a stymie.

So I congratulated him.

"Thanks awfully, old man," he said. "It's a bit premature, but I fancy it's going to be all right. Come along in here, and I'll tell you about it."

"What do you want in this place? It looks a rummy spot?"

"Oh, that's part of the story. I'll tell you the whole thing."

We opened the door marked "Waiting Room." I never saw such a crowded place in my life. The room was packed till the walls bulged.

Gussie explained.

"Pros," he said, "music-hall artistes, you know, waiting to see old Abe Riesbitter. This is September the first, vaudeville's opening day. The early fall," said Gussie, who is a bit of a poet in his way, "is vaudeville's springtime. All over the country, as August wanes, sparkling comediennes burst into bloom, the sap stirs in the veins of tramp cyclists, and last year's contortionists, waking from their summer sleep, tie themselves tentatively into knots. What I mean is, this is the beginning of the new season, and everybody's out hunting for bookings."

"But what do you want here?"

"Oh, I've just got to see Abe about something. If you see a fat man with about fifty-seven chins come out of that door there grab him, for that'll be Abe. He's one of those fellows who advertise each step up they take in the world by growing another chin. I'm told that way back in the nineties he only had two. If you do grab Abe, remember that he knows me as George Wilson."

"You said that you were going to explain that George Wilson business to me, Gussie, old man."

"Well, it's this way——"

At this juncture dear old Gussie broke off short, rose from his seat, and sprang with indescribable vim at an extraordinarily stout chappie who had suddenly appeared. There was the deuce of a rush for him, but Gussie had got away to a good start, and the rest of the singers, dancers, jugglers, acrobats, and refined sketch teams seemed to recognize that he had won the trick, for they ebbed back into their places again, and Gussie and I went into the inner room.

Mr. Riesbitter lit a cigar, and looked at us solemnly over his zareba of chins.

"Now, let me tell ya something," he said to Gussie. "You lizzun t' me."

Gussie registered respectful attention. Mr. Riesbitter mused for a moment and shelled the cuspidor with indirect fire over the edge of the desk.

"Lizzun t' me," he said again. "I seen you rehearse, as I promised Miss Denison I would. You ain't bad for an amateur. You gotta lot to learn, but it's in you. What it comes to is that I can fix you up in the four-a-day, if you'll take thirty-five per. I can't do better than that, and I wouldn't have done that if the little lady hadn't of kep' after me. Take it or leave it. What do you say?"

"I'll take it," said Gussie, huskily. "Thank you."

'In the passage outside, Gussie gurgled with joy and slapped me on the back. " Bertie, old man, it's all right. I'm the happiest man in New York."

" Now what ? "

" Well, you see, as I was telling you when Abe came in, Ray's father used to be in the profession. He was before our time, but I remember hearing about him—Joe Danby. He used to be well known in London before he came over to America. Well, he's a fine old boy, but as obstinate as a mule, and he didn't like the idea of Ray marrying me because I wasn't in the profession. Wouldn't hear of it. Well, you remember at Oxford I could always sing a song pretty well ; so Ray got hold of old Riesbitter and made him promise to come and hear me rehearse and get me bookings if he liked my work. She stands high with him. She coached me for weeks, the darling. And now, as you heard him say, he's booked me in the small time at thirty-five dollars a week."

I steadied myself against the wall. The effects of the restoratives supplied by my pal at the hotel bar were beginning to work off, and I felt a little weak. Through a sort of mist I seemed to have a vision of Aunt Agatha hearing that the head of the Mannering-Phippses was about to appear on the vaudeville stage. Aunt Agatha's worship of the family name amounts to an obsession. The Mannering-Phippses were an old-established clan when William the Conqueror was a small boy going round with bare legs and a catapult. For centuries they have called kings by their first names and helped dukes with their weekly rent ; and there's practically nothing a Mannering-Phipps can do that doesn't blot his escutcheon. So what Aunt Agatha would say—beyond saying that it was all my fault—when she learned the horrid news, it was beyond me to imagine.

" Come back to the hotel, Gussie," I said. " There's a sportsman there who mixes things he calls ' lightning whizzers.' Something tells me I need one now. And excuse me for one minute, Gussie. I want to send a cable."

It was clear to me by now that Aunt Agatha had

picked the wrong man for this job of disentangling Gussie from the clutches of the American vaudeville profession. What I needed was reinforcements. For a moment I thought of cabling Aunt Agatha to come over, but reason told me that this would be overdoing it. I wanted assistance, but not so badly as that. I hit what seemed to me the happy mean. I cabled to Gussie's mother and made it urgent.

"What were you cabling about?" asked Gussie, later.

"Oh, just to say I had arrived safely, and all that sort of tosh," I answered.

Gussie opened his vaudeville career on the following Monday at a rummy sort of place uptown where they had moving pictures some of the time and, in between, one or two vaudeville acts. It had taken a lot of careful handling to bring him up to scratch. He seemed to take my sympathy and assistance for granted, and I couldn't let him down. My only hope, which grew as I listened to him rehearsing, was that he would be such a frightful frost at his first appearance that he would never dare to perform again; and, as that would automatically squash the marriage, it seemed best to me to let the thing go on.

He wasn't taking any chances. On the Saturday and Sunday we practically lived in a beastly little music-room at the offices of the publishers whose songs he proposed to use. A little chappie with a hooked nose sucked a cigarette and played the piano all day. Nothing could tire that lad. He seemed to take a personal interest in the thing.

Gussie would clear his throat and begin:

"There's a great big choo-choo waiting at the deepo."

THE CHAPPIE (playing chords): "Is that so? What's it waiting for?"

GUSSIE (rather rattled at the interruption): "Waiting for me."

THE CHAPPIE (surprised): "For you?"

GUSSIE (sticking to it): "Waiting for me—e—ee!"

THE CHAPPIE (sceptically): "You don't say!"

GUSSIE : " For I'm off to Tennessee."

THE CHAPPIE (*conceding a point*) : " Now, I live at Yonkers."

He did this all through the song. At first poor old Gussie asked him to stop, but the chappie said, No, it was always done. It helped to get pep into the thing. He appealed to me whether the thing didn't want a bit of pep, and I said it wanted all the pep it could get. And the chappie said to Gussie, " There you are ! " So Gussie had to stand it.

The other song that he intended to sing was one of those moon songs. He told me in a hushed voice that he was using it because it was one of the songs that the girl Ray sang when lifting them out of their seats at Mosenstein's and elsewhere. The fact seemed to give it sacred associations for him.

You will scarcely believe me, but the management expected Gussie to show up and start performing at one o'clock in the afternoon. I told him they couldn't be serious, as they must know that he would be rolling out for a bit of lunch at that hour, but Gussie said this was the usual thing in the four-a-day, and he didn't suppose he would ever get any lunch again until he landed on the big time. I was just condoling with him, when I found that he was taking it for granted that I should be there at one o'clock, too. My idea had been that I should look in at night, when—if he survived—he would be coming up for the fourth time ; but I've never deserted a pal in distress, so I said good-bye to the little lunch I'd been planning at a rather decent tavern I'd discovered on Fifth Avenue, and trailed along. They were showing pictures when I reached my seat. It was one of those Western films, where the cowboy jumps on his horse and rides across country at a hundred and fifty miles an hour to escape the sheriff, not knowing, poor chump ! that he might just as well stay where he is, the sheriff having a horse of his own which can do three hundred miles an hour without coughing. I was just going to close my eyes and try to forget till they put Gussie's name up when I discovered that I was sitting next to a deucedly pretty girl.

No, let me be honest. When I went in I had seen that there was a deucedly pretty girl sitting in that particular seat, so I had taken the next one. What happened now was that I began, as it were, to drink her in. I wished they would turn the lights up so that I could see her better. She was rather small, with great big eyes and a ripping smile. It was a shame to let all that run to seed, so to speak, in semi-darkness.

Suddenly the lights did go up, and the orchestra began to play a tune which, though I haven't much of an ear for music, seemed somehow familiar. The next instant out pranced old Gussie from the wings in a purple frock-coat and a brown top-hat, grinned feebly at the audience, tripped over his feet, blushed, and began to sing the Tennessee song.

It was rotten. The poor nut had got stage fright so badly that it practically eliminated his voice. He sounded like some far-off echo of the past "yodeling" through a woollen blanket.

For the first time since I had heard that he was about to go into vaudeville I felt a faint hope creeping over me. I was sorry for the wretched chap, of course, but there was no denying that the thing had its bright side. No management on earth would go on paying thirty-five dollars a week for this sort of performance. This was going to be Gussie's first and only. He would have to leave the profession. The old boy would say, "Unhand my daughter." And, with decent luck, I saw myself leading Gussie on to the next England-bound liner and handing him over intact to Aunt Agatha.

He got through the song somehow and limped off amidst roars of silence from the audience. There was a brief respite, then out he came again.

He sang this time as if nobody loved him. As a song, it was not a very pathetic song, being all about coons spooning in June under the moon, and so on and so forth, but Gussie handled it in such a sad, crushed way that there was genuine anguish in every line. By the time he reached the refrain I was nearly in tears. It seemed such a rotten sort of world with all that kind of thing going on in it.

He started the refrain, and then the most frightful thing happened. The girl next me got up in her seat, chucked her head back, and began to sing too. I say "too," but it wasn't really too, because her first note stopped Gussie dead, as if he had been pole-axed.

I never felt so bally conspicuous in my life. I huddled down in my seat and wished I could turn my collar up. Everybody seemed to be looking at me.

In the midst of my agony I caught sight of Gussie. A complete change had taken place in the old lad. He was looking most frightfully bucked. I must say the girl was singing most awfully well, and it seemed to act on Gussie like a tonic. When she came to the end of the refrain, he took it up, and they sang it together, and the end of it was that he went off the popular hero. The audience yelled for more, and were only quieted when they turned down the lights and put on a film.

When I had recovered I tottered round to see Gussie. I found him sitting on a box behind the stage, looking like one who had seen visions.

"Isn't she a wonder, Bertie?" he said, devoutly. "I hadn't a notion she was going to be there. She's playing at the Auditorium this week, and she can only just have had time to get back to her *matinée*. She risked being late, just to come and see me through. She's my good angel, Bertie. She saved me. If she hadn't helped me out I don't know what would have happened. I was so nervous I didn't know what I was doing. Now that I've got through the first show I shall be all right."

I was glad I had sent that cable to his mother. I was going to need her. The thing had got beyond me.

During the next week I saw a lot of old Gussie, and was introduced to the girl. I also met her father, a formidable old boy with thick eyebrows and a sort of determined expression. On the following Wednesday Aunt Julia arrived. Mrs. Mannering-Phipps, my Aunt Julia, is, I think, the most dignified person I know. She lacks Aunt Agatha's punch, but in a quiet way she has always contrived to make me feel, from boyhood up, that I was a poor worm. Not that she harries me like Aunt Agatha. The difference between the two is that Aunt Agatha conveys the impression that she considers me personally responsible for all the sin and sorrow in the world, while Aunt Julia's manner seems to suggest that I am more to be pitied then censured.

If it wasn't that the thing was a matter of historical fact, I should be inclined to believe that Aunt Julia had never been on the vaudeville stage. She is like a stage duchess.

She always seems to me to be in a perpetual state of being about to desire the butler to instruct the head footman to serve lunch in the blue-room overlooking the west terrace. She exudes dignity. Yet, twenty-five years ago, so I've been told by old boys who were lads about town in those days, she was knocking them cold at the Tivoli in a double act called "Fun in a Tea-Shop," in which she wore tights and sang a song with a chorus that began "Rumpty-tiddley-umpty-ay."

There are some things a chappie's mind absolutely refuses to picture, and Aunt Julia singing "Rumpty-tiddley-umpty-ay" is one of them.

She got straight to the point within five minutes of our meeting.

"What is this about Gussie? Why did you cable for me, Bertie?"

"It's rather a long story," I said, "and complicated. If you don't mind, I'll let you have it in a series of motion pictures. Suppose we look in at the Auditorium for a few minutes."

The girl, Ray, had been re-engaged for a second week at the Auditorium, owing to the big success of her first week. Her act consisted of three songs. She did herself well in the matter of costume and scenery. She had a ripping voice. She looked most awfully pretty; and altogether the act was, broadly speaking, a pippin.

Aunt Julia didn't speak till we were in our seats. Then she gave a sort of sigh.

"It's twenty-five years since I was in a music-hall!"

She didn't say any more, but sat there with her eyes glued on the stage.

After about half an hour the johnnies who work the card-index system at the side of the stage put up the name of Ray Denison, and there was a good deal of applause.

"Watch this act, Aunt Julia," I said.

She didn't seem to hear me.

"Twenty-five years! What did you say, Bertie?"

"Watch this act and tell me what you think of it."

"Who is it? Ray. Oh!"

"Exhibit A," I said. "The girl Gussie's engaged to."

The girl did her act, and the house rose at her. They didn't want to let her go. She had to come back again and again. When she had finally disappeared I turned to Aunt Julia.

"Well?" I said.

"I like her work. She's an artist."

"We will now, if you don't mind, step a goodish way uptown."

And we took the subway to where Gussie, the human film, was earning his thirty-five per. As luck would have it, we hadn't been in the place ten minutes when out he came.

"Exhibit B," I said. "Gussie."

I don't quite know what I had expected her to do, but I certainly didn't expect her to sit there without a word. She did not move a muscle, but just stared at Gussie as he drooled on about the moon. I was sorry for the woman, for it must have been a shock to her to see her only son in a mauve frock-coat and a brown top-hat, but I thought it best to let her get a strangle-hold on the intricacies of the situation as quickly as possible. If I had tried to explain the affair without the aid of illustrations I should have talked all day and left her muddled up as to who was going to marry whom, and why.

I was astonished at the improvement in dear old Gussie. He had got back his voice and was putting the stuff over well. It reminded me of the night at Oxford when, then but a lad of eighteen, he sang "Let's All Go Down the Strand" after a bump supper, standing the while up to his knees in the college fountain. He was putting just the same zip into the thing now.

When he had gone off Aunt Julia sat perfectly still for a long time, and then she turned to me. Her eyes shone queerly.

"What does this mean, Bertie?"

She spoke quite quietly, but her voice shook a bit.

"Gussie went into the business," I said, "because the girl's father wouldn't let him marry her unless he did. If you feel up to it perhaps you wouldn't mind tottering round to One Hundred and Thirty-third Street and having a chat with him. He's an old boy with eyebrows, and he's Exhibit C on my list. When I've put you in touch with him I rather fancy my share of the business is concluded, and it's up to you."

The Danbys lived in one of those big apartments uptown which look as if they cost the earth and really cost about half as much as a hall-room down in the forties. We were shown into the sitting-room, and presently old Danby came in.

"Good afternoon, Mr. Danby," I began.

I had got as far as that when there was a kind of gasping cry at my elbow.

"Joe!" cried Aunt Julia, and staggered against the sofa.

For a moment old Danby stared at her, and then his mouth fell open and his eyebrows shot up like rockets.

"Julie!"

And then they had got hold of each other's hands and were shaking them till I wondered their arms didn't come unscrewed.

I'm not equal to this sort of thing at such short notice. The change in Aunt Julia made me feel quite dizzy. She had shed her *grande-dame* manner completely, and was blushing and smiling. I don't like to say such things of any aunt of mine, or I would go further and put it on record that she was giggling. And old Danby, who usually looked like a cross between a Roman emperor and Napoleon Bonaparte in a bad temper, was behaving like a small boy.

"Joe!"

"Julie!"

"Dear old Joe! Fancy meeting you again!"

"Wherever have you come from, Julie?"

Well, I didn't know what it was all about, but I felt a bit out of it. I butted in:

"Aunt Julia wants to have a talk with you, Mr. Danby."

"I knew you in a second, Joe!"

"It's twenty-five years since I saw you, kid, and you don't look a day older."

"Oh, Joe! I'm an old woman!"

"What are you doing over here? I suppose"—old Danby's cheerfulness waned a trifle—"I suppose your husband is with you?"

"My husband died a long, long while ago, Joe."

Old Danby shook his head.

"You never ought to have married out of the profession, Julie. I'm not saying a word against the late—I can't remember his name; never could—but you shouldn't have done it, an artist like you. Shall I ever forget the way you used to knock them with 'Rumpty-tiddley-umpty-ay'?"

"Ah! how wonderful you were in that act, Joe." Aunt Julia sighed. "Do you remember the back-fall you used to do down the steps? I always have said that you did the best back-fall in the profession."

"I couldn't do it now!"

"Do you remember how we put it across at the Canterbury, Joe? Think of it! The Canterbury's a moving-picture house now, and the old Mogul runs French revues."

"I'm glad I'm not there to see them."

"Joe, tell me, why did you leave England?"

"Well, I—I wanted a change. No, I'll tell you the truth, kid. I wanted you, Julie. You went off and married that—whatever that stage-door johnny's name was—and it broke me all up."

Aunt Julia was staring at him. She is what they call a well-preserved woman. It's easy to see that, twenty-five years ago, she must have been something quite extraordinary to look at. Even now she's almost beautiful. She has very large brown eyes, a mass of soft grey hair, and the complexion of a girl of seventeen.

"Joe, you aren't going to tell me you were fond of me yourself!"

"Of course I was fond of you. Why did I let you have all the fat in 'Fun in a Tea-Shop'? Why did I hang about up-stage while you sang 'Rumpty-tiddley-umpty-ay'? Do you remember my giving you a bag of buns when we were on the road at Bristol?"

"Yes, but——"

"Do you remember my giving you the ham sandwiches at Portsmouth?"

"Joe!"

"Do you remember my giving you a seed-cake at Birmingham? What did you think all that meant, if not that I loved you? Why, I was working up by degrees to telling you straight out when you suddenly went off and married that cane-sucking dude. That's why I wouldn't let my daughter marry this young chap, Wilson, unless he went into the profession. She's an artist——"

"She certainly is, Joe."

"You've seen her? Where?"

"At the Auditorium just now. But, Joe, you mustn't stand in the way of her marrying the man she's in love with. He's an artist, too."

"In the small time."

"You were in the small time once, Joe. You mustn't look down on him because he's a beginner. I know you feel that your daughter is marrying beneath her, but——"

"How on earth do you know anything about young Wilson?"

"He's my son."

"Your son?"

"Yes, Joe. And I've just been watching him work. Oh, Joe, you can't think how proud I was of him! He's got it in him. It's fate. He's my son and he's in the profession! Joe, you don't know what I've been through for his sake. They made a lady of me. I never worked so hard in my life as I did to become a real lady. They kept telling me I had got to put it across, no matter what it cost, so that he wouldn't be ashamed of me. The study was something terrible. I had to watch myself every minute for years, and I never knew when I might fluff in my lines or fall down on some bit of business. But I did it, because I didn't want him to be ashamed of me, though all the time I was just aching to be back where I belonged."

Old Danby made a jump at her, and took her by the shoulders.

"Come back where you belong, Julie!" he cried. "Your husband's dead, your son's a pro. Come back! It's twenty-five years ago, but I haven't changed. I want you still. I've always wanted you. You've got to come back, kid, where you belong."

Aunt Julia gave a sort of gulp and looked at him.

"Joe!" she said in a kind of whisper.

"You're here, kid," said Old Danby, huskily. "You've come back. . . . Twenty-five years! . . . You've come back and you're going to stay!"

She pitched forward into his arms, and he caught her.

"Oh, Joe! Joe! Joe!" she said. "Hold me. Don't let me go. Take care of me."

And I edged for the door and slipped from the room. I felt weak. The old bean will stand a certain amount, but this was too much. I groped my way out into the street and wailed for a taxi.

Gussie called on me at the hotel that night. He curveted into the room as if he had bought it and the rest of the city.

"Bertie," he said, "I feel as if I were dreaming."

"I wish I could feel like that, old top," I said, and I took another glance at a cable that had arrived half an hour ago from Aunt Agatha. I had been looking at it at intervals ever since.

"Ray and I got back to her flat this evening. Who do you think was there? The mater! She was sitting hand in hand with old Danby."

"Yes?"

"He was sitting hand in hand with her."

"Really?"

"They are going to be married."

"Exactly."

"Ray and I are going to be married."

"I suppose so."

"Bertie, old man, I feel immense. I look round me, and everything seems to be absolutely corking. The change in the mater is marvellous. She is twenty-five years younger. She and old Danby are talking of reviving 'Fun in a Tea-Shop,' and going out on the road with it."

I got up.

"Gussie, old top," I said, "leave me for awhile. I would be alone. I think I've got brain fever or something."

"Sorry, old man; perhaps New York doesn't agree with you. When do you expect to go back to England?"

I looked again at Aunt Agatha's cable.

"With luck," I said, "in about ten years."

When he was gone I took up the cable and read it again.

"What is happening?" it read. "Shall I come over?"

I sucked a pencil for a while, and then I wrote the reply. It was not an easy cable to word, but I managed it.

"No," I wrote, "stay where you are. Profession overcrowded."

WILTON'S HOLIDAY

WHEN Jack Wilton first came to Marois Bay, none of us dreamed that he was a man with a hidden sorrow in his life. There was something about the man which made the idea absurd, or would have made it absurd if he himself had not been the authority for the story. He looked so thoroughly pleased with life and with himself. He was one of those men whom you instinctively label in your mind as "strong." He was so healthy, so fit, and had such a confident, yet sympathetic, look about him that you felt directly you saw him that here was the one person you would have selected as the recipient of that hard-luck story of yours. You felt that his kindly strength would have been something to lean on.

As a matter of fact, it was by trying to lean on it that Spencer Clay got hold of the facts of the case; and when young Clay got hold of anything, Marois Bay at large had it hot and fresh a few hours later; for Spencer was one of those slack-jawed youths who are constitutionally incapable of preserving a secret.

Within two hours, then, of Clay's chat with Wilton, every one in the place knew that, and jolly and hearty as the new-comer might seem, there was that gnawing at his heart which made his outward cheeriness simply heroic.

Clay, it seems, who is the worst specimen of self-pitier, had gone to Wilton, in whom, as a new-comer, he naturally saw a fine fresh repository for his tales of woe, and had opened with a long yarn of some misfortune or other. I forget which it was; it might have been any one of a dozen or so which he had constantly in stock, and it is immaterial which it was. The point is that, having heard him out very politely and patiently, Wilton came back at him with a story which silenced even Clay. Spencer was equal to most things, but even he could not go on whining about how he had foozled his putting and been snubbed at the bridge-table, or whatever it was that he was pitying himself about just then, when a man was telling him the story of a wrecked life.

"He told me not to let it go any further," said Clay to every one he met, "but of course it doesn't matter telling *you*. It is a thing he doesn't like to have known. He told me because he said there was something about me that seemed to extract confidences—a kind of strength, he said. You wouldn't think it to look at him, but his life is an absolute blank. Absolutely ruined, don't you know. He told me the whole thing so simply and frankly that it broke me all up. It seems that he was engaged to be married a few years ago, and on the wedding morning—absolutely on the wedding morning—the girl was taken suddenly ill, and——"

"And died?"

"And died. Died in his arms. Absolutely in his arms, old top."

"What a terrible thing!"

"Absolutely. He's never got over it. You won't let it go any further, will you, old man?"

And off sped Spencer, to tell the tale to some one else.

Every one was terribly sorry for Wilton. He was such a good fellow, such a sportsman, and, above all, so young, that one hated the thought that, laugh as he might, beneath his laughter there lay the pain of that awful memory. He seemed so happy, too. It was only in moments of confidence, in those heart-to-heart talks when men reveal their deeper feelings, that he ever gave a hint that all was not well with him. As, for example, when Ellerton, who is always in love with some one, backed him into a corner one evening and began to tell him the story of his latest affair, he had hardly begun when such a look of pain came over Wilton's face that he ceased instantly. He said afterwards that the sudden realization of the horrible break he was making hit him like a bullet, and the manner in which he turned the conversation practically without pausing from love to a discussion of the best method of getting out of the bunker at the seventh hole was, in the circumstances, a triumph of tact.

Marois Bay is a quiet place even in the summer, and the Wilton tragedy was naturally the subject of much talk. It is a sobering thing to get a glimpse of the underlying sadness of life like that, and there was a disposition at first on the part of the community to behave in his presence in a manner reminiscent of pall-bearers at a funeral. But things soon adjusted themselves. He was outwardly so cheerful that it seemed ridiculous for the rest of us to step softly and speak with hushed voices. After all, when you came to examine it, the thing was his affair, and it was for him to dictate the lines on which it should be treated. If he elected to hide his pain under a bright smile and a laugh like that of a hyena with a more than usually keen sense of humour, our line was obviously to follow his lead.

We did so; and by degrees the fact that his life was permanently blighted became almost a legend. At the back of our minds we were aware of it, but it did not obtrude itself into the affairs of every day. It was only when some one, forgetting, as Ellerton had done, tried to enlist his sympathy for some misfortune of his own that the look of pain in his eyes and the sudden tightening of his lips reminded us that he still remembered.

Matters had been at this stage for perhaps two weeks when Mary Campbell arrived.

Sex attraction is so purely a question of the taste of the individual that the wise man never argues about it. He accepts its vagaries as part of the human mystery, and leaves it at that. To me there was no charm whatever about Mary Campbell. It may have been that, at the moment, I was in love with Grace Bates, Heloise Miller, and Clarice Wembley—for at Marois Bay, in the summer, a man who is worth his salt is more than equal to three love affairs simultaneously—but anyway, she left me cold. Not one thrill could she awake in me. She was small and, to my mind, insignificant. Some men said that she had fine eyes. They seemed to me just ordinary eyes. And her hair was just ordinary hair. In fact, ordinary was the word that described her.

But from the first it was plain that she seemed wonderful with Wilton, which was all the more remarkable, seeing that he was the one man of us all who could have got any girl in Marois Bay that he wanted. When a man is six foot high, is a combination of Hercules and Apollo, and plays tennis, golf, and the banjo with almost superhuman vim, his path with the girls of a summer seaside resort is pretty smooth. But, when you add to all these things a tragedy like Wilton's, he can only be described as having a walk-over.

Girls love a tragedy. At least, most girls do. It makes a man interesting to them. Grace Bates was always going on about how interesting Wilton was. So was Heloise Miller. So was Clarice Wembley. But it was not until Mary Campbell came that he displayed any real enthusiasm at all for the feminine element of Marois Bay. We put it down to the fact that he could not forget, but the real reason, I now know, was that he considered that girls were a nuisance on the links and in the tennis-court. I suppose a plus two golfer and a Wildingesque tennis-player, such as Wilton was, does feel like that. Personally, I think that girls add to the fun of the thing. But then, my handicap is twelve, and, though I have been playing tennis for many years, I doubt if I have got my first serve—the fast one—over the net more than half a dozen times.

But Mary Campbell overcame Wilton's prejudices in twenty-four hours. He seemed to feel lonely on the links without her, and he positively egged her to be his partner in the doubles. What Mary thought of him we did not know. She was one of those inscrutable girls.

And so things went on. If it had not been that I knew Wilton's story, I should have classed the thing as one of those summer love-affairs to which the Marois Bay air is so peculiarly conducive. The only reason why anyone comes away from a summer at Marois Bay unbetrothed is because there are so many girls that he falls in love with that his holiday is up before he can, so to speak, concentrate.

But in Wilton's case this was out of the question. A man does not get over the sort of blow he had had, not, at any rate, for many years: and we had gathered that his tragedy was comparatively recent.

I doubt if I was ever more astonished in my life than the night when he confided in me. Why he should have chosen me as a confidant I cannot say. I am inclined to think that I happened to be alone with him at the psychological moment when a man must confide in somebody or burst; and Wilton chose the lesser evil.

I was strolling along the shore after dinner, smoking a cigar and thinking of Grace Bates, Heloise Miller, and Clarice Wembley, when I happened upon him. It was a beautiful night, and we sat down and drank it in for awhile. The first intimation I had that all was not well with him was when he suddenly emitted a hollow groan.

The next moment he had begun to confide.

"I'm in the deuce of a hole," he said. "What would *you* do in my position?"

"Yes?" I said.

"I proposed to Mary Campbell this evening."

"Congratulations."

"Thanks. She refused me."

"Refused you!"

"Yes—because of Amy."

It seemed to me that the narrative required foot-notes.

"Who is Amy?" I said.

"Amy is the girl——"

"Which girl?"

"The girl who died, you know. Mary had got hold of the whole story. In fact, it was the tremendous sympathy she showed that encouraged me to propose. If it hadn't been for that, I shouldn't have had the nerve. I'm not fit to black her shoes."

Odd, the poor opinion a man always has—when he is in love—of his personal attractions. There were times, when I thought of Grace Bates, Heloise Miller, and Clarice Wembley, when I felt like one of the beasts that perish. But then, I'm nothing to write home about, whereas the smallest gleam of intelligence should have told Wilton that he was a kind of Ouida guardsman.

"This evening I managed somehow to do it. She was tremendously nice about it—said she was very fond of me and all that—but it was quite out of the question because of Amy."

"I don't follow this. What did she mean?"

"It's perfectly clear, if you bear in mind that Mary is the most sensitive, spiritual, highly strung girl that ever drew breath," said Wilton, a little coldly. "Her position is this: she feels that, because of Amy, she can never have my love completely; between us there would always be Amy's memory. It would be the same as if she married a widower."

"Well, widowers marry."

"They don't marry girls like Mary."

I couldn't help feeling that this was a bit of luck for the widowers; but I didn't say so. One has always got to remember that opinions differ about girls. One man's peach, so to speak, is another man's poison. I have met men who didn't like Grace Bates, men who, if Heloise Miller or Clarice Wembley had given them their photographs, would have used them to cut the pages of a novel.

"Amy stands between us," said Wilton.

I breathed a sympathetic snort. I couldn't think of anything noticeably suitable to say.

"Stands between us," repeated Wilton. "And the damn silly part of the whole thing is that there isn't any Amy. I invented her."

"You—what!"

"Invented her. Made her up. No, I'm not mad. I had a reason. Let me see, you come from London, don't you?"

"Yes."

"Then you haven't any friends. It's different with me. I live in a small country town, and every one's my friend. I don't know what it is about me, but for some reason, ever since I can remember, I've been looked on as the strong man of my town, the man who's *all right*. Am I making myself clear?"

"Not quite."

"Well, what I am trying to get at is this. Either because I'm a strong sort of fellow to look at, and have obviously never been sick in my life, or because I can't help looking pretty cheerful, the whole of Bridley-in-the-Wold seems to take it for granted that I can't possibly have any troubles of my own, and that I am consequently fair game for anyone who has any sort of worry. I have the sympathetic manner, and they come to me to be cheered up. If a fellow's in love, he makes a bee-line for me, and tells me all about it. If anyone has had a bereavement, I am the rock on which he leans for support. Well, I'm a patient sort of man, and, as far as Bridley-in-the-Wold is concerned, I am willing to play the part. But a strong man does need an occasional holiday, and I made up my mind that I would get it. Directly I got here I saw that the same old game was going to start. Spencer Clay swooped down on me at once. I'm as big a draw with the Spencer Clay type of maudlin idiot as catnip is with a cat. Well, I could stand it at home, but I was hanged if I was going to have my holiday spoiled. So I invented Amy. Now do you see?"

"Certainly I see. And I perceive something else which you appear to have overlooked. If Amy doesn't exist—or, rather, never did exist—she cannot stand between you and Miss Campbell. Tell her what you have told me, and all will be well."

He shook his head.

"You don't know Mary. She would never forgive me. You don't know what sympathy, what angelic sympathy, she has poured out on me about Amy. I can't possibly tell her the whole thing was a fraud. It would make her feel so foolish."

"You must risk it. At the worst, you lose nothing."

He brightened a little.

"No, that's true," he said. "I've half a mind to do it."

"Make it a whole mind," I said, "and you win out."

I was wrong. Sometimes I am. The trouble was, apparently, that I didn't know Mary. I am sure Grace Bates, Heloise Miller, or Clarice Wembley would not have acted as she did. They might have been a trifle stunned at first, but they would soon have come round, and all would have been joy. But with Mary, no. What took place at the interview I do not know; but it was swiftly perceived by Marois Bay that the Wilton-Campbell alliance was off. They no longer walked together, golfed together, and played tennis on the same side of the net. They did not even speak to each other.

The rest of the story I can speak of only from hearsay. How it became public property, I do not know. But there was a confiding strain in Wilton, and I imagine he confided in some one, who confided in some one else. At any rate, it is recorded in Marois Bay's unwritten archives, from which I now extract it.

For some days after the breaking-off of diplomatic relations, Wilton seemed too pulverized to resume the offensive. He mooned about the links by himself, playing a shocking game, and generally comported himself like a man who has looked for the escape of gas with a lighted candle. In affairs of love the strongest men generally behave with the most spineless lack of resolution. Wilton weighed thirteen stone, and his muscles were like steel cables; but he could not have shown less pluck in this crisis in his life if he had been a poached egg. It was pitiful to see him.

Mary, in these days, simply couldn't see that he was on the earth. She looked round him, above him, and through him, but never at him; which was rotten from Wilton's point of view, for he had developed a sort of wistful expression—I am convinced that he practised it before the mirror after his bath—which should have worked wonders, if only he could have got action with it. But she avoided his eye as if he had been a creditor whom she was trying to slide past on the street.

She irritated me. To let the breach widen in this way was absurd. Wilton, when I said as much to him, said that it was due to her wonderful sensitiveness and highly strungness, and that it was just one more proof to him of the loftiness of her soul and her shrinking horror of any form of deceit. In fact, he gave me the impression that, though the affair was rending his vitals, he took a mournful pleasure in contemplating her perfection.

Now one afternoon Wilton took his misery for a long walk along the seashore. He tramped over the sand for some considerable time, and finally pulled up in a little cove, backed by high cliffs and dotted with rocks. The shore around Marois Bay is full of them.

By this time the afternoon sun had begun to be too warm for comfort, and it struck Wilton that he could be a great deal more comfortable nursing his wounded heart with his back against one of the rocks than tramping any farther over the sand. Most of the Marois Bay scenery is simply made as a setting for the nursing of a wounded heart. The cliffs are a sombre indigo, sinister and forbidding ; and even on the finest days the sea has a curious sullen look. You have only to get away from the crowd near the bathing-machines and reach one of these small coves and get your book against a rock and your pipe well alight, and you can simply wallow in misery. I have done it myself. The day when Helois Miller went golfing with Teddy Bingley I spent the whole afternoon in one of these retreats. It is true that, after twenty minutes of contemplating the breakers, I fell asleep ; but that is bound to happen.

It happened to Wilton. For perhaps half an hour he brooded, and then his pipe fell from his mouth and he dropped off into a peaceful slumber. And time went by.

It was a touch of cramp that finally woke him. He jumped up with a yell, and stood there massaging his calf. And he had hardly got rid of the pain, when a startled exclamation broke the primeval stillness ; and there, on the other side of the rock, was Mary Campbell.

Now, if Wilton had had any inductive reasoning in his composition at all, he would have been tremendously elated. A girl does not creep out to a distant cove at Marois Bay unless she is unhappy ; and if Mary Campbell was unhappy she must be unhappy about him ; and if she was unhappy about him all he had to do was to show a bit of determination and get the whole thing straightened out. But Wilton, whom grief had reduced to the mental level of an oyster, did not reason this out ; and the sight of her deprived him of practically all his faculties, including speech. He just stood there and yammered.

"Did you follow me here, Mr. Wilton?" said Mary, very coldly.

He shook his head. Eventually he managed to say that he had come there by chance, and had fallen asleep under the rock. As this was exactly what Mary had done, she could not reasonably complain. So that concluded the conversation for the time being. She walked away in the direction of Marois Bay without another word, and presently he lost sight of her round a bend in the cliffs.

His position now was exceedingly unpleasant. If she had such a distaste for his presence, common decency made it imperative that he should give her a good start on the homeward journey. He could not tramp along a couple of yards in the rear all the way. So he had to remain where he was till she had got well off the mark. And as he was wearing a thin flannel suit, and the sun had gone in, and a chilly breeze had sprung up, his mental troubles were practically swamped in physical discomfort.

Just as he had decided that he could now make a move, he was surprised to see her coming back.

Wilton really was elated at this. The construction he put on it was that she had relented and was coming back to fling her arms round his neck. He was just bracing himself for the clash, when he caught her eye, and it was as cold and unfriendly as the sea.

"I must go round the other way," she said. "The water has come up too far on that side."

And she walked past him to the other end of the cove.

The prospect of another wait chilled Wilton to the marrow. The wind had now grown simply freezing, and it came through his thin suit and roamed about all over him in a manner that caused him exquisite discomfort. He began to jump to keep himself warm.

He was leaping heavenwards for the hundredth time, when, chancing to glance to one side, he perceived Mary again returning. By this time his physical misery had so completely overcome the softer emotions in his bosom that his only feeling now was one of thorough irritation. It was not fair, he felt, that she should jockey at the start in this way and keep him hanging about here catching cold. He looked at her, when she came within range, quite balefully.

"It is impossible," she said, "to get round that way either."

One grows so accustomed in this world to everything going smoothly, that the idea of actual danger had not yet come home to her. From where she stood in the middle of the cove, the sea looked so distant that the fact that it had closed the only ways of getting out was at the moment merely annoying. She felt much the same as she would have felt if she had arrived at a station to catch a train and had been told that the train was not running.

She therefore seated herself on a rock, and contemplated the ocean. Wilton walked up and down. Neither showed any disposition to exercise that gift of speech which places Man in a class of his own, above the ox, the ass, the common wart-hog, and the rest of the lower animals. It was only when a wave swished over the base of her rock that Mary broke the silence.

"The tide is coming *in*," she faltered.

She looked at the sea with such altered feelings that it seemed a different sea altogether.

There was plenty of it to look at. It filled the entire mouth of the little bay, swirling up the sand and lashing among the rocks in a fashion which made one thought stand out above all the others in her mind—the recollection that she could not swim.

"Mr. Wilton!"

Wilton bowed coldly.

"Mr. Wilton, the tide. It's coming IN."

Wilton glanced superciliously at the sea.

"So," he said, "I perceive."

"But what shall we do?"

Wilton shrugged his shoulders. He was feeling at war with Nature and Humanity combined. The wind had shifted a few points to the east, and was exploring his anatomy with the skill of a qualified surgeon.

"We shall drown," cried Miss Campbell. "We shall drown. We shall drown. We shall drown."

All Wilton's resentment left him. Until he heard that pitiful wail his only thoughts had been for himself.

"Mary!" he said, with a wealth of tenderness in his voice.

She came to him as a little child comes to its mother, and he put his arm around her.

"Oh, Jack!"

"My darling!"

"I'm frightened!"

"My precious!"

It is in moments of peril, when the chill breath of fear blows upon our souls, clearing them of pettiness, that we find ourselves.

She looked about her wildly.

"Could we climb the cliffs?"

"I doubt it."

"If we called for help——"

"We could do that."

They raised their voices, but the only answer was the crashing of the waves and the cry of the sea-birds. The water was swirling at their feet, and they drew back to the shelter of the cliffs. There they stood in silence, watching.

"Mary," said Wilton in a low voice, "tell me one thing."

"Yes, Jack?"

"Have you forgiven me?"

"Forgiven you! How can you ask at a moment like this? I love you with all my heart and soul."

He kissed her, and a strange look of peace came over his face.

"I am happy."

"I, too."

A fleck of foam touched her face, and she shivered.

"It was worth it," he said quietly. "If all misunderstandings are cleared away and nothing can come between us again, it is a small price to pay—unpleasant as it will be when it comes."

"Perhaps—perhaps it will not be very unpleasant. They say that drowning is an easy death."

"I didn't mean drowning, dearest. I meant a cold in the head."

"A cold in the head!"

He nodded gravely.

"I don't see how it can be avoided. You know how chilly it gets these late summer nights. It will be a long time before we can get away."

She laughed a shrill, unnatural laugh.

"You are talking like this to keep my courage up. You know in your heart that there is no hope for us. Nothing can save us now. The water will come creeping—creeping——"

"Let it creep! It can't get past that rock there."

"What do you mean?"

"It can't. The tide doesn't come up any farther. I know, because I was caught here last week."

For a moment she stood looking at him without speaking. Then she uttered a cry in which relief, surprise, and indignation were so nicely blended that it would have been impossible to say which predominated.

He was eyeing the approaching waters with an indulgent smile.

"Why didn't you tell me?" she cried.

"I did tell you."

"You know what I mean. Why did you let me go on thinking we were in danger, when——"

"We *were* in danger. We shall probably get pneumonia."

"Isch!"

"There! You're sneezing already."

"I am not sneezing. That was an exclamation of disgust."

"It sounded like a sneeze. It must have been, for you've every reason to sneeze, but why you should utter exclamations of disgust I cannot imagine."

"I'm disgusted with you—with your meanness. You deliberately tricked me into saying——"

"Saying——"

She was silent.

"What you said was that you loved me with all your heart and soul. You can't get away from that, and it's good enough for me."

"Well, it's not true any longer."

"Yes, it is," said Wilton, comfortably; "bless it."

"It is not. I'm going right away now, and I shall never speak to you again."

She moved away from him, and prepared to sit down.

"There's a jelly-fish just where you're going to sit," said Wilton.

"I don't care."

"It will. I speak from experience, as one on whom you have sat so often."

"I'm not amused."

"Have patience. I can be funnier than that."

"Please don't talk to me."

"Very well."

She seated herself with her back to him. Dignity demanded reprisals, so he seated himself with his back to her; and the futile ocean raged towards them, and the wind grew chillier every minute.

Time passed. Darkness fell. The little bay became a black cavern, dotted here and there with white, where the breeze whipped the surface of the water.

Wilton sighed. It was lonely sitting there all by himself. How much jollier it would have been if——

A hand touched his shoulder, and a voice spoke—meekly.

"Jack, dear, it—it's awfully cold. Don't you think if we were to—snuggle up——"

He reached out and folded her in an embrace which would have aroused the professional enthusiasm of Hackenschmidt and drawn guttural congratulations from Zbysco. She creaked, but did not crack, beneath the strain.

"That's much nicer," she said, softly. "Jack, I don't think the tide's started even to think of going down yet."

"I hope not," said Wilton.

THE MIXER

I. He Meets a Shy Gentleman

LOOKING back, I always consider that my career as a dog proper really started when I was bought for the sum of half a crown by the Shy Man. That event marked the end of my puppyhood. The knowledge that I was worth actual cash to somebody filled me with a sense of new responsibilities. It sobered me. Besides, it was only after that half-crown changed hands that I went out into the great world; and, however interesting life may be in an East End public-house, it is only when you go out into the world that you really broaden your mind and begin to see things.

Within its limitations, my life had been singularly full and vivid. I was born, as I say, in a public-house in the East End, and however lacking a public-house may be in refinement and the true culture, it certainly provides plenty of excitement. Before I was six weeks old, I had upset three policemen by getting between their legs when they came round to the side-door, thinking they had heard suspicious noises; and I can still recall the interesting sensation of being chased seventeen times round the yard with a broom-handle after a well-planned and completely successful raid on the larder. These and other happenings of a like nature soothed for the moment but could not cure the restlessness which has always been so marked a trait in my character. I have always been restless, unable to settle down in one place and anxious to get on to the next thing. This may be due to a gipsy strain in my ancestry—one of my uncles travelled with a circus—or it may be the Artistic Temperament, acquired from a grandfather who, before dying of a surfeit of paste in the property-room of the Bristol Coliseum, which he was visiting in the course of a professional tour, had an established reputation on the music-hall stage as one of Professor Pond's Performing Poodles.

I owe the fulness and variety of my life to this restlessness of mine, for I have repeatedly left comfortable homes in order to follow some perfect stranger who looked as if he were on his way to somewhere interesting. Sometimes I think I must have cat blood in me.

The Shy Man came into our yard one afternoon in April, while I was sleeping with mother in the sun on an old sweater which we had borrowed from Fred, one of the barmen. I heard mother growl, but I didn't take any notice. Mother is what they call a good watch-dog, and she growls at everybody except master. At first, when she used to do it, I would get up and bark my head off, but not now. Life's too short to bark at everybody who comes into our yard. It is behind the public-house, and they keep empty bottles and things there, so people are always coming and going.

Besides, I was tired. I had had a very busy morning, helping the men bring in a lot of cases of beer, and running into the saloon to talk to Fred and generally looking after things. So I was just dozing off again, when I heard a voice say, "Well, he's ugly enough?" Then I knew that they were talking about me.

I have never disguised it from myself, and nobody has ever disguised it from me, that I am not a handsome dog. Even mother never thought me beautiful. She was no Gladys Cooper herself, but she never hesitated to criticize my appearance. In fact, I have yet to meet anyone who did. The first thing strangers say about me is, "What an ugly dog!"

I don't know what I am. I have a bulldog kind of a face, but the rest of me is terrier. I have a long tail which sticks straight up in the air. My hair is wiry. My eyes are brown. I am jet black, with a white chest. I once overheard Fred saying that I was a Gorgonzola cheese-hound, and I have generally found Fred reliable in his statements.

When I found that I was under discussion, I opened my eyes. Master was standing there, looking down at me, and by his side the man who had just said I was ugly enough. The man was a thin man, about the age of a barman and smaller than a policeman. He had patched brown shoes and black trousers.

"But he's got a sweet nature," said master.

This was true, luckily for me. Mother always said, "A dog without influence or private means, if he is to make his way in the world, must have either good looks or amiability." But, according to her, I overdid it. "A dog," she used to say, "can have a good heart, without chumming with every Tom, Dick, and Harry he meets. Your behaviour is sometimes quite un-dog-like." Mother prided herself on being a one-man dog. She kept herself to herself, and wouldn't kiss anybody except master—not even Fred.

Now, I'm a mixer. I can't help it. It's my nature. I like men. I like the taste of their boots, the smell of their legs, and the sound of their voices. It may be weak of me, but a man has only to speak to me and a sort of thrill goes right down my spine and sets my tail wagging.

I wagged it now. The man looked at me rather distantly. He didn't pat me. I suspected—what I afterwards found to be the case—that he was shy, so I jumped up at him to put him at his ease. Mother growled again. I felt that she did not approve.

"Why, he's took quite a fancy to you already," said master.

The man didn't say a word. He seemed to be brooding on something. He was one of those silent men. He reminded me of Joe, the old dog down the street at the grocer's shop, who lies at the door all day, blinking and not speaking to anybody.

Master began to talk about me. It surprised me, the way he praised me. I hadn't a suspicion he admired me so much. From what he said you would have thought I had won prizes and ribbons at the Crystal Palace. But the man didn't seem to be impressed. He kept on saying nothing.

When master had finished telling him what a wonderful dog I was till I blushed, the man spoke.

"Less of it," he said. "Half a crown is my bid, and if he was an angel from on high you couldn't get another ha'penny out of me. What about it?"

A thrill went down my spine and out at my tail, for of course I saw now what was happening. The man wanted to buy me and take me away. I looked at master hopefully.

"He's more like a son to me than a dog," said master, sort of wistful.

"It's his face that makes you feel that way," said the man, unsympathetically. "If you had a son that's just how he would look. Half a crown is my offer, and I'm in a hurry."

All right," said master, with a sigh, "though it's giving him away, a valuable dog like that. Where's your half-crown?"

The man got a bit of rope and tied it round my neck.

I could hear mother barking advice and telling me to be a credit to the family, but I was too excited to listen.

"Good-bye, mother," I said. "Good-bye, master. Good-bye, Fred. Good-bye everybody. I'm off to see life. The Shy Man has bought me for half a crown. Wow!"

I kept running round in circles and shouting, till the man gave me a kick and told me to stop it.

So I did.

I don't know where we went, but it was a long way. I had never been off our street before in my life and I didn't know the whole world was half as big as that. We walked on and on, and the man jerking at my rope whenever I wanted to stop and look at anything. He wouldn't even let me pass the time of the day with dogs we met.

When we had gone about a hundred miles and were just going to turn in at a dark doorway, a policeman suddenly stopped the man. I could feel by the way the man pulled at my rope and tried to hurry on that he didn't want to speak to the policeman. The more I saw of the man, the more I saw how shy he was.

"Hi!" said the policeman, and we had to stop.

"I've got a message for you, old pal," said the policeman. "It's from the Board of Health. They told me to tell you you needed a change of air. See?"

"All right!" said the man.

"And take it as soon as you like. Else you'll find you'll get it given you. See?"

I looked at the man with a good deal of respect. He was evidently some one very important, if they worried so about his health.

"I'm going down to the country to-night," said the man.

The policeman seemed pleased.

"That's a bit of luck for the country," he said. "Don't go changing your mind."

And we walked on, and went in at the dark doorway, and climbed about a million stairs and went into a room that smelt of rats. The man sat down and swore a little, and I sat and looked at him.

Presently I couldn't keep it in any longer.

"Do we live here?" I said. "Is it true we're going to the country? Wasn't that policeman a good sort? Don't you like policemen? I knew lots of policemen at the public-house. Are there any other dogs here? What is there for dinner? What's in that cupboard? When are you going to take me out for another run? May I go out and see if I can find a cat?"

"Stop that yelping," he said.

"When we go to the country, where shall we live? Are you going to be a caretaker at a house? Fred's father is a caretaker at a big house in Kent. I've heard Fred talk about it. You didn't meet Fred when you came to the public-house, did you? You would like Fred. I like Fred. Mother likes Fred. We all like Fred."

I was going on to tell him a lot more about Fred, who had always been one of my warmest friends, when he suddenly got hold of a stick and walloped me with it.

"You keep quiet when you're told," he said.

He really was the shyest man I had ever met. It seemed to hurt him to be spoken to. However, he was the boss, and I had to humour him, so I didn't say any more.

We went down to the country that night, just as the man had told the policeman we would. I was all worked up, for I had heard so much about the country from Fred that I had always wanted to go there. Fred used to go off on a motor-bicycle sometimes to spend the night with his father in Kent, and once he brought back a squirrel with him, which I thought was for me to eat, but mother said no. "The first thing a dog has to learn," mother used often to say, "is that the whole world wasn't created for him to eat."

It was quite dark when we got to the country, but the man seemed to know where to go. He pulled at my rope, and we began to walk along a road with no people in it at all. We walked on and on, but it was all so new to me that I forgot how tired I was. I could feel my mind broadening with every step I took.

Every now and then we would pass a very big house, which looked as if it was empty, but I knew that there was a caretaker inside, because of Fred's father. These big houses belong to very rich people, but they don't want to live in them till the summer, so they put in caretakers, and the caretakers have a dog to keep off burglars. I wondered if that was what I had been brought here for.

"Are you going to be a caretaker?" I asked the man.

"Shut up," he said.

So I shut up.

After we had been walking a long time, we came to a cottage. A man came out. My man seemed to know him, for he called him Bill. I was quite surprised to see the man was not at all shy with Bill. They seemed very friendly.

"Is that him?" said Bill, looking at me.

"Bought him this afternoon," said the man.

"Well," said Bill, "he's ugly enough. He looks fierce. If you want a dog, he's the sort of dog you want. But what do you want one for? It seems to me it's a lot of trouble to take, when there's no need of any trouble at all. Why not do what I've always wanted to do? What's wrong with just fixing the dog, same as it's always done, and walking in and helping yourself?"

"I'll tell you what's wrong," said the man. "To start with, you can't get at the dog to fix him except by day, when they let him out. At night he's shut up inside the house. And suppose you do fix him during the day, what happens then? Either the bloke gets another before night, or else he sits up all night with a gun. It isn't like as if these blokes was ordinary blokes. They're down here to look after the house. That's their job, and they don't take any chances."

It was the longest speech I had ever heard the man make, and it seemed to impress Bill. He was quite humble.

"I didn't think of that," he said. "We'd best start in to train this tyke at once."

Mother often used to say, when I went on about wanting to go out into the world and see life, "You'll be sorry when you do. The world isn't all bones and liver." And I hadn't been living with the man and Bill in their cottage long before I found out how right she was.

It was the man's shyness that made all the trouble. It seemed as if he hated to be taken notice of.

It started on my very first night at the cottage. I had fallen asleep in the kitchen, tired out after all the excitement of the day and the long walks I had had, when something woke me with a start. It was somebody scratching at the window, trying to get in.

Well, I ask you, I ask any dog, what would you have done in my place? Ever since I was old enough to listen, mother had told me over and over again what I must do in a case like this. It is the A B C of a dog's education. "If you are in a room and you hear anyone trying to get in," mother used to say, "bark. It may be some one who has business there, or it may not. Bark first, and inquire afterwards. Dogs were made to be heard and not seen."

I lifted my head and yelled. I have a good, deep voice, due to a hound strain in my pedigree, and at the public-house, when there was a full moon, I have often had people leaning out of the windows and saying things all down the street. I took a deep breath and let it go.

"Man!" I shouted. "Bill! Man! Come quick! Here's a burglar getting in!"

Then somebody struck a light, and it was the man himself. He had come in through the window.

He picked up a stick, and he walloped me. I couldn't understand it. I couldn't see where I had done the wrong thing. But he was the boss, so there was nothing to be said.

If you'll believe me, that same thing happened every night. Every single night! And sometimes twice or three times before morning. And every time I would bark my loudest, and the man would strike a light and wallop me. The thing was baffling. I couldn't possibly have mistaken what mother had said to me. She said it too often for that. Bark! Bark! Bark! It was the main plank of her whole system of education. And yet, here I was, getting walloped every night for doing it.

I thought it out till my head ached, and finally I got it right. I began to see that mother's outlook was narrow. No doubt, living with a man like master at the public-house, a man without a trace of shyness in his composition, barking was all right. But circumstances alter cases. I belonged to a man who was a mass of nerves, who got the jumps if you spoke to him. What I had to do was to forget the training I had had from mother, sound as it no doubt was as a general thing, and to adapt myself to the needs of the particular man who had happened to buy me. I had tried mother's way, and all it had brought me was walloping, so now I would think for myself.

So next night, when I heard the window go, I lay there without a word, though it went against all my better feelings. I didn't even growl. Some one came in and moved about in the dark, with a lantern, but, though I smelt that it was the man, I didn't ask him a single question. And presently the man lit a light and came over to me and gave me a pat, which was a thing he had never done before.

"Good dog!" he said. "Now you can have this."

And he let me lick out the saucepan in which the dinner had been cooked.

After that, we got on fine. Whenever I heard anyone at the window I just kept curled up and took no notice, and every time I got a bone or something good. It was easy, once you had got the hang of things.

It was about a week after that the man took me out one morning, and we walked a long way till we turned in at some big gates and went along a very smooth road till we came to a great house, standing all by itself in the middle of a whole lot of country. There was a big lawn in front of it, and all round there were fields and trees, and at the back a great wood.

The man rang a bell, and the door opened, and an old man came out.

"Well?" he said, not very cordially.

"I thought you might want to buy a good watch-dog," said the man.

"Well, that's queer, your saying that," said the caretaker. "It's a coincidence. That's exactly what I do want to buy. I was just thinking of going along and trying to get one. My old dog picked up something this morning that he oughtn't to have, and he's dead, poor feller."

"Poor feller," said the man. "Found an old bone with phosphorus on it, I guess."

"What do you want for this one?"

"Five shillings."

"Is he a good watch-dog?"

"He's a grand watch-dog."

"He looks fierce enough."

"Ah!"

So the caretaker gave the man his five shillings, and the man went off and left me.

At first the newness of everything and the unaccustomed smells and getting to know the caretaker, who was a nice old man, prevented my missing the man, but as the day went on and I began to realize that he had gone and would never come back, I got very depressed. I pattered all over the house, whining. It was a most interesting house, bigger than I thought a house could possibly be, but it couldn't cheer me up. You may think it strange that I should pine for the man, after all the wallopings he had given me, and it is odd, when you come to think of it. But dogs are dogs, and they are built like that. By the time it was evening I was thoroughly miserable. I found a shoe and an old clothes-brush in one of the rooms, but could eat nothing. I just sat and moped.

It's a funny thing, but it seems as if it always happened that just when you are feeling most miserable, something nice happens. As I sat there, there came from outside the sound of a motor-bicycle, and somebody shouted.

It was dear old Fred, my old pal Fred, the best old boy that ever stepped. I recognized his voice in a second, and I was scratching at the door before the old man had time to get up out of his chair.

Well, well, well! That was a pleasant surprise! I ran five times round the lawn without stopping, and then I came back and jumped up at him.

"What are you doing down here, Fred?" I said. "Is this caretaker your father? Have you seen the rabbits in the wood? How long are you going to stop? How's mother? I like the country. Have you come all the way from the public-house? I'm living here now. Your father gave five shillings for me. That's twice as much as I was worth when I saw you last."

"Why, it's young Nigger!" That was what they called me at the saloon. "What are you doing here? Where did you get this dog, father?"

"A man sold him to me this morning Poor old Bob got poisoned. This one ought to be just as good a watch-dog. He barks loud enough."

"He should be. His mother is the best watch-dog in London. This cheese-hound used to belong to the boss. Funny him getting down here."

We went into the house and had supper. And after supper we sat and talked. Fred was only down for the night, he said, because the boss wanted him back next day.

"And I'd sooner have my job, than yours, dad," he said. "Of all the lonely places! I wonder you aren't scared of burglars."

"I've my shot-gun, and there's the dog. I might be

scared if it wasn't for him, but he kind of gives me confidence. Old Bob was the same. Dogs are a comfort in the country."

"Get many tramps here?"

"I've only seen one in two months, and that's the feller who sold me the dog here."

As they were talking about the man, I asked Fred if he knew him. They might have met at the public-house, when the man was buying me from the boss.

"You would like him," I said. "I wish you could have met."

They both looked at me.

"What's he growling at?" asked Fred. "Think he heard something?"

The old man laughed.

"He wasn't growling. He was talking in his sleep. You're nervous, Fred. It comes of living in the city."

"Well, I am. I like this place in the daytime, but it gives me the pip at night. It's so quiet. How you can stand it here all the time, I can't understand. Two nights of it would have me seeing things."

His father laughed.

"If you feel like that, Fred, you had better take the gun to bed with you. I shall be quite happy without it."

"I will," said Fred. "I'll take six if you've got them."

And after that they went upstairs. I had a basket in the hall, which had belonged to Bob, the dog who had got poisoned. It was a comfortable basket, but I was so excited at having met Fred again that I couldn't sleep. Besides, there was a smell of mice somewhere, and I had to move around, trying to place it.

I was just sniffing at a place in the wall, when I heard a scratching noise. At first I thought it was the mice working in a different place, but, when I listened, I found that the sound came from the window. Somebody was doing something to it from outside.

If it had been mother, she would have lifted the roof off right there, and so should I, if it hadn't been for what the man had taught me. I didn't think it possible that this could be the man come back, for he had gone away and said nothing about ever seeing me again. But I didn't bark. I stopped where I was and listened. And presently the window came open, and somebody began to climb in.

I gave a good sniff, and I knew it was the man.

I was so delighted that for a moment I nearly forgot myself and shouted with joy, but I remembered in time how shy he was, and stopped myself. But I ran to him and jumped up quite quietly, and he told me to lie down. I was disappointed that he didn't seem more pleased to see me. I lay down.

It was very dark, but he had brought a lantern with him, and I could see him moving about the room, picking things up and putting them in a bag which he had brought with him. Every now and then he would stop and listen, and then he would start moving round again. He was very quick about it, but very quiet. It was plain that he didn't want Fred or his father to come down and find him.

I kept thinking about this peculiarity of his while I watched him. I suppose, being chummy myself, I find it hard to understand that everybody else in the world isn't chummy too. Of course, my experience at the public-house had taught me that men are just as different from each other as dogs. If I chewed master's shoe, for instance, he used to kick me; but if I chewed Fred's, Fred would tickle me under the ear. And, similarly, some men are shy and some men are mixers. I quite appreciated that, but I couldn't help feeling that the man carried shyness to a point where it became morbid. And he didn't give himself a chance to cure himself of it. That was the point. Imagine a man hating to meet people so much that he never visited their houses till the middle of the night, when they were in bed and asleep. It was silly. Shyness has always been something so outside my nature that I suppose I have never really been able to look at it sympathetically. I have always held the view that you can get over it if you make an effort. The trouble with the man was that he wouldn't make an effort. He went out of his way to avoid meeting people.

I was fond of the man. He was the sort of person you never get to know very well, but we had been together for quite a while, and I wouldn't have been a dog if I hadn't got attached to him.

As I sat and watched him creep about the room, it suddenly came to me that here was a chance of doing him a real good turn in spite of himself. Fred was upstairs, and Fred, as I knew by experience, was the easiest man to get along with in the world. Nobody could be shy with Fred. I felt that if only I could bring him and the man together, they would get along splendidly, and it would teach the man not to be silly and avoid people. It would help to give him the confidence which he needed. I had seen him with Bill, and I knew that he could be perfectly natural and easy when he liked.

It was true that the man might object at first, but after awhile he would see that I had acted simply for his good, and would be grateful.

The difficulty was, how to get Fred down without scaring the man. I knew that if I shouted he wouldn't wait, but would be out of the window and away before Fred could get there. What I had to do was to go to Fred's room, explain the whole situation quietly to him, and ask him to come down and make himself pleasant.

The man was far too busy to pay any attention to me. He was kneeling in a corner with his back to me, putting something in his bag. I seized the opportunity to steal softly from the room.

Fred's door was shut, and I could hear him snoring. I scratched gently, and then harder, till I heard the snores stop. He got out of bed and opened the door.

"Don't make a noise," I whispered. "Come on downstairs I want you to meet a friend of mine."

At first he was quite peevish.

"What's the idea," he said, "coming and spoiling a man's beauty-sleep? Get out."

He actually started to go back into the room.

"No, honestly, Fred," I said, "I'm not fooling you.

There *is* a man downstairs. He got in through the window. I want you to meet him. He's very shy, and I think it will do him good to have a chat with you."

"What are you whining about?" Fred began, and then he broke off suddenly and listened. We could both hear the man's footsteps as he moved about.

Fred jumped back into the room. He came out, carrying something. He didn't say any more but started to go downstairs, very quiet, and I went after him.

There was the man, still putting things in his bag. I was just going to introduce Fred, when Fred, the silly ass, gave a great yell.

I could have bitten him.

"What did you want to do that for, you chump?" I said. "I told you he was shy. Now you've scared him."

He certainly had. The man was out of the window quicker than you would have believed possible. He just flew out. I called after him that it was only Fred and me, but at that moment a gun went off with a tremendous bang, so he couldn't have heard me.

I was pretty sick about it. The whole thing had gone wrong. Fred seemed to have lost his head entirely. He was behaving like a perfect ass. Naturally the man had been frightened with him carrying on in that way. I jumped out of the window to see if I could find the man and explain, but he was gone. Fred jumped out after me, and nearly squashed me.

It was pitch dark out there. I couldn't see a thing. But I knew the man could not have gone far, or I should have heard him. I started to sniff round on the chance of picking up his trail. It wasn't long before I struck it.

Fred's father had come down now, and they were running about. The old man had a light. I followed the trail, and it ended at a large cedar-tree, not far from the house. I stood underneath it and looked up, but of course I could not see anything.

"Are you up there?" I shouted. "There's nothing to be scared at. It was only Fred. He's an old pal of mine. He works at the place where you bought me. His gun went off by accident. He won't hurt you."

There wasn't a sound. I began to think I must have made a mistake.

"He's got away," I heard Fred say to his father, and just as he said it I caught a faint sound of some one moving in the branches above me.

"No he hasn't!" I shouted. "He's up this tree."

"I believe the dog's found him, dad!"

"Yes, he's up here. Come along and meet him."

Fred came to the foot of the tree.

"You up there," he said, "come along down."

Not a sound from the tree.

"It's all right," I explained, "he *is* up there, but he's very shy. Ask him again."

"All right," said Fred. "stay there if you want to. But I'm going to shoot off this gun into the branches just for fun."

And then the man started to come down. As soon as he touched the ground I jumped up at him.

"This is fine!" I said. "Here's my friend Fred. You'll like him."

But it wasn't any good. They didn't get along together at all. They hardly spoke. The man went into the house, and Fred went after him, carrying his gun. And when they got into the house it was just the same. The man sat in one chair, and Fred sat in another, and after a long time some men came in a motor-car, and the man went away with them. He didn't say good-bye to me.

When he had gone, Fred and his father made a great fuss of me. I couldn't understand it. Men are so odd. The man wasn't a bit pleased that I had brought him and Fred together, but Fred seemed as if he couldn't do enough for me for having introduced him to the man. However, Fred's father produced some cold ham—my favourite dish—and gave me quite a lot of it, so I stopped worrying over the thing. As mother used to say, "Don't bother your head about what doesn't concern you. The only thing a dog need concern himself with is the bill-of-fare. Eat your bun, and don't make yourself busy about other people's affairs." Mother's was in some ways a narrow outlook, but she had a great fund of sterling common sense.

THE MIXER

II. He Moves in Society

IT was one of those things which are really nobody's fault. It was not the chauffeur's fault, and it was not mine. I was having a friendly turn-up with a pal of mine on the side-walk; he ran across the road; I ran after him; and the car came round the corner and hit me. It must have been going pretty slow, or I should have been killed. As it was, I just had the breath knocked out of me. You know how you feel when the butcher catches you just as you are edging out of the shop with a bit of meat. It was like that.

I wasn't taking much interest in things for awhile, but when I did I found that I was the centre of a group of three—the chauffeur, a small boy, and the small boy's nurse.

The small boy was very well-dressed, and looked delicate. He was crying.

"Poor doggie," he said, "poor doggie."

"It wasn't my fault, Master Peter," said the chauffeur respectfully. "He run out into the road before I seen him."

"That's right," I put in, for I didn't want to get the man into trouble.

"Oh, he's not dead," said the small boy. "He barked."

"He growled," said the nurse. "Come away, Master Peter. He might bite you."

Women are trying sometimes. It is almost as if they deliberately misunderstood.

"I won't come away. I'm going to take him home with me and send for the doctor to come and see him. He's going to be my dog."

This sounded all right. Goodness knows I am no

snob, and can rough it when required, but I do like comfort when it comes my way, and it seemed to me that this was where I got it. And I liked the boy. He was the right sort.

The nurse, a very unpleasant woman, had to make objections.

"Master Peter! You can't take him home, a great, rough, fierce, common dog! What would your mother say?"

"I'm going to take him home," repeated the child, with a determination which I heartily admired, "and he's going to be my dog. I shall call him Fido."

There's always a catch in these good things. Fido is a name I particularly detest. All dogs do. There was a dog called that that I knew once, and he used to get awfully sick when we shouted it out after him in the street. No doubt there have been respectable dogs called Fido, but to my mind it is a name like Aubrey or Clarence. You may be able to live it down, but you start handicapped. However, one must take the rough with the smooth, and I was prepared to yield the point.

"If you wait, Master Peter, your father will buy you a beautiful, lovely dog . . ."

"I don't want a beautiful, lovely dog. I want this dog."

The slur did not wound me. I have no illusions about my looks. Mine is an honest, but not a beautiful, face.

"It's no use talking," said the chauffeur, grinning. "He means to have him. Shove him in, and let's be getting back, or they'll be thinking His Nibs has been kidnapped."

So I was carried to the car. I could have walked, but I had an idea that I had better not. I had made my hit as a crippled dog, and a crippled dog I intended to remain till things got more settled down.

The chauffeur started the car off again. What with the shock I had had and the luxury of riding in a motor-car, I was a little distrait, and I could not say how far we went. But it must have been miles and miles, for it seemed a long time afterwards that we stopped at the biggest house I have ever seen. There were smooth lawns and flower-beds, and men in overalls, and fountains and trees, and, away to the right, kennels with about a million dogs in them, all pushing their noses through the bars and shouting. They all wanted to know who I was and what prizes I had won, and then I realized that I was moving in high society.

I let the small boy pick me up and carry me into the house, though it was all he could do, poor kid, for I was some weight. He staggered up the steps and along a great hall, and then let me flop on the carpet of the most beautiful room you ever saw. The carpet was a yard thick.

There was a woman sitting in a chair, and as soon as she saw me she gave a shriek.

"I told Master Peter you would not be pleased, m'lady," said the nurse, who seemed to have taken a positive dislike to me, "but he would bring the nasty brute home."

"He's not a nasty brute, mother. He's my dog, and his name's Fido. John ran over him in the car, and I brought him home to live with us. I love him."

This seemed to make an impression. Peter's mother looked as if she were weakening.

"But, Peter, dear, I don't know what your father will say. He's so particular about dogs. All his dogs are prize-winners, pedigree dogs. This is such a mongrel."

"A nasty, rough, ugly, common dog, m'lady," said the nurse, sticking her oar in in an absolutely uncalled-for way.

Just then a man came into the room.

"What on earth?" he said, catching sight of me.

"It's a dog Peter has brought home. He says he wants to keep him."

"I'm *going* to keep him," corrected Peter firmly.

I do like a child that knows his own mind. I was getting fonder of Peter every minute. I reached up and licked his hand.

"See! He knows he's my dog, don't you, Fido? He licked me."

"But, Peter, he looks so fierce." This, unfortunately, is true. I do look fierce. It is rather a misfortune for a perfectly peaceful dog. "I'm sure it's not safe your having him."

"He's my dog, and his name's Fido. I am going to tell cook to give him a bone."

His mother looked at his father, who gave rather a nasty laugh.

"My dear Helen," he said, "ever since Peter was born, ten years ago, he has not asked for a single thing, to the best of my recollection, which he has not got. Let us be consistent. I don't approve of this caricature of a dog, but if Peter wants him, I suppose he must have him."

"Very well. But the first sign of viciousness he shows, he shall be shot. He makes me nervous."

So they left it at that, and I went off with Peter to get my bone.

After lunch, he took me to the kennels to introduce me to the other dogs. I had to go, but I knew it would not be pleasant, and it wasn't. Any dog will tell you what these prize-ribbon dogs are like. Their heads are so swelled they have to go into their kennels backwards.

It was just as I had expected. There were mastiffs, terriers, poodles, spaniels, bulldogs, sheepdogs, and every other kind of dog you can imagine, all prize-winners at a hundred shows, and every single dog in the place just shoved his head back and laughed himself sick. I never felt so small in my life, and I was glad when it was over and Peter took me off to the stables.

I was just feeling that I never wanted to see another dog in my life, when a terrier ran out, shouting. As soon as he saw me, he came up inquiringly, walking very stiff-legged, as terriers do when they see a stranger.

"Well," I said, "and what particular sort of a prize-winner are you? Tell me all about the ribbons they gave you at the Crystal Palace, and let's get it over."

He laughed in a way that did me good.

"Guess again!" he said. "Did you take me for

one of the nuts in the kennels? My name's Jack, and I belong to one of the grooms."

"What!" I cried. "You aren't Champion Bowlegs Royal or anything of that sort! I'm glad to meet you."

So we rubbed noses as friendly as you please. It was a treat meeting one of one's own sort. I had had enough of those high-toned dogs who look at you as if you were something the garbage-man had forgotten to take away.

"So you've been talking to the swells, have you?" said Jack.

"He would take me," I said, pointing to Peter.

"Oh, you're his latest, are you? Then you're all right—while it lasts."

"How do you mean, while it lasts?"

"Well, I'll tell you what happened to me. Young Peter took a great fancy to me once. Couldn't do enough for me for awhile. Then he got tired of me, and out I went. You see, the trouble is that while he's a perfectly good kid, he has always had everything he wanted since he was born, and he gets tired of things pretty easy. It was a toy railway that finished me. Directly he got that, I might not have been on the earth. It was lucky for me that Dick, my present old man, happened to want a dog to keep down the rats, or goodness knows what might not have happened to me. They aren't keen on dogs here unless they've pulled down enough blue ribbons to sink a ship, and mongrels like you and me—no offence—don't last long. I expect you noticed that the grown-ups didn't exactly cheer when you arrived?"

"They weren't chummy."

"Well, take it from me, your only chance is to make them chummy. If you do something to please them, they might let you stay on, even though Peter was tired of you."

"What sort of thing?"

"That's for you to think out. I couldn't find one. I might tell you to save Peter from drowning. You don't need a pedigree to do that. But you can't drag the kid to the lake and push him in. That's the trouble. A dog gets so few opportunities. But, take it from me, if you don't do something within two weeks to make yourself solid with the adults, you can make your will. In two weeks Peter will have forgotten all about you. It's not his fault. It's the way he has been brought up. His father has all the money on earth, and Peter's the only child. You can't blame him. All I say is, look out for yourself. Well, I'm glad to have met you. Drop in again when you can. I can give you some good ratting, and I have a bone or two put away. So long."

It worried me badly what Jack had said. I couldn't get it out of my mind. If it hadn't been for that, I should have had a great time, for Peter certainly made a lot of fuss of me. He treated me as if I were the only friend he had.

And, in a way, I was. When you are the only son of a man who has all the money in the world, it seems that you aren't allowed to be like an ordinary kid. They coop you up, as if you were something precious that would be contaminated by contact with other children. In all the time that I was at the house I never met another child. Peter had everything in the world, except someone of his own age to go round with; and that made him different from any of the kids I had known.

He liked talking to me. I was the only person round who really understood him. He would talk by the hour and I would listen with my tongue hanging out and nod now and then.

It was worth listening to, what he used to tell me. He told me the most surprising things. I didn't know, for instance, that there were any Red Indians in England but he said there was a chief named Big Cloud who lived in the rhododendron bushes by the lake. I never found him, though I went carefully through them one day. He also said that there were pirates on the island in the lake. I never saw them either.

What he liked telling me about best was the city of gold and precious stones which you came to if you walked far enough through the woods at the back of the stables. He was always meaning to go off there some day, and, from the way he described it, I didn't blame him. It was certainly a pretty good city. It was just right for dogs, too, he said, having bones and liver and sweet cakes there and everything else a dog could want. It used to make my mouth water to listen to him.

We were never apart. I was with him all day, and I slept on the mat in his room at night. But all the time I couldn't get out of my mind what Jack had said. I nearly did once, for it seemed to me that I was so necessary to Peter that nothing could separate us ; but just as I was feeling safe his father gave him a toy aeroplane, which flew when you wound it up. The day he got it, I might not have been on the earth. I trailed along, but he hadn't a word to say to me.

Well, something went wrong with the aeroplane the second day, and it wouldn't fly, and then I was in solid again ; but I had done some hard thinking and I knew just where I stood. I was the newest toy, that's what I was, and something newer might come along at any moment, and then it would be the finish for me. The only thing for me was to do something to impress the adults, just as Jack had said.

Goodness knows I tried. But everything I did turned out wrong. There seemed to be a fate about it. One morning, for example, I was trotting round the house early, and I met a fellow I could have sworn was a burglar. He wasn't one of the family, and he wasn't one of the servants, and he was hanging round the house in a most suspicious way. I chased him up a tree, and it wasn't till the family came down to breakfast, two hours later, that I found that he was a guest who had arrived overnight, and had come out early to enjoy the freshness of the morning and the sun shining on the lake, he being that sort of man. That didn't help me much.

Next, I got in wrong with the boss, Peter's father. I don't know why. I met him out in the park with another man, both carrying bundles of sticks and looking very serious and earnest. Just as I reached him, the boss lifted one of the sticks and hit a small white ball with it. He had never seemed to want to play with me before, and I took it as a great compliment. I raced after the ball, which he had hit quite a long way, picked it up in my mouth, and brought it back to him. I laid it at his feet, and smiled up at him.

"Hit it again," I said.

He wasn't pleased at all. He said all sorts of things and tried to kick me, and that night, when he thought I was not listening, I heard him telling his wife that I was a pest and would have to be got rid of. That made me think.

And then I put the lid on it. With the best intentions in the world I got myself into such a mess that I thought the end had come.

It happened one afternoon in the drawing-room. There were visitors that day—women; and women seem fatal to me. I was in the background, trying not to be seen, for, though I had been brought in by Peter, the family never liked my coming into the drawing-room. I was hoping for a piece of cake and not paying much attention to the conversation, which was all about somebody called Toto, whom I had not met. Peter's mother said Toto was a sweet little darling, he was; and one of the visitors said Toto had not been at all himself that day and she was quite worried. And a good lot more about how all that Toto would ever take for dinner was a little white meat of chicken, chopped up fine. It was not very interesting, and I had allowed my attention to wander.

And just then, peeping round the corner of my chair to see if there were any signs of cake, what should I see but a great beastly brute of a rat. It was standing right beside the visitor, drinking milk out of a saucer, if you please!

I may have my faults, but procrastination in the presence of rats is not one of them. I didn't hesitate for a second. Here was my chance. If there is one thing women hate, it is a rat. Mother always used to say, "If you want to succeed in life, please the women. They are the real bosses. The men don't count." By eliminating this rodent I should earn the gratitude and esteem of Peter's mother, and, if I did that, it did not matter what Peter's father thought of me.

I sprang.

The rat hadn't a chance to get away. I was right on to him. I got hold of his neck, gave him a couple of shakes, and chucked him across the room. Then I ran across to finish him off.

Just as I reached him, he sat up and barked at me. I was never so taken aback in my life. I pulled up short and stared at him.

"I'm sure I beg your pardon, sir," I said apologetically. "I thought you were a rat."

And then everything broke loose. Somebody got me by the collar, somebody else hit me on the head with a parasol, and somebody else kicked me in the ribs. Everybody talked and shouted at the same time.

"Poor darling Toto!" cried the visitor, snatching up the little animal. "Did the great savage brute try to murder you!"

"So absolutely unprovoked!"

"He just flew at the poor little thing!"

It was no good my trying to explain. Any dog in my place would have made the same mistake. The creature was a toy-dog of one of those extraordinary breeds—a prize-winner and champion, and so on, of course, and worth his weight in gold. I would have done better to bite the visitor than Toto. That much I gathered from the general run of the conversation, and then, having discovered that the door was shut, I edged under the sofa. I was embarrassed.

"That settles it!" said Peter's mother. "The dog is not safe. He must be shot."

Peter gave a yell at this, but for once he didn't swing the voting an inch.

"Be quiet, Peter," said his mother. "It is not safe for you to have such a dog. He may be mad."

Women are very unreasonable.

Toto, of course, wouldn't say a word to explain how the mistake arose. He was sitting on the visitor's lap, shrieking about what he would have done to me if they hadn't separated us.

Somebody felt cautiously under the sofa. I recognized the shoes of Weeks, the butler. I suppose they had rung for him to come and take me, and I could see that he wasn't half liking it. I was sorry for Weeks, who was a friend of mine, so I licked his hand, and that seemed to cheer him up a whole lot.

"I have him now, madam," I heard him say.

"Take him to the stables and tie him up, Weeks, and tell one of the men to bring his gun and shoot him. He is not safe."

A few minutes later I was in an empty stall, tied up to the manger.

It was all over. It had been pleasant while it lasted, but I had reached the end of my tether now. I don't think I was frightened, but a sense of pathos stole over me. I had meant so well. It seemed as if good intentions went for nothing in this world. I had tried so hard to please everybody, and this was the result—tied up in a dark stable, waiting for the end.

The shadows lengthened in the stable-yard, and still nobody came. I began to wonder if they had forgotten me, and presently, in spite of myself, a faint hope began to spring up inside me that this might mean that I was not to be shot after all Perhaps Toto at the eleventh hour had explained everything.

And then footsteps sounded outside, and the hope died away. I shut my eyes.

Somebody put his arms round my neck, and my nose touched a warm cheek. I opened my eyes. It was not the man with the gun come to shoot me. It was Peter. He was breathing very hard, and he had been crying.

"Quiet!" he whispered.

He began to untie the rope.

"You must keep quite quiet, or they will hear us, and then we shall be stopped. I'm going to take you into the woods, and we'll walk and walk until we come to the city I told you about that's all gold and diamonds, and we'll live there for the rest of our lives, and no one will be able to hurt us. But you must keep very quiet."

He went to the stable-gate and looked out. Then

he gave a little whistle to me to come after him. And we started out to find the city.

The woods were a long way away, down a hill of long grass and across a stream ; and we went very carefully, keeping in the shadows and running across the open spaces. And every now and then we would stop and look back, but there was nobody to be seen. The sun was setting, and everything was very cool and quiet.

Presently we came to the stream and crossed it by a little wooden bridge, and then we were in the woods, where nobody could see us.

I had never been in the woods before, and everything was very new and exciting to me. There were squirrels and rabbits and birds, more than I had ever seen in my life, and little things that buzzed and flew and tickled my ears. I wanted to rush about and look at everything, but Peter called to me, and I came to heel. He knew where we were going, and I didn't, so I let him lead.

We went very slowly. The wood got thicker and thicker the farther we got into it. There were bushes that were difficult to push through, and long branches, covered with thorns, that reached out at you and tore at you when you tried to get away. And soon it was quite dark, so dark that I could see nothing, not even Peter, though he was so close. We went slower and slower, and the darkness was full of queer noises. From time to time Peter would stop, and I would run to him and put my nose in his hand. At first he patted me, but after awhile he did not pat me any more, but just gave me his hand to lick, as if it was too much for him to lift it. I think he was getting very tired. He was quite a small boy and not strong, and we had walked a long way.

It seemed to be getting darker and darker. I could hear the sound of Peter's footsteps, and they seemed to drag as he forced his way through the bushes. And then, quite suddenly, he sat down without any warning, and when I ran up I heard him crying.

I suppose there are lots of dogs who would have known exactly the right thing to do, but I could not think of anything except to put my nose against his cheek and whine. He put his arm round my neck, and for a long time we stayed like that, saying nothing. It seemed to comfort him, for after a time he stopped crying.

I did not bother him by asking about the wonderful city where we were going, for he was so tired. But I could not help wondering if we were near it. There was not a sign of any city, nothing but darkness and odd noises and the wind singing in the trees. Curious little animals, such as I had never smelt before, came creeping out of the bushes to look at us. I would have chased them, but Peter's arm was round my neck and I could not leave him. But when something that smelt like a rabbit came so near that I could have reached out a paw and touched it, I turned my head and snapped; and then they all scurried back into the bushes and there were no more noises.

There was a long silence. Then Peter gave a great gulp.

"I'm not frightened," he said. "I'm not!"

I shoved my head closer against his chest. There was another silence for a long time.

"I'm going to pretend we have been captured by brigands," said Peter at last. "Are you listening? There were three of them, great big men with beards, and they crept up behind me and snatched me up and took me out here to their lair. This is their lair. One was called Dick, the other's names were Ted and Alfred. They took hold of me and brought me all the way through the wood till we got here, and then they went off, meaning to come back soon. And while they were away, you missed me and tracked me through the woods till you found me here. And then the brigands came back, and they didn't know you were here, and you kept quite quiet till Dick was quite near, and then you jumped out and bit him and he ran away. And then you bit Ted and you bit Alfred, and they ran away too. And so we were left all alone, and I was quite safe because you were here to look after me. And then—— And then——"

His voice died away, and the arm that was round my neck went limp, and I could hear by his breathing that he was asleep. His head was resting on my back, but I didn't move. I wriggled a little closer to make him as comfortable as I could, and then I went to sleep myself.

I didn't sleep very well. I had funny dreams all the time, thinking these little animals were creeping up close enough out of the bushes for me to get a snap at them without disturbing Peter.

If I woke once, I woke a dozen times, but there was never anything there. The wind sang in the trees and the bushes rustled, and far away in the distance the frogs were calling.

And then I woke once more with the feeling that this time something really was coming through the bushes. I lifted my head as far as I could, and listened. For a little while nothing happened, and then, straight in front of me, I saw lights. And there was a sound of trampling in the undergrowth.

It was no time to think about not waking Peter. This was something definite, something that had to be attended to quick. I was up with a jump, yelling. Peter rolled off my back and woke up, and he sat there listening, while I stood with my front paws on him and shouted at the men. I was bristling all over. I didn't know who they were or what they wanted, but the way I looked at it was that anything could happen in those woods at that time of night, and, if anybody was coming along to start something, he had got to reckon with me.

Somebody called, "Peter! Are you there, Peter?"

There was a crashing in the bushes, the lights came nearer and nearer, and then somebody said "Here he is!" and there was a lot of shouting. I stood where I was, ready to spring if necessary, for I was taking no chances.

"Who are you?" I shouted. "What do you want?"

A light flashed in my eyes.

"Why, it's that dog!"

Somebody came into the light, and I saw it was the

boss. He was looking very anxious and scared, and he scooped Peter up off the ground and hugged him tight.

Peter was only half awake. He looked up at the boss drowsily, and began to talk about brigands, and Dick and Ted and Alfred, the same as he had said to me. There wasn't a sound till he had finished. Then the boss spoke.

"Kidnappers! I thought as much. And the dog drove them away!"

For the first time in our acquaintance he actually patted me.

"Good old man!" he said.

"He's my dog," said Peter sleepily, "and he isn't to be shot."

"He certainly isn't, my boy," said the boss. "From now on he's the honoured guest. He shall wear a gold collar and order what he wants for dinner. And now let's be getting home. It's time you were in bed."

Mother used to say, "If you're a good dog, you will be happy. If you're not, you won't," but it seems to me that in this world it is all a matter of luck. When I did everything I could to please people, they wanted to shoot me; and when I did nothing except run away, they brought me back and treated me better than the most valuable prize-winner in the kennels. It was puzzling at first, but one day I heard the boss talking to a friend who had come down from the city.

The friend looked at me and said, "What an ugly mongrel! Why on earth do you have him about? I thought you were so particular about your dogs?"

And the boss replied, "He may be a mongrel, but he can have anything he wants in this house. Didn't you hear how he saved Peter from being kidnapped?"

And out it all came about the brigands.

"The kid called them brigands," said the boss. "I suppose that's how it would strike a child of that age. But he kept mentioning the name Dick, and that put the police on the scent. It seems there's a kidnapper well-known to the police all over the country as Dick the Snatcher. It was almost certainly that scoundrel and his gang. How they spirited the child away, goodness knows, but they managed it, and the dog tracked them and scared them off. We found him and Peter together in the woods. It was a narrow escape, and we have to thank this animal here for it."

What could I say? It was no more use trying to put them right than it had been when I mistook Toto for a rat. Peter had gone to sleep that night pretending about the brigands to pass the time, and when he awoke he still believed in them. He was that sort of child. There was nothing that I could do about it.

Round the corner, as the boss was speaking, I saw the kennel-man coming with a plate in his hand. It smelt fine, and he was headed straight for me.

He put the plate down before me. It was liver, which I love.

"Yes," went on the boss, "if it hadn't been for him, Peter would have been kidnapped and scared half to death, and I should be poorer, I suppose, by whatever the scoundrels had chosen to hold me up for."

I am an honest dog, and hate to obtain credit under false pretences, but—liver is liver. I let it go at that.

CROWNED HEADS

KATIE had never been more surprised in her life than when the serious young man with the brown eyes and the Charles Dana Gibson profile spirited her away from his friend and Genevieve. Till that moment she had looked on herself as playing a sort of "villager and retainer" part to the brown-eyed young man's hero and Genevieve's heroine. She knew she was not pretty, though somebody (unidentified) had once said that she had nice eyes; whereas Genevieve was notoriously a beauty, incessantly pestered, so report had it, by musical comedy managers to go on the stage.

Genevieve was tall and blonde, a destroyer of masculine peace of mind. She said "harf" and "rahther," and might easily have been taken for an English duchess instead of a cloak-model at Macey's. You would have said, in short, that, in the matter of personable young men, Genevieve would have swept the board. Yet, here was this one deliberately selecting her, Katie, for his companion. It was almost a miracle.

He had managed it with the utmost dexterity at the merry-go-round. With winning politeness he had assisted Genevieve on her wooden steed, and then, as the machinery began to work, had grasped Katie's arm and led her at a rapid walk out into the sunlight. Katie's last glimpse of Genevieve had been the sight of her amazed and offended face as it whizzed round the corner, while the steam melodeon drowned protests with a spirited plunge into "Alexander's Ragtime Band."

Katie felt shy. This young man was a perfect stranger. It was true she had had a formal introduction to him, but only from Genevieve, who had scraped acquaintance with him exactly two minutes previously. It had happened on the ferry-boat on the way to Palisades Park. Genevieve's bright eye, roving among the throng on the lower deck, had singled out this young man and his companion as suitable cavaliers for the expedition. The young man pleased her, and his friend, with the broken nose and the face like a good-natured bulldog, was obviously suitable for Katie.

Etiquette is not rigid on New York ferry-boats. Without fuss or delay she proceeded to make their acquaintance—to Katie's concern, for she could never get used to Genevieve's short way with strangers. The quiet life she had led had made her almost prudish, and there were times when Genevieve's conduct shocked her. Of course, she knew there was no harm in Genevieve. As the latter herself had once put it, "The feller that tries to get gay with me is going to get a call-down that'll make him holler for his winter overcoat." But all the same she could not approve. And the net result of her disapproval was to make her shy and silent as she walked by this young man's side.

The young man seemed to divine her thoughts.

"Say, I'm on the level," he observed. "You want to get that. Right on the square. See?"

"Oh, yes," said Katie, relieved but yet embarrassed. It was awkward to have one's thoughts read like this.

"You ain't like your friend. Don't think I don't see that."

"Genevieve's a sweet girl," said Katie, loyally.

"A darned sight too sweet. Somebody ought to tell her mother."

"Why did you speak to her if you did not like her?"

"Wanted to get to know you," said the young man simply

They walked on in silence. Katie's heart was beating with a rapidity that forbade speech. Nothing like this very direct young man had ever happened to her before She had grown so accustomed to regarding herself as something too insignificant and unattractive for the notice of the lordly male that she was overwhelmed. She had a vague feeling that there was a mistake somewhere. It surely could not be she who was proving so alluring to this fairy prince. The novelty of the situation frightened her.

"Come here often?" asked her companion.

"I've never been here before."

"Often go to Coney?"

"I've never been."

He regarded her with astonishment.

"You've never been to Coney Island! Why, you don't know what this sort of thing is till you've taken in Coney. This place isn't on the map with Coney. Do you mean to say you've never seen Luna Park, or Dreamland, or Steeplechase, or the diving ducks? Haven't you had a look at the Mardi Gras stunts? Why, Coney during Mardi Gras is the greatest thing on earth. It's a knockout. Just about a million boys and girls having the best time that ever was. Say, I guess you don't go out much, do you?"

"Not much."

"If it's not a rude question, what do you do? I been trying to place you all along. Now I reckon your friend works in a store, don't she?"

"Yes. She's a cloak-model. She has a lovely figure, hasn't she?"

"Didn't notice it. I guess so, if she's what you say. It's what they pay her for, ain't it? Do you work in a store, too?"

"Not exactly. I keep a little shop."

"All by yourself?"

"I do all the work now. It was my father's shop, but he's dead. It began by being my grandfather's. He started it. But he's so old now that, of course, he can't work any longer, so I look after things."

"Say, you're a wonder! What sort of a shop?"

"It's only a little second-hand bookshop. There really isn't much to do."

"Where is it?"

"Sixth Avenue. Near Washington Square."

"What name?"

"Bennett."

"That's your name, then?"

"Yes."

"Anything besides Bennett?"

"My name's Kate."

The young man nodded.

"I'd make a pretty good district attorney," he said, disarming possible resentment at this cross-examination. "I guess you're wondering if I'm ever going to stop asking you questions. Well, what would you like to do?"

"Don't you think we ought to go back and find your friend and Genevieve? They will be wondering where we are."

"Let 'em," said the young man briefly. "I've had all I want of Jenny."

"I can't understand why you don't like her."

"I like you. Shall we have some ice-cream, or would you rather go on the Scenic Railway?"

Katie decided on the more peaceful pleasure. They resumed their walk, socially licking two cones. Out of the corner of her eyes Katie cast swift glances at her friend's face. He was a very grave young man. There was something important as well as handsome about him. Once, as they made their way through the crowds, she saw a couple of boys look almost reverently at him. She wondered who he could be, but was too shy to inquire. She had got over her nervousness to a great extent, but there were still limits to what she felt herself equal to saying. It did not strike her that it was only fair that she should ask a few questions in return for those which he had put. She had always repressed herself, and she did so now. She was content to be with him without finding out his name and history.

He supplied the former just before he finally consented to let her go.

They were standing looking over the river. The sun had spent its force, and it was cool and pleasant in the breeze which was coming up the Hudson. Katie was conscious of a vague feeling that was almost melancholy. It had been a lovely afternoon, and she was sorry that it was over.

The young man shuffled his feet on the loose stones. "I'm mighty glad I met you," he said. "Say, I'm coming to see you. On Sixth Avenue. Don't mind, do you?"

He did not wait for a reply.

"Brady's my name. Ted Brady, Glencoe Athletic Club," he paused. "I'm on the level," he added, and paused again. "I like you a whole lot. There's your friend, Genevieve. Better go after her, hadn't you? Good-bye." And he was gone, walking swiftly through the crowd about the band-stand.

Katie went back to Genevieve, and Genevieve was simply horrid. Cold and haughty, a beautiful iceberg of dudgeon, she refused to speak a single word during the whole long journey back to Sixth Avenue. And Katie, whose tender heart would at other times have been tortured by this hostility, leant back in her seat, and was happy. Her mind was far away from Genevieve's frozen gloom, living over again the wonderful happenings of the afternoon.

Yes, it had been a wonderful afternoon, but trouble was waiting for her in Sixth Avenue. Trouble was never absent for very long from Katie's unselfish life. Arriving at the little bookshop, she found Mr. Murdoch, the glazier, preparing for departure. Mr. Murdoch came in on Mondays, Wednesdays, and Fridays to play draughts with her grandfather, who was paralysed from the waist, and unable to leave the house except when Katie took him for his outing in Washington Square each morning in his bath-chair.

Mr. Murdoch welcomed Katie with joy.

"I was wondering whenever you would come back, Katie. I'm afraid the old man's a little upset."

"Not ill?"

"Not ill. Upset. And it was my fault, too. Thinking he'd be interested, I read him a piece from the paper where I seen about these English Suffragettes, and he just went up in the air. I guess he'll be all right now you've come back. I was a fool to read it, I reckon. I kind of forgot for the moment."

"Please don't worry yourself about it, Mr. Murdoch. He'll be all right soon. I'll go to him."

In the inner room the old man was sitting. His face was flushed, and he gesticulated from time to time.

"I won't have it," he cried as Katie entered. "I tell you I won't have it. If Parliament can't do anything, I'll send Parliament about its business."

"Here I am, grandpapa," said Katie quickly. "I've had the greatest time. It was lovely up there. I——"

"I tell you it's got to stop. I've spoken about it before. I won't have it."

"I expect they're doing their best. It's your being so far away that makes it hard for them. But I do think you might write them a very sharp letter."

"I will. I will. Get out the paper. Are you ready?" He stopped, and looked piteously at Katie. "I don't know what to say. I don't know how to begin."

Katie scribbled a few lines.

"How would this do? 'His Majesty informs his Government that he is greatly surprised and indignant that no notice has been taken of his previous communications. If this goes on, he will be reluctantly compelled to put the matter in other hands.'"

She read it glibly as she had written it. The formula had been a favourite one of her late father, when roused to fall upon offending patrons of the bookshop.

The old man beamed. His resentment was gone. He was soothed and happy.

"That'll wake 'em up," he said. "I won't have these goings on while I'm king, and if they don't like it, they know what to do. You're a good girl, Katie."

He chuckled.

"I beat Lord Murdoch five games to nothing," he said.

It was now nearly two years since the morning when old Matthew Bennett had announced to an audience consisting of Katie and a smoky blue cat, which had wandered in from Washington Square to take pot-luck, that he was the King of England.

This was a long time for any one delusion of the old man's to last. Usually they came and went with a rapidity which made it hard for Katie, for all her tact, to keep abreast of them. She was not likely to forget the time when he went to bed President Roosevelt and woke up the Prophet Elijah. It was the only occasion in all the years they had passed together when she had felt like giving way and indulging in the fit of hysterics which most girls of her age would have had as a matter of course.

She had handled that crisis, and she handled the present one with equal smoothness. When her grandfather made his announcement, which he did rather as one stating a generally recognized fact than as if the information were in any way sensational, she neither screamed nor swooned, nor did she rush to the neighbours for advice. She merely gave the old man his breakfast, not forgetting to set aside a suitable portion for the smoky cat, and then went round to notify Mr. Murdoch of what had happened.

Mr. Murdoch, excellent man, received the news without any fuss or excitement at all, and promised to look in on Schwartz, the stout saloon-keeper, who was Mr. Bennett's companion and antagonist at draughts on Tuesdays, Thursdays, and Saturdays, and, as he expressed it, put him wise.

Life ran comfortably in the new groove. Old Mr. Bennett continued to play draughts and pore over his second-hand classics. Every morning he took his outing in Washington Square where, from his invalid's chair, he surveyed somnolent Italians and roller-skating children with his old air of kindly approval. Katie, whom circumstances had taught to be thankful for small mercies, was perfectly happy in the shadow of the throne. She liked her work; she liked looking after her grandfather; and now that Ted Brady had come into her life, she really began to look on herself as an exceptionally lucky girl, a spoilt favourite of Fortune.

For Ted Brady had called, as he said he would, and from the very first he had made plain in his grave, direct way the objects of his visits. There was no subtlety about Ted, no finesse. He was as frank as a music-hall love song.

On his first visit, having handed Katie a large bunch of roses with the stolidity of a messenger boy handing over a parcel, he had proceeded, by way of establishing his *bona fides*, to tell her all about himself. He supplied the facts in no settled order, just as they happened to occur to him in the long silences with which his speech was punctuated. Small facts jostled large facts. He spoke of his morals and his fox-terrier in the same breath.

"I'm on the level. Ask anyone who knows me. They'll tell you that. Say, I got the cutest little dog you ever seen. Do you like dogs? I've never been a fellow that's got himself mixed up with girls. I don't like 'em as a general thing. A fellow's got too much to do keeping himself in training, if his club expects him to do things. I belong to the Glencoe Athletic. I ran the hundred yards dash in evens last sports there was. They expect me to do it at the Glencoe, so I've never got myself mixed up with girls. Till I seen you that afternoon I reckon I'd hardly looked at a girl, honest. They didn't seem to kind to make any hit with me. And then I seen you, and I says to myself, 'That's the one.' It sort of came over me in a flash. I fell for you directly I seen you. And I'm on the level. Don't forget that."

And more in the same strain, leaning on the counter and looking into Katie's eyes with a devotion that added emphasis to his measured speech.

Next day he came again, and kissed her respectfully but firmly, making a sort of shuffling dive across the counter. Breaking away, he fumbled in his pocket and produced a ring, which he proceeded to place on her finger with the serious air which accompanied all his actions.

"That looks pretty good to me," he said, as he stepped back and eyed it.

It struck Katie, when he had gone, how differently different men did things. Genevieve had often related stories of men who had proposed to her, and according to Genevieve, they always got excited and emotional, and sometimes cried. Ted Brady had fitted her with the ring more like a glover's assistant than anything else, and he had hardly spoken a word from beginning to end. He had seemed to take her acquiescence for granted. And yet there had been nothing flat or disappointing about the proceedings. She had been thrilled throughout. It is to be supposed that Mr. Brady had the force of character which does not require the aid of speech.

It was not till she took the news of her engagement to old Mr. Bennett that it was borne in upon Katie that fate did not intend to be so wholly benevolent to her as she supposed.

That her grandfather could offer any opposition had not occurred to her as a possibility. She took his approval for granted. Never, as long as she could remember, had he been anything but kind to her. And the only possible objections to marriage from a grandfather's point of view—badness of character, insufficient means, or inferiority of social position—were in this case gloriously absent.

She could not see how anyone, however hypercritical, could find a flaw in Ted. His character was spotless. He was comfortably off. And so far from being in any way inferior socially, it was he who condescended. For Ted, she had discovered from conversation with Mr. Murdoch, the glazier, was no ordinary young man. He was a celebrity. So much so that for a moment, when told the news of the engagement, Mr. Murdoch, startled out of his usual tact, had exhibited frank surprise that the great Ted Brady should not have aimed higher.

"You're sure you've got the name right, Katie?" he had said. "It's really Ted Brady? No mistake about the first name? Well-built, good-looking young chap with brown eyes? Well, this beats me. Not," he went on hurriedly, "that any young fellow mightn't think himself lucky to get a wife like you, Katie, but Ted Brady! Why, there isn't a girl in this part of the town, or in Harlem or the B onx, for that matter, who wouldn't give her eyes to be in your place. Why, Ted Brady is the big nose. He's the star of the Glencoe."

"He told me he belonged to the Glencoe Athletic."

"Don't you believe it. It belongs to him. Why, the way that boy runs and jumps is the real limit. There's only Billy Burton, of the Irish-American, that can touch him. You've certainly got the pick of the bunch, Katie."

He stared at her admiringly, as if for the first time realizing her true worth. For Mr. Murdoch was a great patron of sport.

With these facts in her possession Katie had approached the interview with her grandfather with a good deal of confidence.

The old man listened to her recital of Mr. Brady's qualities in silence. Then he shook his head.

"It can't be, Katie. I couldn't have it."

"Grandpapa!"

"You're forgetting, my dear."

"Forgetting?"

"Who ever heard of such a thing? The granddaughter of the King of England marrying a commoner! It wouldn't do at all."

Consternation, surprise, and misery kept Katie dumb. She had learned in a hard school to be prepared for sudden blows from the hand of fate, but this one was so entirely unforeseen that it found her unprepared, and she was crushed by it. She knew her grandfather's obstinacy too well to argue against the decision.

"Oh, no, not at all," he repeated. "Oh, no, it wouldn't do."

Katie said nothing, she was beyond speech. She stood there wide-eyed and silent among the ruins of her little air-castle. The old man patted her hand affectionately. He was pleased at her docility. It was the right attitude, becoming in one of her high rank.

"I am very sorry, my dear, but—oh, no! oh, no! oh, no——" His voice trailed away into an unintelligible mutter He was a very old man, and he was not always able to concentrate his thoughts on a subject for any length of time.

So little did Ted Brady realize at first the true complexity of the situation that he was inclined, when he heard of the news, to treat the crisis in the jaunty, dashing, love-laughs-at-locksmith fashion so popular with young men of spirit when thwarted in their loves by the interference of parents and guardians.

It took Katie some time to convince him that, just because he had the licence in his pocket, he could not snatch her up on his saddle-bow and carry her off to the nearest clergyman after the manner of young Lochinvar.

In the first flush of his resentment at restraint he saw no reason why he should differentiate between old Mr. Bennett and the conventional banns-forbidding father of the novelettes with which he was accustomed to sweeten his hours of idleness. To him, till Katie explained the intricacies of the position, Mr. Bennett was simply the proud millionaire who would not hear of his daughter marrying the artist.

"But, Ted, dear, you don't understand," Katie said. "We simply couldn't do that. There's no one but me to look after him, poor old man. How could I run away like that and get married? What would become of him?"

"You wouldn't be away long," urged Mr. Brady, a man of many parts, but not a rapid thinker. "The minister would have us fixed up inside of half an hour. Then we'd look in at Mouquin's for a steak and fried, just to make a sort of wedding breakfast. And then back we'd come, hand-in-hand, and say, 'Well, here we are. Now what?'"

"He would never forgive me."

"That," said Ted judicially, "would be up to him."

"It would kill him. Don't you see, we know that it's all nonsense, this idea of his; but he really thinks he is the king, and he's so old that the shock of my disobeying him would be too much. Honest, Ted, dear, I couldn't."

Gloom unutterable darkened Ted Brady's always serious countenance. The difficulties of the situation were beginning to come home to him.

"Maybe if I went and saw him——" he suggested at last.

"You *could*," said Katie doubtfully.

Ted tightened his belt with an air of determination, and bit resolutely on the chewing-gum which was his inseparable companion.

"I will," he said.

"You'll be nice to him, Ted?"

He nodded. He was the man of action, not words.

It was perhaps ten minutes before he came out of the inner room in which Mr. Bennett passed his days. When he did, there was no sign of jubilation on his face. His brow was darker than ever.

Katie looked at him anxiously. He returned the look with a sombre shake of the head.

"Nothing doing," he said shortly. He paused. "Unless," he added, "you count it anything that he's made me an earl."

In the next two weeks several brains busied themselves with the situation. Genevieve, reconciled to Katie after a decent interval of wounded dignity, said she supposed there was a way out, if one could only think of it, but it certainly got past her. The only approach to a plan of action was suggested by the broken-nosed individual who had been Ted's companion that day at Palisades Park, a gentleman of some eminence in the boxing world, who rejoiced in the name of the Tennessee Bear-Cat.

What they ought to do, in the Bear-Cat's opinion, was to get the old man out into Washington Square one morning. He of Tennessee would then sasshay up in a flip manner and make a break. Ted, waiting close by, would resent his insolence. There would be words, followed by blows.

"See what I mean?" pursued the Bear-Cat. "There's you and me mixing it. I'll square the cop on the beat to leave us be; he's a friend of mine. Pretty soon you land me one on the plexus, and I take th' count. Then there's you hauling me up by th' collar to the old gentleman, and me saying I quits and apologizing. See what I mean?"

The whole, presumably, to conclude with warm expressions of gratitude and esteem from Mr. Bennett, and an instant withdrawal of the veto.

Ted himself approved of the scheme. He said it was a cracker-jaw, and he wondered how one so notoriously ivory-skulled as the other could have had such an idea. The Bear-Cat said modestly that he had 'em sometimes.

And it is probable that all would have been well, had it not been necessary to tell the plan to Katie, who was horrified at the very idea, spoke warmly of the danger to her grandfather's nervous system, and said she did not think the Bear-Cat could be a nice friend for Ted. And matters relapsed into their old state of hopelessness.

And then, one day, Katie forced herself to tell Ted that she thought it would be better if they did not see each other for a time. She said that these meetings were only a source of pain to both of them. It would really be better if he did not come round for—well, quite some time.

It had not been easy for her to say it. The decision was the outcome of many wakeful nights. She had asked herself the question whether it was fair for her to keep Ted chained to her in this hopeless fashion, when, left to himself and away from her, he might so easily find some other girl to make him happy.

So Ted went, reluctantly, and the little shop on Sixth Avenue knew him no more. And Katie spent her time looking after old Mr. Bennett (who had completely forgotten the affair by now, and sometimes wondered why Katie was not so cheerful as she had been), and—for, though unselfish, she was human—hating those unknown girls whom in her mind's eye she could see clustering round Ted, smiling at him, making much of him, and driving the bare recollection of her out of his mind.

The summer passed. July came and went, making New York an oven. August followed, and one wondered why one had complained of July's tepid advances.

It was on the evening of September the eleventh that Katie, having closed the little shop, sat in the dusk on the steps, as many thousands of her fellow-townsmen and townswomen were doing, turning her face to the first breeze which New York had known for two months. The hot spell had broken abruptly that afternoon, and the city was drinking in the coolness as a flower drinks water.

From round the corner, where the yellow cross of the Judson Hotel shone down on Washington Square, came the shouts of children, and the strains, mellowed by distance, of the indefatigable barrel-organ which had played the same tunes in the same place since the spring.

Katie closed her eyes, and listened. It was very peaceful this evening, so peaceful that for an instant she forgot even to think of Ted. And it was just during this instant that she heard his voice.

" That you, kid ? "

He was standing before her, his hands in his pockets, one foot on the pavement, the other in the road ; and if he was agitated, his voice did not show it.

" Ted ! "

" That's me. Can I see the old man for a minute, Katie ? "

This time it did seem to her that she could detect a slight ring of excitement.

" It's no use, Ted. Honest."

" No harm in going in and passing the time of day, is there ? I've got something I want to say to him."

" What ? "

" Tell you later, maybe. Is he in his room ? "

He stepped past her, and went in. As he went, he caught her arm and pressed it, but he did not stop. She saw him go into the inner room and heard through the door as he closed it behind him, the murmur of voices. And almost immediately, it seemed to her, her name was called. It was her grandfather's voice which called, high and excited. The door opened, and Ted appeared.

" Come here a minute, Katie, will you ? " he said. " You're wanted."

The old man was leaning forward in his chair. He was in a state of extraordinary excitement. He quivered and jumped. Ted, standing by the wall, looked as stolid as ever ; but his eyes glittered.

" Katie," cried the old man, " this is a most remarkable piece of news. This gentleman has just been telling me—extraordinary. He——"

He broke off, and looked at Ted, as he had looked at Katie when he had tried to write the letter to the Parliament of England.

Ted's eye, as it met Katie's, was almost defiant.

" I want to marry you," he said.

"Yes, yes," broke in Mr. Bennett, impatiently, "but——"

"And I'm a king."

"Yes, yes, that's it, that's it, Katie. This gentleman is a king."

Once more Ted's eye met Katie's, and this time there was an imploring look in it.

"That's right," he said, slowly. "I've just been telling your grandfather I'm the King of Coney Island."

"That's it. Of Coney Island."

"So there's no objection now to us getting married, kid—Your Royal Highness. It's a royal alliance, see?"

"A royal alliance," echoed Mr. Bennett.

Out in the street, Ted held Katie's hand, and grinned a little sheepishly.

"You're mighty quiet, kid," he said. "It looks as if it don't make much of a hit with you, the notion of being married to me."

"Oh, Ted! But——'

He squeezed her hand.

"I know what you're thinking. I guess it was raw work pulling a tale like that on the old man. I hated to do it, but, gee! when a fellow's up against it like I was, he's apt to grab most any chance that comes along. Why, say, kid, it kind of looked to me as if it was sort of *meant*. Coming just now, like it did, just when it was wanted, and just when it didn't seem possible it could happen. Why, a week ago I was nigh on two hundred votes behind Billy Burton. The Irish-American put him up, and everybody thought he'd be King at the Mardi Gras. And then suddenly they came pouring in for me, till at the finish I had Billy looking like a regular has-been.

"It's funny the way the voting jumps about every year in this Coney election. It was just Providence, and it didn't seem right to let it go by. So I went in to the old man, and told him. Say, I tell you I was just sweating when I got ready to hand it to him. It was an outside chance he'd remember all about what the Mardi Gras at Coney was, and just what being a king at it amounted to. Then I remembered you telling me you'd never been to Coney, so I figured your grandfather wouldn't be what you'd call well fixed in his information about it, so I took the chance.

" I tried him out first. I tried him with Brooklyn. Why, say, from the way he took it, he'd either never heard of the place, or else he'd forgotten what it was. I guess he don't remember much, poor old fellow. Then I mentioned Yonkers. He asked me what Yonkers were. Then I reckoned it was safe to bring on Coney, and he fell for it right away, I felt mean, but it had to be done."

He caught her up, and swung her into the air with a perfectly impassive face. Then, having kissed her, he lowered her gently to the ground again. The action seemed to have relieved his feelings, for when he spoke again it was plain that his conscience no longer troubled him.

" And say," he said, " come to think of it, I don't see where there's so much call for me to feel mean. I'm not so far short of being a regular king. Coney's just as big as some of those kingdoms you read about on the other side ; and, from what you see in the papers about the goings-on there, it looks to me that, having a whole week on the throne like I'm going to have, amounts to a pretty steady job as kings go."

AT GEISENHEIMER'S

AS I walked to Geisenheimer's that night I was feeling blue and restless, tired of New York, tired of dancing, tired of everything. Broadway was full of people hurrying to the theatres. Cars rattled by. All the electric lights in the world were blazing down on the Great White Way. And it all seemed stale and dreary to me.

Geisenheimer's was full as usual. All the tables were occupied, and there were several couples already on the dancing-floor in the centre. The band was playing "Michigan":

> I want to go back, I want to go back
> To the place where I was born.
> Far away from harm
> With a milk-pail on my arm.

I suppose the fellow who wrote that would have called for the police if anyone had ever really tried to get him on to a farm, but he has certainly put something into the tune which makes you think he meant what he said. It's a home-sick tune, that.

I was just looking round for an empty table, when a man jumped up and came towards me, registering joy as if I had been his long-lost sister.

He was from the country. I could see that. It was written all over him, from his face to his shoes.

He came up with his hand out, beaming.

"Why, Miss Roxborough!"

"Why not?" I said.

"Don't you remember me?"

I didn't.

"My name is Ferris."

"It's a nice name, but it means nothing in my young life."

"I was introduced to you last time I came here. We danced together."

This seemed to bear the stamp of truth. If he was introduced to me, he probably danced with me. It's what I'm at Geisenheimer's for.

"When was it?"

"A year ago last April."

You can't beat these rural charmers. They think New York is folded up and put away in camphor when they leave, and only taken out again when they pay their next visit. The notion that anything could possibly have happened since he was last in our midst to blur the memory of that happy evening had not occurred to Mr. Ferris. I suppose he was so accustomed to dating things from "when I was in New York" that he thought everybody else must do the same.

"Why, sure, I remember you," I said. "Algernon Clarence, isn't it?"

"Not Algernon Clarence. My name's Charlie."

"My mistake. And what's the great scheme, Mr. Ferris? Do you want to dance with me again?"

He did. So we started. Mine not to reason why, mine but to do and die, as the poem says. If an elephant had come into Geisenheimer's and asked me to dance, I'd have had to do it. And I'm not saying that Mr. Ferris wasn't the next thing to it. He was one of those earnest, persevering dancers—the kind that have taken twelve correspondence lessons.

I guess I was about due that night to meet some one from the country. There still come days in the spring when the country seems to get a stranglehold on me and start in pulling. This particular day had been one of them. I got up in the morning and looked out of the window, and the breeze just wrapped me round and began whispering about pigs and chickens. And when I went out on Fifth Avenue there seemed to be flowers everywhere. I headed for the Park, and there was the grass all green, and the trees coming out, and a sort of something in the air—why, say, if there hadn't have been a big policeman keeping an eye on me, I'd have flung myself down and bitten chunks out of the turf.

And as soon as I got to Geisenheimer's they played that "Michigan" thing.

Why, Charlie from Squeedunk's "entrance" couldn't have been better worked up if he'd been a star in a Broadway show. The stage was just waiting for him.

But somebody's always taking the joy out of life. I ought to have remembered that the most metropolitan thing in the metropolis is a rustic who's putting in a week there. We weren't thinking on the same plane, Charlie and me. The way I had been feeling all day, what I wanted to talk about was last season's crops. The subject he fancied was this season's chorus-girls. Our souls didn't touch by a mile and a half.

"This is the life!" he said.

There's always a point when that sort of man says that.

"I suppose you come here quite a lot?" he said.

"Pretty often."

I didn't tell him that I came there every night, and that I came because I was paid for it. If you're a professional dancer at Geisenheimer's, you aren't supposed to advertise the fact. The management thinks that if you did it might send the public away thinking too hard when they saw you win the Great Contest for the Love—r—ly Silver Cup which they offer later in the evening. Say, that Love—r—ly Cup's a joke. I win it on Mondays, Wednesdays, and Fridays, and Mabel Francis wins it on Tuesdays, Thursdays, and Saturdays. It's all perfectly fair and square, of course. It's purely a matter of merit who wins the Love—r—ly Cup. Anybody could win it. Only somehow they don't. And the coincidence of the fact that Mabel and I always do has kind of got on the management's nerves, and they don't like us to tell people we're employed there. They prefer us to blush unseen."

"It's a great place," said Mr. Ferris, "and New York's a great place. I'd like to live in New York."

"The loss is ours. Why don't you?"

"Some city! But dad's dead now, and I've got the drug-store, you know."

He spoke as if I ought to remember reading about it in the papers.

"And I'm making good with it, what's more. I've got push and ideas. Say, I got married since I saw you last."

"You did, did you?" I said. "Then what are you doing, may I ask, dancing on Broadway like a gay bachelor? I suppose you have left your wife at Hicks' Corners, singing 'Where is my wandering boy to-night?'"

"Not Hicks' Corners. Ashley, Maine. That's where I live. My wife comes from Rodney. . . . Pardon me, I'm afraid I stepped on your foot."

"My fault," I said; "I lost step. Well, I wonder you aren't ashamed even to think of your wife, when you've left her all alone out there while you come whooping it up in New York. Haven't you got any conscience?"

"But I haven't left her. She's here."

"In New York?"

"In this restaurant. That's her up there."

I looked up at the balcony. There was a face hanging over the red plush rail. It looked to me as if it had some hidden sorrow. I'd noticed it before, when we were dancing around, and I had wondered what the trouble was. Now I began to see.

"Why aren't you dancing with her and giving her a good time, then?" I said.

"Oh, she's having a good time."

"She doesn't look it. She looks as if she would like to be down here, treading the measure."

"She doesn't dance much."

"Don't you have dances at Ashley?"

"It's different at home. She dances well enough for Ashley, but—well, this isn't Ashley."

"I see. But *you're* not like that?"

He gave a kind of smirk.

"Oh, I've been in New York before."

I could have bitten him, the sawn-off little rube! It made me mad. He was ashamed to dance in public with his wife—didn't think her good enough for him. So he had dumped her in a chair, given her a lemonade, and told her to be good, and then gone off to have a good time. They could have had me arrested for what I was thinking just then.

The band began to play something else.

"This is the life!" said Mr. Ferris. "Let's do it again."

"Let somebody else do it," I said. "I'm tired. I'll introduce you to some friends of mine."

So I took him off, and whisked him on to some girls I knew at one of the tables.

"Shake hands with my friend Mr. Ferris," I said. "He wants to show you the latest steps. He does most of them on your feet."

I could have betted on Charlie, the Debonair Pride of Ashley. Guess what he said? He said, "This is the life!"

And I left him, and went up to the balcony.

She was leaning with her elbows on the red plush, looking down on the dancing-floor. They had just started another tune, and hubby was moving around with one of the girls I'd introduced him to. She didn't have to prove to me that she came from the country. I knew it. She was a little bit of a thing, old-fashioned looking. She was dressed in grey, with white muslin collar and cuffs, and her hair done simple. She had a black hat.

I kind of hovered for awhile. It isn't the best thing I do, being shy; as a general thing I'm more or less there with the nerve; but somehow I sort of hesitated to charge in.

Then I braced up, and made for the vacant chair.

"I'll sit here, if you don't mind," I said.

She turned in a startled way. I could see she was wondering who I was, and what right I had there, but wasn't certain whether it might not be city etiquette for strangers to come and dump themselves down and start chatting. "I've just been dancing with your husband," I said, to ease things along.

"I saw you."

She fixed me with a pair of big brown eyes. I took one look at them, and then I had to tell myself that it might be pleasant, and a relief to my feelings, to take something solid and heavy and drop it over the rail on to hubby, but the management wouldn't like it. That was how I felt about him just then. The poor kid was doing everything with those eyes except crying. She looked like a dog that's been kicked.

She looked away, and fiddled with the string of the electric light. There was a hatpin lying on the table. She picked it up, and began to dig at the red plush.

"Ah, come on, sis," I said; "tell me all about it."

"I don't know what you mean."

"You can't fool me. Tell me your troubles."

"I don't know you."

"You don't have to know a person to tell her your troubles. I sometimes tell mine to the cat that camps out on the wall opposite my room. What did you want to leave the country for, with the summer coming on?"

She didn't answer, but I could see it coming, so I sat still and waited. And presently she seemed to make up her mind that, even if it was no business of mine, it would be a relief to talk about it.

"We're on our honeymoon. Charlie wanted to come to New York. I didn't want to, but he was set on it. He's been here before."

"So he told me."

"He's wild about New York."

"But you're not."

"I hate it."

"Why?"

She dug away at the red plush with the hatpin, picking out little bits and dropping them over the edge. I could see she was bracing herself to put me wise to the whole trouble. There's a time comes when things aren't going right, and you've had all you can stand, when you have got to tell somebody about it, no matter who it is.

"I hate New York," she said, getting it out at last with a rush. "I'm scared of it. It—it isn't fair Charlie bringing me here. I didn't want to come. I knew what would happen. I felt it all along."

"What do you think will happen, then?"

She must have picked away at least an inch of the red plush before she answered. It's lucky Jimmy, the balcony waiter, didn't see her; it would have broken his heart; he's as proud of that red plush as if he had paid for it himself.

"When I first went to live at Rodney," she said, "two years ago—we moved there from Illinois—there was a man there named Tyson—Jack Tyson. He lived all alone and didn't seem to want to know anyone. I couldn't understand it till somebody told me all about him. I can understand it now. Jack Tyson married a Rodney girl, and they came to New York for their honeymoon, just like us. And when they got there I guess she got to comparing him with the fellows she saw, and comparing the city with Rodney, and when she got home she just couldn't settle down."

"Well?"

"After they had been back in Rodney for a little while she ran away. Back to the city, I guess."

"I suppose he got a divorce?"

"No, he didn't. He still thinks she may come back to him."

"He still thinks she will come back?" I said. "After she has been away three years!"

"Yes. He keeps her things just the same as she left them when she went away, everything just the same."

"But isn't he angry with her for what she did? If I was a man and a girl treated me that way, I'd be apt to murder her if she tried to show up again."

"He wouldn't. Nor would I, if—if anything like that happened to me; I'd wait and wait, and go on hoping all the time. And I'd go down to the station to meet the train every afternoon, just like Jack Tyson."

Something splashed on the tablecloth. It made me jump.

"For goodness' sake," I said, "what's your trouble? Brace up. I know it's a sad story, but it's not your funeral."

"It is. It is. The same thing's going to happen to me."

"Take a hold on yourself. Don't cry like that."

"I can't help it. Oh! I knew it would happen. It's happening right now. Look—look at him."

I glanced over the rail, and I saw what she meant. There was her Charlie, dancing about all over the floor as if he had just discovered that he hadn't lived till then. I saw him say something to the girl he was dancing with. I wasn't near enough to hear it, but I bet it was "This is the life!" If I had been his wife, in the same position as this kid, I guess I'd have felt as bad as she did, for if ever a man exhibited all the symptoms of incurable Newyorkitis, it was this Charlie Ferris.

"I'm not like these New York girls," she choked. "I can't be smart. I don't want to be. I just want to live at home and be happy. I knew it would happen if we came to the city. He doesn't think me good enough for him. He looks down on me."

"Pull yourself together."

"And I do love him so!"

Goodness knows what I should have said if I could have thought of anything to say. But just then the music stopped, and somebody on the floor below began to speak.

"Ladeez 'n' gemmen," he said, "there will now take place our great Numbah Contest. This gen—u—ine sporting contest——"

It was Izzy Baermann making his nightly speech, introducing the Love—r—ly Cup; and it meant that, for me, duty called. From where I sat I could see Izzy looking about the room, and I knew he was looking for me. It's the management's nightmare that one of these evenings Mabel or I won't show up, and somebody else will get away with the Love—r—ly Cup.

"Sorry I've got to go," I said. "I have to be in this."

And then suddenly I had the great idea. It came to me like a flash. I looked at her, crying there, and I looked over the rail at Charlie the Boy Wonder, and I knew that this was where I got a stranglehold on my place in the Hall of Fame, along with the great thinkers of the age.

"Come on," I said. "Come along. Stop crying and powder your nose and get a move on. You're going to dance this."

"But Charlie doesn't want to dance with me."

"It may have escaped your notice," I said, "but your Charlie is not the only man in New York, or even in this restaurant. I'm going to dance with Charlie myself, and I'll introduce you to some one who can go through the movements. Listen!"

"The lady of each couple"—this was Izzy, getting it off his diaphragm—"will receive a ticket containing a num—bah. The dance will then proceed, and the num—bahs will be eliminated one by one, those called out by the judge kindly returning to their seats as their num—bah is called. The num—bah finally remaining is the winning num—bah. The contest is a genuine sporting contest, decided purely by the skill of the holders of the various num—bahs." (Izzy stopped blushing at the age of six.) "Will ladies now kindly step forward and receive their num—bahs. The winner, the holder of the num—bah left on the floor when the other num—bahs have been eliminated" (I could see Izzy getting more and more uneasy, wondering where on earth I'd got to) "will receive this Love—r—ly Silver Cup, presented by the management. Ladies will now kindly step forward and receive their num—bahs."

I turned to Mrs. Charlie. "There," I said, "don't you want to win a Love—r—ly Silver Cup?"

"But I couldn't."

"You never know your luck."

"But it isn't luck. Didn't you hear him say it's a contest decided purely by skill?"

"Well, try your skill, then." I felt as if I could have shaken her. "For goodness' sake," I said, "show a little grit. Aren't you going to stir a finger to keep your Charlie? Suppose you win, think what it will mean. He will look up to you for the rest of your life. When he starts talking about New York, all you will have to say is, 'New York? Ah, yes, that was the town I won that Love—r—ly Silver Cup in, was it not?' and he'll drop as if you had hit him behind the ear with a sand-bag. Pull yourself together and try."

I saw those brown eyes of hers flash, and she said, "I'll try."

"Good for you," I said. "Now you get those tears dried, and fix yourself up, and I'll go down and get the tickets."

Izzy was mighty relieved when I bore down on him.

"Gee!" he said, "I thought you had run away, or was sick or something. Here's your ticket."

"I want two, Izzy. One's for a friend of mine. And I say, Izzy, I'd take it as a personal favour if you would let her stop on the floor as one of the last two couples. There's a reason. She's a kid from the country, and she wants to make a hit."

"Sure, that'll be all right. Here are the tickets. Yours is thirty-six, hers is ten." He lowered his voice. "Don't go mixing them."

I went back to the balcony. On the way I got hold of Charlie.

"We're dancing this together," I said.

He grinned all across his face.

I found Mrs. Charlie looking as if she had never shed a tear in her life. She certainly had pluck, that kid.

"Come on," I said. "Stick to your ticket like wax and watch your step."

I guess you've seen these sporting contests at Geisenheimer's. Or, if you haven't seen them at Geisenheimer's, you've seen them somewhere else. They're all the same.

When we began, the floor was so crowded that there was hardly elbow-room. Don't tell me there aren't any optimists nowadays. Every one was looking as if they were wondering whether to have the Love—r—ly Cup in the sitting-room or the bedroom. You never saw such a hopeful gang in your life.

Presently Izzy gave tongue. The management expects him to be humorous on these occasions, so he did his best.

"Num—bahs seven, eleven, and twenty-one will kindly rejoin their sorrowing friends."

This gave us a little more elbow-room, and the band started again.

A few minutes later, Izzy once more: "Num—bahs thirteen, sixteen, and seventeen—good-bye."

Off we went again.

"Num—bah twelve, we hate to part with you, but—back to your table!"

A plump girl in a red hat, who had been dancing with a kind smile, as if she were doing it to amuse the children, left the floor.

"Num—bahs six, fifteen, and twenty, thumbs down!"

And pretty soon the only couples left were Charlie and me, Mrs. Charlie and the fellow I'd introduced her to, and a bald-headed man and a girl in a white hat. He was one of your stick-at-it performers. He had been dancing all the evening. I had noticed him from the balcony. He looked like a hard-boiled egg from up there.

He was a trier all right, that fellow, and had things been otherwise, so to speak, I'd have been glad to see him win. But it was not to be. Ah, no!

"Num—bah nineteen, you're getting all flushed. Take a rest."

So there it was, a straight contest between me and Charlie and Mrs. Charlie and her man. Every nerve in my system was tingling with suspense and excitement, was it not? It was not.

Charlie, as I've already hinted, was not a dancer who took much of his attention off his feet while in action. He was there to do his durnedest, not to inspect objects of interest by the wayside. The correspondence college he'd attended doesn't guarantee to teach you to do two things at once. It won't bind itself to teach you to look round the room while you're dancing. So Charlie hadn't the least suspicion of the state of the drama. He was breathing heavily down my neck in a determined sort of way, with his eyes glued to the floor. All he knew was that the competition had thinned out a bit, and the honour of Ashley, Maine, was in his hands.

You know how the public begins to sit up and take notice when these dance-contests have been narrowed down to two couples. There are evenings when I quite forget myself, when I'm one of the last two left in, and get all excited. There's a sort of hum in the air, and, as you go round the room, people at the tables start applauding. Why, if you didn't know about the inner workings of the thing, you'd be all of a twitter.

It didn't take my practised ear long to discover that it wasn't me and Charlie that the great public was cheering for. We would go round the floor without getting a hand, and every time Mrs. Charlie and her guy got to a corner there was a noise like election night. She sure had made a hit.

I took a look at her across the floor, and I didn't wonder. She was a different kid from what she'd been upstairs. I never saw anybody look so happy and pleased with herself. Her eyes were like lamps, and her cheeks all pink, and she was going at it like a champion. I knew what had made a hit with the people. It was the look of her. She made you think of fresh milk and new-laid eggs and birds singing. To see her was like getting away to the country in August. It's funny about people who live in the city. They chuck out their chests, and talk about little old New York being good enough for them, and there's a street in heaven they call Broadway, and all the rest of it; but it seems to me that what they really live for is that three weeks in the summer when they get away into the country. I knew exactly why they were cheering so hard for Mrs. Charlie. She made them think of their holidays which were coming along, when they would go and board at the farm and drink out of the old oaken bucket, and call the cows by their first names.

Gee! I felt just like that myself. All day the country had been tugging at me, and now it tugged worse than ever.

I could have smelled the new-mown hay if it wasn't that when you're in Geisenheimer's you have to smell Geisenheimer's, because it leaves no chance for competition.

"Keep working," I said to Charlie. "It looks to me as if we were going back in the betting."

"Uh, huh!" he says, too busy to blink.

"Do some of those fancy steps of yours. We need them in our business."

And the way that boy worked—it was astonishing!

Out of the corner of my eye I could see Izzy Baermann, and he wasn't looking happy. He was nerving himself for one of those quick referee's decisions—the sort you make and then duck under the ropes, and run five miles, to avoid the incensed populace. It was this kind of thing happening every now and then that prevented his job being perfect. Mabel Francis told me that one night when Izzy declared her the winner of the great sporting contest, it was such raw work that she thought there'd have been a riot. It looked pretty much as if he was afraid the same thing was going to happen now. There wasn't a doubt which of us two couples was the one that the customers wanted to see win that Love—r—ly Silver Cup. It was a walk-over for Mrs. Charlie, and Charlie and I were simply among those present.

But Izzy had his duty to do, and drew a salary for doing it, so he moistened his lips, looked round to see that his strategic railways weren't blocked, swallowed twice, and said in a husky voice:

"Num—bah ten, please re—tiah!"

I stopped at once.

"Come along," said I to Charlie. "That's our exit cue."

And we walked off the floor amidst applause.

"Well," says Charlie, taking out his handkerchief and attending to his brow, which was like the village blacksmith's, "we didn't do so bad, did we? We didn't do so bad, I guess! We——"

And he looked up at the balcony, expecting to see the dear little wife, draped over the rail, worshipping him; when, just as his eye is moving up, it gets caught by the sight of her a whole heap lower down than he had expected—on the floor, in fact.

She wasn't doing much in the worshipping line just at that moment. She was too busy.

It was a regular triumphal progress for the kid. She and her partner were doing one or two rounds now for exhibition purposes, like the winning couple always do at Geisenheimer's, and the room was fairly rising at them. You'd have thought from the way they were clapping that they had been betting all their spare cash on her.

Charlie gets her well focussed, then he lets his jaw drop, till he pretty near bumped it against the floor.

"But—but—but——" he begins.

"I know," I said. "It begins to look as if she could dance well enough for the city after all. It begins to look as if she had sort of put one over on somebody, don't it? It begins to look as if it were a pity you didn't think of dancing with her yourself."

"I—I—I——"

"You come along and have a nice cold drink," I said, "and you'll soon pick up."

He tottered after me to a table, looking as if he had been hit by a street-car. He had got his.

I was so busy looking after Charlie, flapping the towel and working on him with the oxygen, that, if you'll believe me, it wasn't for quite a time that I thought of glancing around to see how the thing had struck Izzy Baermann.

If you can imagine a fond father whose only son has hit him with a brick, jumped on his stomach, and then gone off with all his money, you have a pretty good notion of how poor old Izzy looked. He was staring at me across the room, and talking to himself and jerking his hands about. Whether he thought he was talking to me, or whether he was rehearsing the scene where he broke it to the boss that a mere stranger had got away with his Love—r—ly Silver Cup, I don't know. Whichever it was, he was being mighty eloquent.

I gave him a nod, as much as to say that it would all come right in the future, and then I turned to Charlie again. He was beginning to pick up.

"She won the cup!" he said in a dazed voice, looking at me as if I could do something about it.

"You bet she did!"

"But—well, what do you know about that?"

I saw that the moment had come to put it straight to him.

"I'll tell you what I know about it," I said. "If you take my advice, you'll hustle that kid straight back to Ashley—or wherever it is that you said you poison the natives by making up the wrong prescriptions—before she gets New York into her system. When I was talking to her upstairs, she was telling me about a fellow in her village who got it in the neck just the same as you're apt to do."

He started. "She was telling you about Jack Tyson?"

"That was his name—Jack Tyson. He lost his wife through letting her have too much New York. Don't you think it's funny she should have mentioned him if she hadn't had some idea that she might act just the same as his wife did?"

He turned quite green.

"You don't think she would do that?"

"Well, if you'd heard her—— She couldn't talk of anything except this Tyson, and what his wife did to him. She talked of it sort of sad, kind of regretful, as if she was sorry, but felt that it had to be. I could see she had been thinking about it a whole lot."

Charlie stiffened in his seat, and then began to melt with pure fright. He took up his empty glass with a shaking hand and drank a long drink out of it. It didn't take much observation to see that he had had the jolt he wanted, and was going to be a whole heap less jaunty and metropolitan from now on. In fact, the way he looked, I should say he had finished with metropolitan jauntiness for the rest of his life.

"I'll take her home to-morrow," he said. "But—will she come?"

"That's up to you. If you can persuade her—— Here she is now. I should start at once."

Mrs. Charlie, carrying the cup, came to the table. I was wondering what would be the first thing she would say. If it had been Charlie, of course he'd have said, "This is the life!" but I looked for something snappier from her. If I had been in her place there were at least ten things I could have thought of to say, each nastier than the other.

She sat down and put the cup on the table. Then she gave the cup a long look. Then she drew a deep breath. Then she looked at Charlie.

"Oh, Charlie, dear," she said, "I do wish I'd been dancing with you!"

Well, I'm not sure that that wasn't just as good as

anything I would have said. Charlie got right off the mark. After what I had told him, he wasn't wasting any time.

"Darling," he said, humbly, "you're a wonder! What will they say about this at home?" He did pause here for a moment, for it took nerve to say it, but then he went right on. "Mary, how would it be if we went home right away—first train to-morrow, and showed it to them?"

"Oh, Charlie!" she said.

His face lit up as if somebody had pulled a switch.

"You will? You don't want to stop on? You aren't wild about New York?"

"If there was a train," she said, "I'd start to-night. But I thought you loved the city so, Charlie?"

He gave a kind of shiver. "I never want to see it again in my life!" he said.

"You'll excuse me," I said, getting up, "I think there's a friend of mine wants to speak to me."

And I crossed over to where Izzy had been standing for the last five minutes, making signals to me with his eyebrows.

You couldn't have called Izzy coherent at first. He certainly had trouble with his vocal chords, poor fellow. There was one of those African explorer men used to come to Geisenheimer's a lot when he was home from roaming the trackless desert, and he used to tell me about tribes he had met who didn't use real words at all, but talked to one another in clicks and gurgles. He imitated some of their chatter one night to amuse me, and, believe me, Izzy Baermann started talking the same language now. Only he didn't do it to amuse me.

He was like one of those gramophone records when it's getting into its stride.

"Be calm, Isadore," I said. "Something is troubling you. Tell me all about it."

He clicked some more, and then he got it out

"Say, are you crazy? What did you do it for? Didn't I tell you as plain as I could; didn't I say it twenty times, when you came for the tickets, that yours was thirty-six?"

"Didn't you say my friends' was thirty-six?"

"Are you deaf? I said hers was ten."

"Then," I said handsomely, "say no more. The mistake was mine. It begins to look as if I must have got them mixed."

He did a few Swedish exercises.

"Say no more? That's good! That's great! You've got nerve. I'll say that."

"It was a lucky mistake, Izzy. It saved your life. The people would have lynched you if you had given me the cup. They were solid for her."

"What's the boss going to say when I tell him?"

"Never mind what the boss will say. Haven't you any romance in your system, Izzy? Look at those two sitting there with their heads together. Isn't it worth a silver cup to have made them happy for life? They are on their honeymoon, Isadore. Tell the boss exactly how it happened, and say that I thought it was up to Geisenheimer's to give them a wedding-present."

He clicked for a spell.

"Ah!" he said. "Ah! now you've done it! Now you've given yourself away! You did it on purpose. You mixed those tickets on purpose. I thought as much. Say, who do you think you are, doing this sort of thing? Don't you know that professional dancers are three for ten cents? I could go out right now and whistle, and get a dozen girls for your job. The boss'll sack you just one minute after I tell him."

"No, he won't, Izzy, because I'm going to resign."

"You'd better!"

"That's what I think. I'm sick of this place, Izzy. I'm sick of dancing. I'm sick of New York. I'm sick of everything. I'm going back to the country. I thought I had got the pigs and chickens clear out of my system, but I hadn't. I've suspected it for a long, long time, and to-night I know it. Tell the boss, with my love, that I'm sorry, but it had to be done. And if he wants to talk back, he must do it by letter: 'Mrs. John Tyson, Rodney, Maine, is the address."

THE MAKING OF MAC'S

MAC'S RESTAURANT—nobody calls it MacFarland's—is a mystery. It is off the beaten track. It is not smart. It does not advertise. It provides nothing nearer to an orchestra than a solitary piano, yet, with all these things against it, it is a success. In theatrical circles especially it holds a position which might turn the white lights of many a supper-palace green with envy.

This is mysterious. You do not expect Soho to compete with and even eclipse Piccadilly in this way. And when Soho does so compete, there is generally romance of some kind somewhere in the background.

Somebody happened to mention to me casually that Henry, the old waiter, had been at Mac's since its foundation.

"Me?" said Henry, questioned during a slack spell in the afternoon. "Rather!"

"Then can you tell me what it was that first gave the place the impetus which started it on its upward course? What causes should you say were responsible for its phenomenal prosperity? What——"

"What gave it a leg-up? Is that what you're trying to get at?"

"Exactly. What gave it a leg-up? Can you tell me?"

"Me?" said Henry. "Rather!"

And he told me this chapter from the unwritten history of the London whose day begins when Nature's finishes.

Old Mr. MacFarland (*said Henry*) started the place fifteen years ago. He was a widower with one son and what you might call half a daughter. That's to say, he had adopted her. Katie was her name, and she was the child of a dead friend of his. The son's name was Andy. A little freckled nipper he was when I first knew him—one of those silent kids that don't say much and have as much obstinacy in them as if they were mules. Many's the time, in them days, I've clumped him on the head and told him to do something; and he didn't run yelling to his pa, same as most kids would have done, but just said nothing and went on not doing whatever it was I had told him to do. That was the sort of disposition Andy had, and it grew on him. Why, when he came back from Oxford College the time the old man sent for him—what I'm going to tell you about soon—he had a jaw on him like the ram of a battleship. Katie was the kid for my money. I liked Katie. We all liked Katie.

Old MacFarland started out with two big advantages. One was Jules, and the Other was me. Jules came from Paris, and he was the greatest cook you ever seen. And me—well, I was just come from ten years as waiter at the "Guelph," and I won't conceal it from you that I gave the place a tone. I gave Soho something to think about over its chop, believe me. It was a come-down in the world for me, maybe, after the "Guelph," but what I said to myself was that, when you get a tip in Soho, it may be only tuppence, but you keep it; whereas at the "Guelph" about ninety-nine hundredths of it goes to helping to maintain some blooming head waiter in the style to which he has been accustomed. It was through my kind of harping on that fact that me and the "Guelph" parted company. The head waiter complained to the management the day I called him a fat-headed vampire.

Well, what with me and what with Jules, MacFarland's—it wasn't Mac's in them days—began to get a move on. Old MacFarland, who knew a good man when he saw one and always treated me more like a brother than anything else, used to say to me, "Henry, if this keeps up, I'll be able to send the boy to Oxford College"; until one day he changed it to, "Henry, I'm going to send the boy to Oxford College"; and next year, sure enough, off he went.

Katie was sixteen then, and she had just been given the cashier job, as a treat. She wanted to do something to help the old man, so he put her on a high chair behind a wire cage with a hole in it, and she gave the customers their change. And let me tell you, mister, that a man that wasn't satisfied after he'd had me serve him a dinner cooked by Jules and then had a chat with Katie through the wire cage would have groused at Paradise. For she was pretty, was Katie, and getting prettier every day. I spoke to the boss about it. I said it was putting temptation in the girl's way to set her up there right in the public eye, as it were. And he told me to hop it. So I hopped it.

Katie was wild about dancing. Nobody knew it till later, but all this while, it turned out, she was attending regular one of them schools. That was where she went to in the afternoons, when we all thought she was visiting girl friends. It all come out after, but she fooled us then. Girls are like monkeys when it comes to artfulness. She called me Uncle Bill, because she said the name Henry always reminded her of cold mutton. If it had been young Andy that had said it I'd have clumped him one ; but he never said anything like that. Come to think of it, he never said anything much at all. He just thought a heap without opening his face.

So young Andy went off to college, and I said to him, "Now then, you young devil, you be a credit to us, or I'll fetch you a clip when you come home." And Katie said, "Oh, Andy, I *shall* miss you." And Andy didn't say nothing to me, and he didn't say nothing to Katie, but he gave her a look, and later in the day I found her crying, and she said she'd got toothache, and I went round the corner to the chemist's and brought her something for it.

It was in the middle of Andy's second year at college that the old man had the stroke which put him out of business. He went down under it as if he'd been hit with an axe, and the doctor tells him he'll never be able to leave his bed again.

So they sent for Andy, and he quit his college, and come back to London to look after the restaurant.

I was sorry for the kid. I told him so in a fatherly kind of way. And he just looked at me and says, "Thanks very much, Henry."

"What must be must be," I says. "Maybe, it's all for the best. Maybe it's better you're here than in among all those young devils in your Oxford school what might be leading you astray."

"If you would think less of me and more of your work, Henry," he says, "perhaps that gentleman over there wouldn't have to shout sixteen times for the waiter."

Which, on looking into it, I found to be the case, and he went away without giving me no tip, which shows what you lose in a hard world by being sympathetic.

I'm bound to say that young Andy showed us all jolly quick that he hadn't come home just to be an ornament about the place. There was exactly one boss in the restaurant, and it was him. It come a little hard at first to have to be respectful to a kid whose head you had spent many a happy hour in clumping for his own good in the past; but he pretty soon showed me I could do it if I tried, and I done it. As for Jules and the two young fellers that had been taken on to help me owing to increase of business, they would jump through hoops and roll over if he just looked at them. He was a boy who liked his own way, was Andy, and, believe me, at MacFarland's Restaurant he got it.

And then, when things had settled down into a steady jog, Katie took the bit in her teeth.

She done it quite quiet and unexpected one afternoon when there was only me and her and Andy in the place. And I don't think either of them knew I was there, for I was taking an easy on a chair at the back, reading a evening paper.

She said, kind of quiet, "Oh, Andy."

"Yes, darling," he said.

And that was the first I knew that there was anything between them.

"Andy, I've something to tell you."

"What is it?"

She kind of hesitated.

"Andy, dear, I shan't be able to help any more in the restaurant."

He looked at her, sort of surprised.

"What do you mean?"

"I'm—I'm going on the stage."

I put down my paper. What do you mean? Did I listen? Of course I listened. What do you take me for?

From where I sat I could see young Andy's face, and I didn't need any more to tell me there was going to be trouble. That jaw of his was right out. I forgot to tell you that the old man had died, poor old feller, maybe six months before, so that now Andy was the real boss instead of just acting boss; and what's more, in the nature of things, he was, in a manner of speaking, Katie's guardian, with power to tell her what she could do and what she couldn't. And I felt that Katie wasn't going to have any smooth passage with this stage business which she was giving him. Andy didn't hold with the stage—not with any girl he was fond of being on it anyway. And when Andy didn't like a thing he said so.

He said so now.

"You aren't going to do anything of the sort."

"Don't be horrid about it, Andy, dear. I've got a big chance. Why should you be horrid about it?"

"I'm not going to argue about it. You don't go."

"But it's such a big chance. And I've been working for it for years."

"How do you mean working for it?"

And then it come out about this dancing-school she'd been attending regular.

When she'd finished telling him about it, he just shoved out his jaw another inch.

"You aren't going on the stage."

"But it's such a chance. I saw Mr. Mandelbaum yesterday, and he saw me dance, and he was very pleased, and said he would give me a solo dance to do in this new piece he's putting on."

"You aren't going on the stage."

What I always say is, you can't beat tact. If you're

smooth and tactful you can get folks to do anything you want; but if you just shove your jaw out at them, and order them about, why, then they get their backs up and sauce you. I knew Katie well enough to know that she would do anything for Andy, if he asked her properly; but she wasn't going to stand this sort of thing. But you couldn't drive that into the head of a feller like young Andy with a steam-hammer.

She flared up, quick, as if she couldn't hold herself in no longer.

"I certainly am," she said.

"You know what it means?"

"What does it mean?"

"The end of—everything."

She kind of blinked as if he'd hit her, then she chucks her chin up.

"Very well," she says. "Good-bye."

"Good-bye," says Andy, the pig-headed young mule; and she walks out one way and he walks out another.

I don't follow the drama much as a general rule, but seeing that it was now, so to speak, in the family, I did keep an eye open for the newspaper notices of "The Rose Girl," which was the name of the piece which Mr. Mandelbaum was letting Katie do a solo dance in; and while some of them cussed the play considerable, they all gave Katie a nice word. One feller said that she was like cold water on the morning after, which is high praise coming from a newspaper man.

There wasn't a doubt about it. She was a success. You see, she was something new, and London always sits up and takes notice when you give it that.

There were pictures of her in the papers, and one evening paper had a piece about "How I Preserve my Youth" signed by her. I cut it out and showed it to Andy.

He gave it a look. Then he gave me a look, and I didn't like his eye.

"Well?" he says.

"Pardon," I says.

"What about it?" he says.

"I don't know," I says.

"Get back to your work," he says.

So I got back.

It was that same night that the queer thing happened. We didn't do much in the supper line at MacFarland's as a rule in them days, but we kept open, of course, in case Soho should take it into its head to treat itself to a welsh rabbit before going to bed; so all hands was on deck, ready for the call if it should come, at half-past eleven that night; but we weren't what you might term sanguine.

Well, just on the half-hour, up drives a taxicab, and in comes a party of four. There was a nut, another nut, a girl, and another girl. And the second girl was Katie.

"Hallo, Uncle Bill!" she says.

"Good evening, madam," I says dignified, being on duty.

"Oh, stop it, Uncle Bill," she says. "Say 'Hallo!' to a pal, and smile prettily, or I'll tell them about the time you went to the White City."

Well, there's some bygones that are best left bygones, and the night at the White City what she was alluding to was one of them. I still maintain, as I always shall maintain, that the constable had no right to—but, there, it's a story that wouldn't interest you. And, anyway, I was glad to see Katie again, so I give her a smile.

"Not so much of it," I says. "Not so much of it. I'm glad to see you, Katie."

"Three cheers! Jimmy, I want to introduce you to my friend, Uncle Bill. Ted, this is Uncle Bill. Violet, this is Uncle Bill."

It wasn't my place to fetch her one on the side of the head, but I'd of liked to have; for she was acting like she'd never used to act when I knew her—all tough and bold. Then it come to me that she was nervous. And natural, too, seeing young Andy might pop out any moment.

And sure enough out he popped from the back room at that very instant. Katie looked at him, and he looked at Katie, and I seen his face get kind of hard; but he didn't say a word. And presently he went out again.

I heard Katie breathe sort of deep.

"He's looking well, Uncle Bill, ain't he?" she says to me, very soft.

"Pretty fair," I says. "Well, kid, I been reading the pieces in the papers. You've knocked 'em."

"Ah, don't, Bill," she says, as if I'd hurt her. And me meaning only to say the civil thing. Girls are rum.

When the party had paid their bill and give me a tip which made me think I was back at the "Guelph" again—only there weren't any Dick Turpin of a head waiter standing by for his share—they hopped it. But Katie hung back and had a word with me.

"He *was* looking well, wasn't he, Uncle Bill?"

"Rather!"

"Does—does he ever speak of me?"

"I ain't heard him."

"I suppose he's still pretty angry with me, isn't he, Uncle Bill? You're sure you've never heard him speak of me?"

So, to cheer her up, I tells her about the piece in the paper I showed him; but it didn't seem to cheer her up any. And she goes out.

The very next night in she come again for supper, but with different nuts and different girls. There was six of them this time, counting her. And they'd hardly sat down at their table, when in come the fellers she had called Jimmy and Ted with two girls. And they sat eating of their suppers and chaffing one another across the floor, all as pleasant and sociable as you please.

"I say, Katie," I heard one of the nuts say, "you were right. He's worth the price of admission."

I don't know who they meant, but they all laughed. And every now and again I'd hear them praising the food, which I don't wonder at, for Jules had certainly done himself proud. All artistic temperament, these Frenchmen are. The moment I told him we had company, so to speak, he blossomed like a flower does when you put it in water.

"Ah, see, at last!" he says, trying to grab me and kiss me. "Our fame has gone abroad in the world which amuses himself, ain't it? For a good supper connection I have always prayed, and he has arrived."

Well, it did begin to look as if he was right. Ten high-class supper-folk in an evening was pretty hot stuff for MacFarland's. I'm bound to say I got excited myself. I can't deny that I missed the "Guelph" at times.

On the fifth night, when the place was fairly packed and looked for all the world like Oddy's or Romano's, and me and the two young fellers helping me was working double tides, I suddenly understood, and I went up to Katie and, bending over her very respectful with a bottle, I whispers, "Hot stuff, kid. This is a jolly fine boom you're working for the old place." And by the way she smiled back at me, I seen I had guessed right.

Andy was hanging round, keeping an eye on things, as he always done, and I says to him, when I was passing, "She's doing us proud, bucking up the old place, ain't she?" And he says, "Get on with your work." And I got on.

Katie hung back at the door, when she was on her way out, and had a word with me.

"Has he said anything about me, Uncle Bill?"

"Not a word," I says.

And she goes out.

You've probably noticed about London, mister, that a flock of sheep isn't in it with the nuts, the way they all troop on each other's heels to supper-places. One month they're all going to one place, next month to another. Some one in the push starts the cry that he's found a new place, and off they all go to try it. The trouble with most of the places is that once they've got the custom they think it's going to keep on coming and all they've got to do is to lean back and watch it come. Popularity comes in at the door, and good food and good service flies out at the window. We wasn't going to have any of that at MacFarland's. Even if it hadn't been that Andy would have come down like half a ton of bricks on the first sign of slackness, Jules and me both of us had our professional reputations to keep up. I didn't give myself no airs when I seen things coming our way. I worked all the harder, and I seen to it that the four young fellers under me—there was four now—didn't lose no time fetching of the orders.

The consequence was that the difference between us and most popular restaurants was that we kept our popularity. We fed them well, and we served them well; and once the thing had started rolling it didn't stop. Soho isn't so very far away from the centre of things, when you come to look at it, and they didn't mind the extra step, seeing that there was something good at the end of it. So we got our popularity, and we kept our popularity; and we've got it to this day. That's how MacFarland's came to be what it is, mister.

With the air of one who has told a well-rounded tale, Henry ceased, and observed that it was wonderful the way Mr. Woodward, of Chelsea, preserved his skill in spite of his advanced years.

I stared at him.

"But, heavens, man!" I cried, "you surely don't think you've finished? What about Katie and Andy? What happened to them? Did they ever come together again?"

"Oh, ah," said Henry, "I was forgetting!"

And he resumed.

As time went on, I begin to get pretty fed up with young Andy. He was making a fortune as fast as any feller could out of the sudden boom in the supper-custom, and he knowing perfectly well that if it hadn't of been for Katie there wouldn't of been any supper-custom at all; and you'd of thought that anyone claiming to be a human being would have had the gratitood to forgive and forget and go over and say a civil word to Katie when she come in. But no, he just hung round looking black at all of them; and one night he goes and fairly does it.

The place was full that night, and Katie was there,

and the piano going, and everybody enjoying themselves, when the young feller at the piano struck up the tune what Katie danced to in the show. Catchy tune it was. "Lum-tum-tum, tiddle-iddle-um." Something like that it went. Well, the young feller struck up with it, and everybody begin clapping and hammering on the tables and hollering to Katie to get up and dance; which she done, in an open space in the middle, and she hadn't hardly started when along come young Andy.

He goes up to her, all jaw, and I seen something that wanted dusting on the table next to 'em, so I went up and began dusting it, so by good luck I happened to hear the whole thing.

He says to her, very quiet, "You can't do that here. What do you think this place is?"

And she says to him, "Oh, Andy!"

"I'm very much obliged to you," he says, "for all the trouble you seem to be taking, but it isn't necessary. MacFarland's got on very well before your well-meant efforts to turn it into a bear-garden."

And him coining the money from the supper-custom! Sometimes I think gratitood's a thing of the past and this world not fit for a self-respecting rattlesnake to live in.

"Andy!" she says.

"That's all. We needn't argue about it. If you want to come here and have supper, I can't stop you. But I'm not going to have the place turned into a night-club."

I don't know when I've heard anything like it. If it hadn't of been that I hadn't of got the nerve, I'd have give him a look.

Katie didn't say another word, but just went back to her table.

But the episode, as they say, wasn't conclooded. As soon as the party she was with seen that she was through dancing, they begin to kick up a row; and one young nut with about an inch and a quarter of forehead and the same amount of chin kicked it up especial.

"No, I say! I say, you know!" he hollered. "That's too bad, you know. Encore! Don't stop. Encore!"

Andy goes up to him.

"I must ask you, please, not to make so much noise," he says, quite respectful. "You are disturbing people."

"Disturbing be damned! Why shouldn't she——"

"One moment. You can make all the noise you please out in the street, but as long as you stay in here you'll be quiet. Do you understand?"

Up jumps the nut. He'd had quite enough to drink. I know, because I'd been serving him.

"Who the devil are you?" he says.

"Sit down," says Andy.

And the young feller took a smack at him. And the next moment Andy had him by the collar and was chucking him out in a way that would have done credit to a real professional down Whitechapel way. He dumped him on the pavement as neat as you please.

That broke up the party.

You can never tell with restaurants. What kills one makes another. I've no doubt that if we had chucked out a good customer from the "Guelph" that would have been the end of the place. But it only seemed to do MacFarland's good. I guess it gave just that touch to the place which made the nuts think that this was real Bohemia. Come to think of it, it does give a kind of charm to a place, if you feel that at any moment the feller at the next table to you may be gathered up by the slack of his trousers and slung into the street.

Anyhow, that's the way our supper-custom seemed to look at it; and after that you had to book a table in advance if you wanted to eat with us. They fairly flocked to the place.

But Katie didn't. She didn't flock. She stayed away. And no wonder, after Andy behaving so bad. I'd of spoke to him about it, only he wasn't the kind of feller you do speak to about things.

One day I says to him to cheer him up, "What price this restaurant now, Mr. Andy?"

"Curse the restaurant," he says.

And him with all that supper-custom! It's a rum world!

Mister, have you ever had a real shock—something that came out of nowhere and just knocked you flat? I have, and I'm going to tell you about it.

When a man gets to be my age, and has a job of work which keeps him busy till it's time for him to go to bed, he gets into the habit of not doing much worrying about anything that ain't shoved right under his nose. That's why, about now, Katie had kind of slipped my mind. It wasn't that I wasn't fond of the kid, but I'd got so much to think about, what with having four young fellers under me and things being in such a rush at the restaurant that, if I thought of her at all, I just took it for granted that she was getting along all right, and didn't bother. To be sure we hadn't seen nothing of her at MacFarland's since the night when Andy bounced her pal with the small size in foreheads, but that didn't worry me. If I'd been her, I'd have stopped away the same as she done, seeing that young Andy still had his hump. I took it for granted, as I'm telling you, that she was all right, and that the reason we didn't see nothing of her was that she was taking her patronage elsewhere.

And then, one evening, which happened to be my evening off, I got a letter, and for ten minutes after I read it I was knocked flat.

You get to believe in fate when you get to be my age, and fate certainly had taken a hand in this game. If it hadn't of been my evening off, don't you see, I wouldn't have got home till one o'clock or past that in the morning, being on duty. Whereas, seeing it was my evening off, I was back at half-past eight.

I was living at the same boarding-house in Bloomsbury what I'd lived at for the past ten years, and when I got there I find her letter shoved half under my door.

I can tell you every word of it. This is how it went:

"DARLING UNCLE BILL,

"Don't be too sorry when you read this. It is nobody's fault, but I am just tired of everything, and I want to end it all. You have been such a dear to me always that I want you to be good to me now. I should not like Andy to know the truth, so I want you to make it seem as if it had happened naturally. You will do this for me, won't you? It will be quite easy. By the time you get this, it will be one, and it will all be over, and you can just come up and open the window and let the gas out and then every one will think I just died naturally. It will be quite easy. I am leaving the door unlocked so that you can get in. I am in the room just above yours. I took it yesterday, so as to be near you. Good-bye, Uncle Bill. You will do it for me, won't you? I don't want Andy to know what it really was.

"KATIE."

That was it, mister, and I tell you it floored me. And then it come to me, kind of as a new idea, that I'd best do something pretty soon, and up the stairs I went quick.

There she was, on the bed, with her eyes closed, and the gas just beginning to get bad.

As I come in, she jumped up, and stood staring at me. I went to the tap, and turned the flow off, and then I gives her a look.

"Now then," I says.

"How did you get here?"

"Never mind how I got here. What have *you* got to say for yourself?"

She just began to cry, same as she used to when she was a kid and some one had hurt her.

"Here," I says, "let's get along out of here, and go where there's some air to breathe. Don't you take on so. You come along out and tell me all about it."

She started to walk to where I was, and suddenly I seen she was limping. So I give her a hand down to my room, and set her on a chair.

"Now then," I says again.

"Don't be angry with me, Uncle Bill," she says.

And she looks at me so pitiful that I goes up to her and puts my arm round her and pats her on the back.

"Don't you worry, dearie," I says, "nobody ain't going to be angry with you. But, for goodness' sake,"

I says, "tell a man why in the name of goodness you ever took and acted so foolish."

"I wanted to end it all."

"But why?"

She burst out a-crying again, like a kid.

"Didn't you read about it in the paper, Uncle Bill?"

"Read about what in the paper?"

"My accident. I broke my ankle at rehearsal ever so long ago, practising my new dance. The doctor says it will never be right again. I shall never be able to dance any more. I shall always limp. I shan't even be able to walk properly. And when I thought of that . . . and Andy . . . and everything . . . I . . ."

I got on to my feet.

"Well, well, well," I says. "Well, well, well! I don't know as I blame you. But don't you do it. It's a mug's game. Look here, if I leave you alone for half an hour, you won't go trying it on again? Promise."

"Very well, Uncle Bill. Where are you going?"

"Oh, just out. I'll be back soon. You sit there and rest yourself."

It didn't take me ten minutes to get to the restaurant in a cab. I found Andy in the back room.

"What's the matter, Henry?" he says.

"Take a look at this," I says.

There's always this risk, mister, in being the Andy type of feller what must have his own way and goes straight ahead and has it; and that is that when trouble does come to him, it comes with a rush. It sometimes seems to me that in this life we've all got to have trouble sooner or later, and some of us gets it bit by bit, spread out thin, so to speak, and a few of us gets it in a lump—*biff!* And that was what happened to Andy, and what I knew was going to happen when I showed him that letter. I nearly says to him, "Brace up, young feller, because this is where you get it."

I don't often go to the theatre, but when I do I like one of those plays with some ginger in them which the papers generally cuss. The papers say that real human beings don't carry on in that way. Take it from me, mister, they do. I seen a feller on the stage read a letter once which didn't just suit him; and he gasped and rolled his eyes and tried to say something and couldn't, and had to get a hold on a chair to keep him from falling. There was a piece in the paper saying that this was all wrong, and that he wouldn't of done them things in real life. Believe me, the paper was wrong. There wasn't a thing that that feller did that Andy didn't do when he read that letter.

"God!" he says. "Is she . . . She isn't . . . Were you in time?" he says.

And he looks at me, and I seen that he had got it in the neck, right enough.

"If you mean is she dead," I says, "no, she ain't dead."

"Thank God!"

"Not yet," I says.

And the next moment we was out of that room and in the cab and moving quick.

He was never much of a talker, wasn't Andy, and he didn't chat in that cab. He didn't say a word till we was going up the stairs.

"Where?" he says.

"Here," I says.

And I opens the door.

Katie was standing looking out of the window. She turned as the door opened, and then she saw Andy. Her lips parted, as if she was going to say something, but she didn't say nothing. And Andy, he didn't say nothing, neither. He just looked, and she just looked.

And then he sort of stumbles across the room, and goes down on his knees, and gets his arms around her.

"Oh, my kid!" he says.

And I seen I wasn't wanted, so I shut the door, and I hopped it. I went and saw the last half of a music-hall. But, I don't know, it didn't kind of have no fascination for me. You've got to give your mind to it to appreciate good music-hall turns.

ONE TOUCH OF NATURE

THE feelings of Mr. J. Wilmot Birdsey, as he stood wedged in the crowd that moved inch by inch towards the gates of the Chelsea Football Ground, rather resembled those of a starving man who has just been given a meal but realizes that he is not likely to get another for many days. He was full and happy. He bubbled over with the joy of living and a warm affection for his fellow-man. At the back of his mind there lurked the black shadow of future privations, but for the moment he did not allow it to disturb him. On this maddest, merriest day of all the glad New Year he was content to revel in the present and allow the future to take care of itself.

Mr. Birdsey had been doing something which he had not done since he left New York five years ago. He had been watching a game of baseball.

New York lost a great baseball fan when Hugo Percy de Wynter Framlinghame, sixth Earl of Carricksteed, married Mae Elinor, only daughter of Mr. and Mrs. J. Wilmot Birdsey of East Seventy-Third Street; for scarcely had that internationally important event taken place when Mrs. Birdsey, announcing that for the future the home would be in England as near as possible to dear Mae and dear Hugo, scooped J. Wilmot out of his comfortable morris chair as if he had been a clam, corked him up in a swift taxicab, and decanted him into a Deck B stateroom on the "Olympic." And there he was, an exile.

Mr. Birdsey submitted to the worst bit of kidnapping since the days of the old press gang with that delightful amiability which made him so popular among his fellows and such a cypher in his home. At an early date in his married life his position had been clearly defined beyond possibility of mistake. It was his business to make money, and, when called upon, to jump through hoops and sham dead at the bidding of his wife and daughter Mae. These duties he had been performing conscientiously for a matter of twenty years.

It was only occasionally that his humble rôle jarred upon him, for he loved his wife and idolized his daughter. The international alliance had been one of these occasions. He had no objection to Hugo Percy, sixth Earl of Carricksteed. The crushing blow had been the sentence of exile. He loved baseball with a love passing the love of women, and the prospect of never seeing a game again in his life appalled him.

And then, one morning, like a voice from another world, had come the news that the White Sox and the Giants were to give an exhibition in London at the Chelsea Football Ground. He had counted the days like a child before Christmas.

There had been obstacles to overcome before he could attend the game, but he had overcome them, and had been seated in the front row when the two teams lined up before King George.

And now he was moving slowly from the ground with the rest of the spectators. Fate had been very good to him. It had given him a great game, even unto two home-runs. But its crowning benevolence had been to allot the seats on either side of him to two men of his own mettle, two god-like beings who knew every move on the board, and howled like wolves when they did not see eye to eye with the umpire. Long before the ninth innings he was feeling towards them the affection of a shipwrecked mariner who meets a couple of boyhood's chums on a desert island.

As he shouldered his way towards the gate he was aware of these two men, one on either side of him. He looked at them fondly, trying to make up his mind which of them he liked best. It was sad to think that they must soon go out of his life again for ever.

He came to a sudden resolution. He would postpone the parting. He would ask them to dinner. Over the best that the Savoy Hotel could provide they would fight the afternoon's battle over again. He did not know who they were or anything about them, but what did that matter? They were brother-fans. That was enough for him.

The man on his right was young, clean-shaven, and of a somewhat vulturine cast of countenance. His face was cold and impassive now, almost forbiddingly so; but only half an hour before it had been a battle-field of conflicting emotions, and his hat still showed the dent where he had banged it against the edge of his seat on the occasion of Mr. Daly's home-run. A worthy guest!

The man on Mr. Birdsey's left belonged to another species of fan. Though there had been times during the game when he had howled, for the most part he had watched in silence so hungrily tense that a less experienced observer than Mr. Birdsey might have attributed his immobility to boredom. But one glance at his set jaw and gleaming eyes had told him that here also was a man and a brother.

This man's eyes were still gleaming, and under their curiously deep tan his bearded cheeks were pale. He was staring straight in front of him with an unseeing gaze.

Mr. Birdsey tapped the young man on the shoulder

"Some game!" he said.

The young man looked at him and smiled.

"You bet," he said.

"I haven't seen a ball-game in five years."

"The last one I saw was two years ago next June."

"Come and have some dinner at my hotel and talk it over," said Mr. Birdsey impulsively.

"Sure!" said the young man.

Mr. Birdsey turned and tapped the shoulder of the man on his left.

The result was a little unexpected. The man gave a start that was almost a leap, and the pallor of his face became a sickly white. His eyes, as he swung round, met Mr. Birdsey's for an instant before they dropped, and there was panic fear in them. His breath whistled softly through clenched teeth.

Mr. Birdsey was taken aback. The cordiality of the clean-shaven young man had not prepared him for the possibility of such a reception. He felt chilled. He was on the point of apologizing with some murmur about a mistake, when the man reassured him by smiling. It was rather a painful smile, but it was enough for Mr. Birdsey. This man might be of a nervous temperament, but his heart was in the right place.

He, too, smiled. He was a small, stout, red-faced little man, and he possessed a smile that rarely failed to set strangers at their ease. Many strenuous years on the New York Stock Exchange had not destroyed a certain childlike amiability in Mr. Birdsey, and it shone out when he smiled at you.

"I'm afraid I startled you," he said soothingly. "I wanted to ask you if you would let a perfect stranger, who also happens to be an exile, offer you dinner to-night."

The man winced. "Exile?"

"An exiled fan. Don't you feel that the Polo Grounds are a good long way away? This gentleman is joining me. I have a suite at the Savoy Hotel, and I thought we might all have a quiet little dinner there and talk about the game. I haven't seen a ball-game in five years."

"Nor have I."

"Then you must come. You really must. We fans ought to stick to one another in a strange land. Do come."

"Thank you," said the bearded man; "I will."

When three men, all strangers, sit down to dinner together, conversation, even if they happen to have a mutual passion for baseball, is apt to be for awhile a little difficult. The first fine frenzy in which Mr. Birdsey had issued his invitations had begun to ebb by the time the soup was served, and he was conscious of a feeling of embarrassment.

There was some subtle hitch in the orderly progress of affairs. He sensed it in the air. Both of his guests were disposed to silence, and the clean-shaven young man had developed a trick of staring at the man with the beard, which was obviously distressing that sensitive person.

"Wine," murmured Mr. Birdsey to the waiter. "Wine, wine!"

He spoke with the earnestness of a general calling up his reserves for the grand attack. The success of this little dinner mattered enormously to him. There were circumstances which were going to make it an oasis in his life. He wanted it to be an occasion to which, in grey days to come, he could look back and be consoled. He could not let it be a failure.

He was about to speak when the young man anticipated him. Leaning forward, he addressed the bearded man, who was crumbling bread with an absent look in his eyes.

"Surely we have met before?" he said. "I'm sure I remember your face."

The effect of these words on the other was as curious as the effect of Mr. Birdsey's tap on the shoulder had been. He looked up like a hunted animal.

He shook his head without speaking.

"Curious," said the young man. "I could have sworn to it, and I am positive that it was somewhere in New York. Do you come from New York?"

"Yes."

"It seems to me," said Mr. Birdsey, "that we ought to introduce ourselves. Funny it didn't strike any of us before. My name is Birdsey, J. Wilmot Birdsey. I come from New York."

"My name is Waterall," said the young man. "I come from New York."

The bearded man hesitated.

"My name is Johnson. I—used to live in New York."

"Where do you live now, Mr. Johnson?" asked Waterall.

The bearded man hesitated again. "Algiers," he said.

Mr. Birdsey was inspired to help matters along with small-talk.

"Algiers," he said. "I have never been there, but I understand that it is quite a place. Are you in business there, Mr. Johnson?"

"I live there for my health."

"Have you been there some time?" inquired Waterall.

"Five years."

"Then it must have been in New York that I saw you, for I have never been to Algiers, and I'm certain I have seen you somewhere. I'm afraid you will think me a bore for sticking to the point like this, but the fact is, the one thing I pride myself on is my memory for faces. It's a hobby of mine. If I think I remember a face, and can't place it, I worry myself into insomnia. It's partly sheer vanity, and partly because in my job a good memory for faces is a mighty fine asset. It has helped me a hundred times."

Mr. Birdsey was an intelligent man, and he could see that Waterall's table-talk was for some reason getting upon Johnson's nerves. Like a good host, he endeavoured to cut in and make things smooth.

"I've heard great accounts of Algiers," he said helpfully. "A friend of mine was there in his yacht last year. It must be a delightful spot."

"It's a hell on earth," snapped Johnson, and slew the conversation on the spot.

Through a grim silence an angel in human form fluttered in—a waiter bearing a bottle. The pop of the cork was more than music to Mr. Birdsey's ears. It was the booming of the guns of the relieving army.

The first glass, as first glasses will, thawed the bearded man, to the extent of inducing him to try and pick up the fragments of the conversation which he had shattered.

"I am afraid you will have thought me abrupt, Mr. Birdsey," he said awkwardly; "but then you haven't lived in Algiers for five years, and I have."

Mr. Birdsey chirruped sympathetically.

"I liked it at first. It looked mighty good to me. But five years of it, and nothing else to look forward to till you die . . ."

He stopped, and emptied his glass. Mr. Birdsey was still perturbed. True, conversation was proceeding in a sort of way, but it had taken a distinctly gloomy turn. Slightly flushed with the excellent champagne which he had selected for this important dinner, he endeavoured to lighten it.

"I wonder," he said, "which of us three fans had

the greatest difficulty in getting to the bleachers to-day. I guess none of us found it too easy."

The young man shook his head.

"Don't count on me to contribute a romantic story to this Arabian Night's Entertainment. My difficulty would have been to stop away. My name's Waterall, and I'm the London correspondent of the "New York Chronicle." I had to be there this afternoon in the way of business."

Mr. Birdsey giggled self-consciously, but not without a certain impish pride.

"The laugh will be on me when you hear my confession. My daughter married an English earl, and my wife brought me over here to mix with his crowd. There was a big dinner-party to-night, at which the whole gang were to be present, and it was as much as my life was worth to side-step it. But when you get the Giants and the White Sox playing ball within fifty miles of you—— Well, I packed a grip and sneaked out the back way, and got to the station and caught the fast train to London. And what is going on back there at this moment I don't like to think. About now," said Mr. Birdsey, looking at his watch, "I guess they'll be pronging the *hors d'œuvres* and gazing at the empty chair. It was a shame to do it, but, for the love of Mike, what else could I have done?"

He looked at the bearded man.

"Did you have any adventures, Mr. Johnson?"

"No. I—I just came."

The young man Waterall leaned forward. His manner was quiet, but his eyes were glittering.

"Wasn't that enough of an adventure for you?" he said.

Their eyes met across the table. Seated between them, Mr. Birdsey looked from one to the other, vaguely disturbed. Something was happening, a drama was going on, and he had not the key to it.

Johnson's face was pale, and the tablecloth crumpled into a crooked ridge under his fingers, but his voice was steady as he replied:

"I don't understand."

"Will you understand if I give you your right name, Mr. Benyon?"

"What's all this?" said Mr. Birdsey feebly.

Waterall turned to him, the vulturine cast of his face more noticeable than ever. Mr. Birdsey was conscious of a sudden distaste for this young man.

"It's quite simple, Mr. Birdsey. If you have not been entertaining angels unawares, you have at least been giving a dinner to a celebrity. I told you I was sure I had seen this gentleman before. I have just remembered where, and when. This is Mr. John Benyon, and I last saw him five years ago when I was a reporter in New York, and covered his trial."

"His trial?"

"He robbed the New Asiatic Bank of a hundred thousand dollars, jumped his bail, and was never heard of again."

"For the love of Mike!"

Mr. Birdsey stared at his guest with eyes that grew momently wider. He was amazed to find that deep down in him there was an unmistakable feeling of elation. He had made up his mind, when he left home that morning, that this was to be a day of days. Well, nobody could call this an anti-climax.

"So that's why you have been living in Algiers?"

Benyon did not reply. Outside, the Strand traffic sent a faint murmur into the warm, comfortable room.

Waterall spoke. "What on earth induced you, Benyon, to run the risk of coming to London, where every second man you meet is a New Yorker, I can't understand. The chances were two to one that you would be recognized. You made a pretty big splash with that little affair of yours five years ago."

Benyon raised his head. His hands were trembling.

"I'll tell you," he said with a kind of savage force, which hurt kindly little Mr. Birdsey like a blow. "It was because I was a dead man, and saw a chance of coming to life for a day; because I was sick of the damned tomb I've been living in for five centuries; because I've been aching for New York ever since I've left it—and here was a chance of being back there for a few hours. I knew there was a risk. I took a chance on it. Well?"

Mr. Birdsey's heart was almost too full for words. He had found him at last, the Super-Fan, the man who would go through fire and water for a sight of a game of baseball. Till that moment he had been regarding himself as the nearest approach to that dizzy eminence. He had braved great perils to see this game. Even in this moment his mind would not wholly detach itself from speculation as to what his wife would say to him when he slunk back into the fold. But what had he risked compared with this man Benyon? Mr. Birdsey glowed. He could not restrain his sympathy and admiration. True, the man was a criminal. He had robbed a bank of a hundred thousand dollars. But, after all, what was that? They would probably have wasted the money in foolishness. And, anyway, a bank which couldn't take care of its money deserved to lose it.

Mr. Birdsey felt almost a righteous glow of indignation against the New Asiatic Bank.

He broke the silence which had followed Benyon's words with a peculiarly immoral remark:

"Well, it's lucky it's only us that's recognized you," he said.

Waterall stared. "Are you proposing that we should hush this thing up, Mr. Birdsey?" he said coldly.

"Oh, well——"

Waterall rose and went to the telephone.

"What are you going to do?"

"Call up Scotland Yard, of course. What did you think?"

Undoubtedly the young man was doing his duty as a citizen, yet it is to be recorded that Mr. Birdsey eyed him with unmixed horror.

"You can't! You mustn't!" he cried.

"I certainly shall."

"But—but—this fellow came all that way to see the ball-game."

It seemed incredible to Mr. Birdsey that this aspect of the affair should not be the one to strike everybody to the exclusion of all other aspects.

"You can't give him up. It's too raw."

"He's a convicted criminal."

"He's a fan. Why, say, he's *the* fan."

Waterall shrugged his shoulders, and walked to the telephone. Benyon spoke.

"One moment."

Waterall turned, and found himself looking into the muzzle of a small pistol. He laughed.

"I expected that. Wave it about all you want."

Benyon rested his shaking hand on the edge of the table.

"I'll shoot if you move."

"You won't. You haven't the nerve. There's nothing to you. You're just a cheap crook, and that's all. You wouldn't find the nerve to pull that trigger in a million years."

He took off the receiver.

"Give me Scotland Yard," he said.

He had turned his back to Benyon. Benyon sat motionless. Then, with a thud, the pistol fell to the ground. The next moment Benyon had broken down. His face was buried in his arms, and he was a wreck of a man, sobbing like a hurt child.

Mr. Birdsey was profoundly distressed. He sat tingling and helpless. This was a nightmare.

Waterall's level voice spoke at the telephone.

"Is this Scotland Yard? I am Waterall, of the 'New York Chronicle.' Is Inspector Jarvis there? Ask him to come to the 'phone. . . . Is that you, Jarvis? This is Waterall. I'm speaking from the Savoy, Mr. Birdsey's rooms. Birdsey. Listen, Jarvis. There's a man here that's wanted by the American police. Send some one here and get him. Benyon. Robbed the New Asiatic Bank in New York. Yes, you've a warrant out for him, five years old. . . . All right."

He hung up the receiver. Benyon sprang to his feet. He stood, shaking, a pitiable sight. Mr. Birdsey had risen with him. They stood looking at Waterall.

"You—skunk!" said Mr. Birdsey.

"I'm an American citizen," said Waterall, "and I happen to have some idea of a citizen's duties. What is more, I'm a newspaper man, and I have some idea of my duty to my paper. Call me what you like, you won't alter that."

Mr. Birdsey snorted.

"You're suffering from ingrowing sentimentality, Mr. Birdsey. That's what's the matter with you. Just because this man has escaped justice for five years, you think he ought to be considered quit of the whole thing."

"But—but——"

"I don't."

He took out his cigarette case. He was feeling a great deal more strung-up and nervous than he would have had the others suspect. He had had a moment of very swift thinking before he had decided to treat that ugly little pistol in a spirit of contempt. Its production had given him a decided shock, and now he was suffering from reaction. As a consequence, because his nerves were strained, he lit his cigarette very languidly, very carefully, and with an offensive superiority which was to Mr. Birdsey the last straw.

These things are matters of an instant. Only an infinitesimal fraction of time elapsed between the spectacle of Mr. Birdsey, indignant but inactive, and Mr. Birdsey berserk, seeing red, frankly and undisguisedly running amok. The transformation took place in the space of time required for the lighting of a match.

Even as the match gave out its flame, Mr. Birdsey sprang.

Aeons before, when the young blood ran swiftly in his veins and life was all before him, Mr. Birdsey had played football. Once a footballer, always a potential footballer, even to the grave. Time had removed the flying tackle as a factor in Mr. Birdsey's life. Wrath brought it back. He dived at young Mr. Waterall's neatly trousered legs as he had dived at other legs, less neatly trousered, thirty years ago. They crashed to the floor together; and with the crash came Mr. Birdsey's shout:

"Run! Run, you fool! Run!"

And, even as he clung to his man, breathless, bruised, feeling as if all the world had dissolved in one vast explosion of dynamite, the door opened, banged to, and feet fled down the passage.

Mr. Birdsey disentangled himself, and rose painfully. The shock had brought him to himself. He was no longer berserk. He was a middle-aged gentleman of high respectability who had been behaving in a very peculiar way.

Waterall, flushed and dishevelled, glared at him speechlessly. He gulped. "Are you crazy?"

Mr. Birdsey tested gingerly the mechanism of a leg which lay under suspicion of being broken. Relieved, he put his foot to the ground again. He shook his head at Waterall. He was slightly crumpled, but he achieved a manner of dignified reproof.

"You shouldn't have done it, young man. It was raw work. Oh, yes, I know all about that duty-of-a-citizen stuff. It doesn't go. There are exceptions to every rule, and this was one of them. When a man risks his liberty to come and root at a ball-game, you've got to hand it to him. He isn't a crook. He's a fan. And we exiled fans have got to stick together."

Waterall was quivering with fury, disappointment, and the peculiar unpleasantness of being treated by an elderly gentleman like a sack of coals. He stammered with rage.

"You damned old fool, do you realize what you've done? The police will be here in another minute."

"Let them come."

"But what am I to say to them? What explanation can I give? What story can I tell them? Can't you see what a hole you've put me in?"

Something seemed to click inside Mr. Birdsey's soul. It was the berserk mood vanishing and reason leaping back on to her throne. He was able now to think calmly, and what he thought about filled him with a sudden gloom.

"Young man," he said, "don't worry yourself. You've got a cinch. You've only got to hand a story to the police. Any old tale will do for them. I'm the man with the really difficult job—I've got to square myself with my wife!"

BLACK FOR LUCK

HE was black, but comely. Obviously in reduced circumstances, he had nevertheless contrived to retain a certain smartness, a certain air—what the French call the *tournure*. Nor had poverty killed in him the aristocrat's instinct of personal cleanliness; for even as Elizabeth caught sight of him he began to wash himself.

At the sound of her step he looked up. He did not move, but there was suspicion in his attitude. The muscles of his back contracted, his eyes glowed like yellow lamps against black velvet, his tail switched a little, warningly.

Elizabeth looked at him. He looked at Elizabeth. There was a pause, while he summed her up. Then he stalked towards her, and, suddenly lowering his head, drove it vigorously against her dress. He permitted her to pick him up and carry him into the hall-way, where Francis, the janitor, stood.

"Francis," said Elizabeth, "does this cat belong to anyone here?"

"No, miss. That cat's a stray, that cat is. I been trying to lo—cate that cat's owner for days."

Francis spent his time trying to locate things. It was the one recreation of his eventless life. Sometimes it was a noise, sometimes a lost letter, sometimes a piece of ice which had gone astray in the dumb-waiter—whatever it was, Francis tried to locate it.

"Has he been round here long, then?"

"I seen him snooping about considerable time."

"I shall keep him."

"Black cats bring luck," said Francis sententiously.

"I certainly shan't object to that," said Elizabeth.

She was feeling that morning that a little luck would be a pleasing novelty. Things had not been going very well with her of late. It was not so much that the usual proportion of her manuscripts had come back with editorial compliments from the magazines to which they had been sent—she accepted that as part of the game; what she did consider scurvy treatment at the hands of fate was the fact that her own pet magazine, the one to which she had been accustomed to fly for refuge, almost sure of a welcome—when coldly treated by all the others—had suddenly expired with a low gurgle for want of public support. It was like losing a kind and open-handed relative, and it made the addition of a black cat to the household almost a necessity.

In her flat, the door closed, she watched her new ally with some anxiety. He had behaved admirably on the journey upstairs, but she would not have been surprised, though it would have pained her, if he had now proceeded to try to escape through the ceiling. Cats were so emotional. However, he remained calm, and, after padding silently about the room for awhile, raised his head and uttered a crooning cry.

"That's right," said Elizabeth, cordially. "If you don't see what you want, ask for it. The place is yours."

She went to the ice-box, and produced milk and sardines. There was nothing finnicky or affected about her guest. He was a good trencher-man, and he did not care who knew it. He concentrated himself on the restoration of his tissues with the purposeful air of one whose last meal is a dim memory. Elizabeth, brooding over him like a Providence, wrinkled her forehead in thought.

"Joseph," she said at last, brightening; "that's your name. Now settle down, and start being a mascot."

Joseph settled down amazingly. By the end of the second day he was conveying the impression that he was the real owner of the apartment, and that it was due to his good nature that Elizabeth was allowed the run of the place. Like most of his species, he was an autocrat. He waited a day to ascertain which was Elizabeth's favourite chair, then appropriated it for his own. If Elizabeth closed a door while he was in a room, he wanted it opened so that he might go out; if she closed it while he was outside, he wanted it opened so that he might come in; if she left it open, he fussed about the draught. But the best of us have our faults, and Elizabeth adored him in spite of his.

It was astonishing what a difference he made in her life. She was a friendly soul, and until Joseph's arrival she had had to depend for company mainly on the footsteps of the man in the flat across the way. Moreover, the building was an old one, and it creaked at night. There was a loose board in the passage which made burglar noises in the dark behind you when you stepped on it on the way to bed; and there were funny scratching sounds which made you jump and hold your breath. Joseph soon put a stop to all that. With Joseph around, a loose board became a loose board, nothing more, and a scratching noise just a plain scratching noise.

And then one afternoon he disappeared.

Having searched the flat without finding him, Elizabeth went to the window, with the intention of making a bird's-eye survey of the street. She was not hopeful, for she had just come from the street, and there had been no sign of him then.

Outside the window was a broad ledge, running the width of the building. It terminated on the left, in a shallow balcony belonging to the flat whose front door faced hers—the flat of the young man whose footsteps she sometimes heard. She knew he was a young man, because Francis had told her so. His name, James Renshaw Boyd, she had learned from the same source.

On this shallow balcony, licking his fur with the tip of a crimson tongue and generally behaving as if he were in his own backyard, sat Joseph.

"Jo—seph!" cried Elizabeth—surprise, joy and reproach combining to give her voice an almost melodramatic quiver.

He looked at her coldly. Worse, he looked at her as

if she had been an utter stranger. Bulging with her meat and drink, he cut her dead; and, having done so, turned and walked into the next flat.

Elizabeth was a girl of spirit. Joseph might look at her as if she were a saucerful of tainted milk, but he was her cat, and she meant to get him back. She went out and rang the bell of Mr. James Renshaw Boyd's flat.

The door was opened by a shirt-sleeved young man. He was by no means an unsightly young man. Indeed, of his type—the rough-haired, clean-shaven, square-jawed type—he was a distinctly good-looking young man. Even though she was regarding him at the moment purely in the light of a machine for returning strayed cats, Elizabeth noticed that.

She smiled upon him. It was not the fault of this nice-looking young man that his sitting-room window was open; or that Joseph was an ungrateful little beast who should have no fish that night.

"Would you mind letting me have my cat, please?" she said pleasantly. "He has gone into your sitting-room through the window."

He looked faintly surprised.

"Your cat?"

"My black cat, Joseph. He is in your sitting-room."

"I'm afraid you have come to the wrong place. I've just left my sitting-room, and the only cat there is my black cat, Reginald."

"But I saw Joseph go in only a minute ago."

"That was Reginald."

For the first time, as one who examining a fair shrub abruptly discovers that it is a stinging-nettle, Elizabeth realized the truth. This was no innocent young man who stood before her, but the blackest criminal known to criminologists—a stealer of other people's cats. Her manner shot down to zero.

"May I ask how long you have had your Reginald?"

"Since four o'clock this afternoon."

"Did he come in through the window?"

"Why, yes. Now you mention it, he did."

"I must ask you to be good enough to give me back my cat," said Elizabeth, icily.

He regarded her defensively.

"Assuming," he said, "purely for the purposes of academic argument, that your Joseph is my Reginald, couldn't we come to an agreement of some sort? Let me buy you another cat. A dozen cats."

"I don't want a dozen cats. I want Joseph."

"Fine, fat, soft cats," he went on persuasively. "Lovely, affectionate Persians and Angoras, and——"

"Of course, if you intend to steal Joseph——"

"These are harsh words. Any lawyer will tell you that there are special statutes regarding cats. To retain a stray cat is not a tort or a misdemeanour. In the celebrated test-case of Wiggins *v.* Bluebody it was established——"

"Will you please give me back my cat?"

She stood facing him, her chin in the air and her eyes shining, and the young man suddenly fell a victim to conscience.

"Look here," he said, "I'll throw myself on your mercy. I admit the cat is your cat, and that I have no right to it, and that I am just a common sneak-thief. But consider. I had just come back from the first rehearsal of my first play; and as I walked in at the door that cat walked in at the window. I'm as superstitious as a coon, and I felt that to give him up would be equivalent to killing the play before ever it was produced. I know it will sound absurd to you. *You* have no idiotic superstitions. You are sane and practical. But, in the circumstances, if you *could* see your way to waiving your rights——"

Before the wistfulness of his eye Elizabeth capitulated. She felt quite overcome by the revulsion of feeling which swept through her. How she had misjudged him! She had taken him for an ordinary soulless purloiner of cats, a snapper-up of cats at random and without reason; and all the time he had been reluctantly compelled to the act by this deep and praiseworthy motive. All the unselfishness and love of sacrifice innate in good women stirred within her.

"Why, of *course* you mustn't let him go! It would mean awful bad luck."

"But how about you——"

"Never mind about me. Think of all the people who are dependent on your play being a success."

The young man blinked.

"This is overwhelming," he said.

"I had no notion why you wanted him. He was nothing to me—at least, nothing much—that is to say—well, I suppose I was rather fond of him—but he was not—not——"

"Vital?"

"That's just the word I wanted. He was just company, you know."

"Haven't you many friends?"

"I haven't any friends."

"You haven't any friends! That settles it. You must take him back."

"I couldn't think of it."

"Of course you must take him back at once."

"I really couldn't."

"You must."

"I won't."

"But, good gracious, how do you suppose I should feel, knowing that you were all alone and that I had sneaked your—your ewe lamb, as it were?"

"And how do you suppose I should feel if your play failed simply for lack of a black cat?"

He started, and ran his fingers through his rough hair in an overwrought manner.

"Solomon couldn't have solved this problem," he said. "How would it be—it seems the only possible way out—if you were to retain a sort of managerial right in him? Couldn't you sometimes step across and chat with him—and me, incidentally—over here? I'm very nearly as lonesome as you are. Chicago is my home. I hardly know a soul in New York."

Her solitary life in the big city had forced upon Elizabeth the ability to form instantaneous judgments on the men she met. She flashed a glance at the young man and decided in his favour.

"It's very kind of you," she said. "I should love to. I want to hear all about your play. I write myself, you know, in a very small way, so a successful playwright is Someone to me."

"I wish I were a successful playwright."

"Well, you are having the first play you have ever written produced on Broadway. That's pretty wonderful."

"'M—yes," said the young man. It seemed to Elizabeth that he spoke doubtfully, and this modesty consolidated the favourable impression she had formed.

The gods are just. For every ill which they inflict they also supply a compensation. It seems good to them that individuals in big cities shall be lonely, but they have so arranged that, if one of these individuals does at last contrive to seek out and form a friendship with another, that friendship shall grow more swiftly than the tepid acquaintanceships of those on whom the icy touch of loneliness has never fallen. Within a week Elizabeth was feeling that she had known this James Renshaw Boyd all her life.

And yet there was a tantalizing incompleteness about his personal reminiscences. Elizabeth was one of those persons who like to begin a friendship with a full statement of their position, their previous life, and the causes which led up to their being in this particular spot at this particular time. At their next meeting, before he had had time to say much on his own account, she had told him of her life in the small Canadian town where she had passed the early part of her life; of the rich and unexpected aunt who had sent her to college for no particular reason that anyone could ascertain except that she enjoyed being unexpected; of the legacy from this same aunt, far smaller than might have been hoped for, but sufficient to send a grateful Elizabeth to New York, to try her luck there; of editors, magazines, manuscripts refused or accepted, plots for stories; of life in general, as lived down where the Arch spans Fifth Avenue and the lighted cross of the Judson shines by night on Washington Square.

Ceasing eventually, she waited for him to begin; and he did not begin—not, that is to say, in the sense the word conveyed to Elizabeth. He spoke briefly of college, still more briefly of Chicago—which city he appeared to regard with a distaste that made Lot's attitude towards the Cities of the Plain almost kindly by comparison. Then, as if he had fulfilled the demands of the most exacting inquisitor in the matter of personal reminiscence, he began to speak of the play.

The only facts concerning him to which Elizabeth could really have sworn with a clear conscience at the end of the second week of their acquaintance were that he was very poor, and that this play meant everything to him.

The statement that it meant everything to him insinuated itself so frequently into his conversation that it weighed on Elizabeth's mind like a burden, and by degrees she found herself giving the play place of honour in her thoughts over and above her own little ventures. With this stupendous thing hanging in the balance, it seemed almost wicked of her to devote a moment to wondering whether the editor of an evening paper, who had half promised to give her the entrancing post of Adviser to the Lovelorn on his journal, would fulfil that half-promise.

At an early stage in their friendship the young man had told her the plot of the piece; and if he had not unfortunately forgotten several important episodes and had to leap back to them across a gulf of one or two acts, and if he had referred to his characters by name instead of by such descriptions as "the fellow who's in love with the girl—not what's-his-name but the other chap"—she would no doubt have got that mental half-Nelson on it which is such a help towards the proper understanding of a four-act comedy. As it was, his précis had left her a little vague; but she said it was perfectly splendid, and he said did she really think so. And she said yes, she did, and they were both happy.

Rehearsals seemed to prey on his spirits a good deal. He attended them with the pathetic regularity of the young dramatist, but they appeared to bring him little balm. Elizabeth generally found him steeped in gloom, and then she would postpone the recital, to which she had been looking forward, of whatever little triumph she might have happened to win, and devote herself to the task of cheering him up. If women were wonderful in no other way, they would be wonderful for their genius for listening to shop instead of talking it.

Elizabeth was feeling more than a little proud of the way in which her judgment of this young man was being justified. Life in Bohemian New York had left her decidedly wary of strange young men, not formally introduced; her faith in human nature had had to undergo much straining. Wolves in sheep's clothing were common objects of the wayside in her unprotected life; and perhaps her chief reason for appreciating this friendship was the feeling of safety which it gave her.

Their relations, she told herself, were so splendidly unsentimental. There was no need for that silent defensiveness which had come to seem almost an inevitable accompaniment to dealings with the opposite sex. James Boyd, she felt, she could trust; and it was wonderful how soothing the reflexion was.

And that was why, when the thing happened, it so shocked and frightened her.

It had been one of their quiet evenings. Of late they had fallen into the habit of sitting for long periods together without speaking. But it had differed from other quiet evenings through the fact that Elizabeth's silence hid a slight but well-defined feeling of injury. Usually she sat happy with her thoughts, but to-night she was ruffled. She had a grievance.

That afternoon the editor of the evening paper, whose angelic status not even a bald head and an absence of wings and harp could conceal, had definitely informed her that the man who had conducted the column hitherto having resigned, the post of Heloise Milton, official adviser to readers troubled with affairs of the heart, was hers; and he looked to her to justify the daring experiment of letting a woman handle so responsible a job. Imagine how Napoleon felt after Austerlitz, picture Colonel Gœthale contemplating the last spadeful of dirt from the Panama Canal, try to visualize a suburban householder who sees a flower emerging from the soil in which he has inserted a packet of guaranteed seeds, and you will have some faint conception how Elizabeth felt as those golden words proceeded from that editor's lips. For the moment Ambition was sated. The years, rolling by, might perchance open out other vistas ; but for the moment she was content.

Into James Boyd's apartment she had walked, stepping on fleecy clouds of rapture, to tell him the great news.

She told him the great news.

He said, "Ah!"

There are many ways of saying "Ah!" You can put joy, amazement, rapture into it ; you can also make it sound as if it were a reply to a remark on the weather. James Boyd made it sound just like that. His hair was rumpled, his brow contracted, and his manner absent. The impression he gave Elizabeth was that he had barely heard her. The next moment he was deep in a recital of the misdemeanours of the actors now rehearsing for his four-act comedy. The star had done this, the leading woman that, the juvenile something else. For the first time Elizabeth listened unsympathetically.

The time came when speech failed James Boyd, and he sat back in his chair, brooding. Elizabeth, cross and wounded, sat in hers, nursing Joseph. And so, in a dim light, time flowed by.

Just how it happened she never knew. One moment, peace ; the next chaos. One moment, stillness ; the next, Joseph hurtling through the air, all claws and expletives, and herself caught in a clasp which shook the breath from her.

One can dimly reconstruct James's train of thought. He is in despair ; things are going badly at the theatre, and life has lost its savour. His eye, as he sits, is caught by Elizabeth's profile. It is a pretty—above all, a soothing—profile. An almost painful sentimentality sweeps over James Boyd. There she sits, his only friend in this cruel city. If you argue that there is no necessity to spring at your only friend and nearly choke her, you argue soundly ; the point is well taken. But James Boyd was beyond the reach of sound argument. Much rehearsing had frayed his nerves to ribbons. One may say that he was not responsible for his actions.

That is the case for James. Elizabeth, naturally, was not in a position to take a wide and understanding view of it. All she knew was that James had played her false, abused her trust in him. For a moment, such was the shock of the surprise, she was not conscious of indignation—or, indeed, of any sensation except the purely physical one of semi-strangulation. Then, flushed, and more bitterly angry than she could ever have imagined herself capable of being, she began to struggle. She tore herself away from him. Coming on top of her grievance, this thing filled her with a sudden, very vivid hatred of James. At the back of her anger, feeding it, was the humiliating thought that it was all her own fault, that by her presence there she had invited this.

She groped her way to the door. Something was writhing and struggling inside her, blinding her eyes, and robbing her of speech. She was only conscious of a desire to be alone, to be back and safe in her own home. She was aware that he was speaking, but the words did not reach her. She found the door, and pulled it open. She felt a hand on her arm, but she shook it off. And then she was back behind her own door, alone and at liberty to contemplate at leisure the ruins of that little temple of friendship which she had built up so carefully and in which she had been so happy.

The broad fact that she would never forgive him was for awhile her only coherent thought. To this succeeded the determination that she would never forgive herself. And having thus placed beyond the pale the only two friends she had in New York, she was free to devote herself without hindrance to the task of feeling thoroughly lonely and wretched.

The shadows deepened. Across the street a sort of bubbling explosion, followed by a jerky glare that shot athwart the room, announced the lighting of the big arc-lamp on the opposite side-walk. She resented it, being in the mood for undiluted gloom; but she had not the energy to pull down the shade and shut it out. She sat where she was, thinking thoughts that hurt.

The door of the apartment opposite opened. There was a single ring at her bell. She did not answer it. There came another. She sat where she was, motionless. The door closed again.

The days dragged by. Elizabeth lost count of time. Each day had its duties, which ended when you went to bed; that was all she knew—except that life had become very grey and very lonely, far lonelier even than in the time when James Boyd was nothing to her but an occasional sound of footsteps.

Of James she saw nothing. It is not difficult to avoid anyone in New York, even when you live just across the way.

It was Elizabeth's first act each morning, immediately on awaking, to open her front door and gather in whatever lay outside it. Sometimes there would be mail; and always, unless Francis, as he sometimes did, got mixed and absent-minded, the morning milk and the morning paper.

One morning, some two weeks after that evening of which she tried not to think, Elizabeth, opening the door, found immediately outside it a folded scrap of paper. She unfolded it.

"I am just off to the theatre. Won't you wish me luck? I feel sure it is going to be a hit. Joseph is purring like a dynamo.—J. R. B."

In the early morning the brain works sluggishly. For an instant Elizabeth stood looking at the words uncomprehendingly; then, with a leaping of the heart, their meaning came home to her. He must have left this at her door on the previous night. The play had been produced! And somewhere in the folded interior of that morning paper at her feet must be the opinion of "One in Authority" concerning it!

Dramatic criticisms have this peculiarity, that if you

are looking for them, they burrow and hide like rabbits. They dodge behind murders; they duck behind baseball scores; they lie up snugly behind the Wall Street news. It was a full minute before Elizabeth found what she sought, and the first words she read smote her like a blow.

In that vein of delightful facetiousness which so endears him to all followers and perpetrators of the drama, the "One in Authority" rent and tore James Boyd's play. He knocked James Boyd's play down, and kicked it; he jumped on it with large feet; he poured cold water on it, and chopped it into little bits. He merrily disembowelled James Boyd's play.

Elizabeth quivered from head to foot. She caught at the door-post to steady herself. In a flash all her resentment had gone, wiped away and annihilated like a mist before the sun. She loved him, and she knew now that she had always loved him.

It took her two seconds to realize that the "One in Authority" was a miserable incompetent, incapable of recognizing merit when it was displayed before him. It took her five minutes to dress. It took her a minute to run downstairs and out to the news-stand on the corner of the street. Here, with a lavishness which charmed and exhilarated the proprietor, she bought all the other papers which he could supply.

Moments of tragedy are best described briefly. Each of the papers noticed the play, and each of them damned it with uncompromising heartiness. The criticisms varied only in tone. One cursed with relish and gusto; another with a certain pity; a third with a kind of wounded superiority, as of one compelled against his will to speak of something unspeakable; but the meaning of all was the same. James Boyd's play was a hideous failure.

Back to the house sped Elizabeth, leaving the organs of a free people to be gathered up, smoothed, and replaced on the stand by the now more than ever charmed proprietor. Up the stairs she sped, and arriving breathlessly at James's door rang the bell.

Heavy footsteps came down the passage; crushed,

disheartened footsteps; footsteps that sent a chill to Elizabeth's heart. The door opened. James Boyd stood before her, heavy-eyed and haggard. In his eyes was despair, and on his chin the blue growth of beard of the man from whom the mailed fist of Fate has smitten the energy to perform his morning shave.

Behind him, littering the floor, were the morning papers; and at the sight of them Elizabeth broke down.

"Oh, Jimmy, darling!" she cried; and the next moment she was in his arms, and for a space time stood still.

How long afterwards it was she never knew; but eventually James Boyd spoke.

"If you'll marry me," he said hoarsely, "I don't care a hang."

"Jimmy, darling!" said Elizabeth, "of course I will."

Past them, as they stood there, a black streak shot silently, and disappeared out of the door. Joseph was leaving the sinking ship.

"Let him go, the fraud," said Elizabeth bitterly. "I shall never believe in black cats again."

But James was not of this opinion.

"Joseph has brought me all the luck I need."

"But the play meant everything to you."

"It did then."

Elizabeth hesitated.

"Jimmy, dear, it's all right, you know. I know you will make a fortune out of your next play, and I've heaps for us both to live on till you make good. We can manage splendidly on my salary from the 'Evening Chronicle.'"

"What! Have you got a job on a New York paper?"

"Yes, I told you about it. I am doing Heloise Milton. Why, what's the matter?"

He groaned hollowly.

"And I was thinking that you would come back to Chicago with me!"

"But I will. Of course I will. What did you think I meant to do?"

"What! Give up a real job in New York!" He blinked. "This isn't really happening. I'm dreaming."

"But, Jimmy, are you sure you can get work in Chicago? Wouldn't it be better to stay on here, where all the managers are, and——"

He shook his head.

"I think it's time I told you about myself," he said. "Am I sure I can get work in Chicago? I am, worse luck. Darling, have you in your more material moments ever toyed with a Boyd's Premier Breakfast-Sausage or kept body and soul together with a slice off a Boyd's Excelsior Home-Cured Ham? My father makes them, and the tragedy of my life is that he wants me to help him at it. This was my position. I loathed the family business as much as dad loved it. I had a notion—a fool notion, as it has turned out—that I could make good in the literary line. I've scribbled in a sort of way ever since I was in college. When the time came for me to join the firm, I put it to dad straight. I said, 'Give me a chance, one good, square chance, to see if the divine fire is really there, or if somebody has just turned on the alarm as a practical joke.' And we made a bargain. I had written this play, and we made it a test-case. We fixed it up that dad should put up the money to give it a Broadway production. If it succeeded, all right; I'm the young Gus Thomas, and may go ahead in the literary game. If it's a fizzle, off goes my coat, and I abandon pipe-dreams of literary triumphs and start in as the guy who put the Co. in Boyd & Co. Well, events have proved that I *am* the guy, and now I'm going to keep my part of the bargain just as squarely as dad kept his. I know quite well that if I refused to play fair and chose to stick on here in New York and try again, dad would go on staking me. That's the sort of man he is. But I wouldn't do it for a million Broadway successes. I've had my chance, and I've foozled; and now I'm going back to make him happy by being a real live member of the firm. And the queer thing about it is that last night I hated the idea, and this morning, now that I've got you, I almost look forward to it."

He gave a little shiver.

"And yet—I don't know. There's something rather gruesome still to my near-artist soul in living in luxury on murdered piggies. Have you ever seen them persuading a pig to play the stellar rôle in a Boyd Premier Breakfast-Sausage? It's pretty ghastly. They string them up by their hind legs, and—b—r—r—r—r!"

"Never mind," said Elizabeth soothingly. "Perhaps they don't mind it really."

"Well, I don't know," said James Boyd, doubtfully. "I've watched them at it, and I'm bound to say they didn't seem any too well pleased."

"Try not to think of it."

"Very well," said James dutifully.

There came a sudden shout from the floor above, and on the heels of it a shock-haired youth in pyjamas burst into the apartment.

"Now what?" said James. "By the way, Miss Herrold, my fiancée; Mr. Briggs—Paul Axworthy Briggs, sometimes known as the Boy Novelist. What's troubling you, Paul?"

Mr. Briggs was stammering with excitement.

"Jimmy," cried the Boy Novelist, "what do you think has happened! A black cat has just come into my apartment. I heard him mewing outside the door, and opened it, and he streaked in. And I started my new novel last night! Say, you *do* believe this thing of black cats bringing luck, don't you?"

"Luck! My lad, grapple that cat to your soul with hoops of steel. He's the greatest little luck-bringer in New York. He was boarding with me till this morning."

"Then—by Jove! I nearly forgot to ask—your play was a hit? I haven't seen the papers yet."

"Well, when you see them, don't read the notices. It was the worst frost Broadway has seen since Columbus's time."

"But—I don't understand."

"Don't worry. You don't have to. Go back and fill that cat with fish, or she'll be leaving you. I suppose you left the door open?"

"My God!" said the Boy Novelist, paling, and dashed for the door.

"Do you think Joseph *will* bring him luck?" said Elizabeth, thoughtfully.

"It depends what sort of luck you mean. Joseph seems to work in devious ways. If I know Joseph's methods, Briggs's new novel will be rejected by every publisher in the city; and then, when he is sitting in his apartment, wondering which of his razors to end himself with, there will be a ring at the bell, and in will come the most beautiful girl in the world, and then—well, then, take it from me, he will be all right."

"He won't mind about the novel?"

"Not in the least."

"Not even if it means that he will have to go away and kill pigs and things."

"About the pig business, dear. I've noticed a slight tendency in you to let yourself get rather morbid about it. I know they string them up by the hind-legs, and all that sort of thing; but you must remember that a pig looks at these things from a different standpoint. My belief is that the pigs like it. Try not to think of it."

"Very well," said Elizabeth, dutifully.

THE ROMANCE OF AN UGLY POLICEMAN

CROSSING the Thames by Chelsea Bridge, the wanderer through London finds himself in pleasant Battersea. Rounding the Park, where the female of the species wanders with its young by the ornamental water where the wild-fowl are, he comes upon a vast road. One side of this is given up to Nature, the other to Intellect. On the right, green trees stretch into the middle distance; on the left, endless blocks of residential flats. It is Battersea Park Road, the home of the cliff-dwellers.

Police-constable Plimmer's beat embraced the first quarter of a mile of the cliffs. It was his duty to pace in the measured fashion of the London policeman along the front of them, turn to the right, turn to the left, and come back along the road which ran behind them. In this way he was enabled to keep the king's peace over no fewer than four blocks of mansions.

It did not require a deal of keeping. Battersea may have its tough citizens, but they do not live in Battersea Park Road. Battersea Park Road's speciality is Brain, not Crime. Authors, musicians, newspaper men, actors, and artists are the inhabitants of these mansions. A child could control them. They assault and batter nothing but pianos; they steal nothing but ideas; they murder nobody except Chopin and Beethoven. Not through these shall an ambitious young constable achieve promotion.

At this conclusion Edward Plimmer arrived within forty-eight hours of his installation. He recognized the flats for what they were—just so many layers of big-brained blamelessness. And there was not even the chance of a burglary. No burglar wastes his time burgling authors. Constable Plimmer reconciled his mind to the fact that his term in Battersea must be looked on as something in the nature of a vacation.

He was not altogether sorry. At first, indeed, he found the new atmosphere soothing. His last beat had been in the heart of tempestuous Whitechapel, where his arms had ached from the incessant hauling of wiry inebriates to the station, and his shins had revolted at the kicks showered upon them by haughty spirits impatient of restraint. Also, one Saturday night, three friends of a gentleman whom he was trying to induce not to murder his wife had so wrought upon him that, when he came out of hospital, his already homely appearance was further marred by a nose which resembled the gnarled root of a tree. All these things had taken from the charm of Whitechapel, and the cloistral peace of Battersea Park Road was grateful and comforting.

And just when the unbroken calm had begun to lose its attraction and dreams of action were once more troubling him, a new interest entered his life; and with its coming he ceased to wish to be removed from Battersea. He fell in love.

It happened at the back of York Mansions. Anything that ever happened, happened there; for it is at the back of these blocks of flats that the real life is. At the front you never see anything, except an occasional tousle-headed young man smoking a pipe; but at the back, where the cooks come out to parley with the tradesmen, there is at certain hours of the day quite a respectable activity. Pointed dialogues about yesterday's eggs and the toughness of Saturday's meat are conducted *fortissimo* between cheerful youths in the road and satirical young women in print dresses, who come out of their kitchen doors on to little balconies. The whole thing has a pleasing Romeo and Juliet touch. Romeo rattles up in his cart. "Sixty-four!" he cries. "Sixty-fower, sixty-fower, sixty-fow——" The kitchen door opens, and Juliet emerges. She eyes Romeo without any great show of affection. "Are you

Perkins & Blissett ?" she inquires coldly. Romeo admits it. "Two of them yesterday's eggs was bad." Romeo protests. He defends his eggs. They were fresh from the hen; he stood over her while she laid them. Juliet listens frigidly. "I *don't* think," she says. "Well, half of sugar, one marmalade, and two of breakfast bacon," she adds, and ends the argument. There is a rattling as of a steamer weighing anchor; the goods go up in the tradesman's lift; Juliet collects them, and exits, banging the door. The little drama is over.

Such is life at the back of York Mansions—a busy, throbbing thing.

The peace of afternoon had fallen upon the world one day towards the end of Constable Plimmer's second week of the simple life, when his attention was attracted by a whistle. It was followed by a musical "Hi!"

Constable Plimmer looked up. On the kitchen balcony of a second-floor flat a girl was standing As he took her in with a slow and exhaustive gaze, he was aware of strange thrills. There was something about this girl which excited Constable Plimmer. I do not say that she was a beauty; I do not claim that you or I would have raved about her; I merely say that Constable Plimmer thought she was All Right.

"Miss ?" he said.

"Got the time about you ?" said the girl. "All the clocks have stopped."

"The time," said Constable Plimmer, consulting his watch, "wants exactly ten minutes to four."

"Thanks."

"Not at all, miss."

The girl was inclined for conversation. It was that gracious hour of the day when you have cleared lunch and haven't got to think of dinner yet, and have a bit of time to draw a breath or two. She leaned over the balcony and smiled pleasantly.

"If you want to know the time, ask a pleeceman," she said. "You been on this beat long ?"

"Just short of two weeks, miss."

"I been here three days."

"I hope you like it, miss."

"So-so. The milkman's a nice boy."

Constable Plimmer did not reply. He was busy silently hating the milkman. He knew him—one of those good-looking blighters; one of those oiled and curled perishers; one of those blooming fascinators who go about the world making things hard for ugly, honest men with loving hearts. Oh, yes, he knew the milkman.

"He's a rare one with his jokes," said the girl.

Constable Plimmer went on not replying. He was perfectly aware that the milkman was a rare one with his jokes. He had heard him. The way girls fell for anyone with the gift of the gab—that was what embittered Constable Plimmer.

"He——" she giggled. "He calls me Little Pansy-Face."

"If you'll excuse me, miss," said Constable Plimmer coldly, "I'll have to be getting along on my beat."

Little Pansy-Face! And you couldn't arrest him for it! What a world! Constable Plimmer paced upon his way, a blue-clad volcano.

It is a terrible thing to be obsessed by a milkman. To Constable Plimmer's disordered imagination it seemed that, dating from this interview, the world became one solid milkman. Wherever he went, he seemed to run into this milkman. If he was in the front road, this milkman—Alf Brooks, it appeared, was his loathsome name—came rattling past with his jingling cans as if he were Apollo driving his chariot. If he was round at the back, there was Alf, his damned tenor doing duets with the balconies. And all this in defiance of the known law of natural history that milkmen do not come out after five in the morning. This irritated Constable Plimmer. You talk of a man "going home with the milk" when you mean that he sneaks in in the small hours of the morning. If all milkmen were like Alf Brooks the phrase was meaningless.

He brooded. The unfairness of Fate was souring him. A man expects trouble in his affairs of the heart from soldiers and sailors, and to be cut out by even a postman is to fall before a worthy foe; but milkmen—no! Only grocers' assistants and telegraph-boys were intended by Providence to fear milkmen.

Yet here was Alf Brooks, contrary to all rules, the established pet of the mansions. Bright eyes shone from balconies when his "Milk—oo—oo" sounded. Golden voices giggled delightedly at his bellowed chaff. And Ellen Brown, whom he called Little Pansy-Face, was definitely in love with him.

They were keeping company. They were walking out. This crushing truth Edward Plimmer learned from Ellen herself.

She had slipped out to mail a letter at the pillar-box on the corner, and she reached it just as the policeman arrived there in the course of his patrol.

Nervousness impelled Constable Plimmer to be arch.

"'Ullo, 'ullo, 'ullo," he said. "Posting love-letters?"

"What, me? This is to the Police Commissioner, telling him you're no good."

"I'll give it to him. Him and me are taking supper to-night."

Nature had never intended Constable Plimmer to be playful. He was at his worst when he rollicked. He snatched at the letter with what was meant to be a debonair gaiety, and only succeeded in looking like an angry gorilla. The girl uttered a startled squeak.

The letter was addressed to Mr. A. Brooks.

Playfulness, after this, was at a discount. The girl was frightened and angry, and he was scowling with mingled jealousy and dismay.

"Ho!" he said. "Ho! Mr. A. Brooks!"

Ellen Brown was a nice girl, but she had a temper, and there were moments when her manners lacked rather noticeably the repose which stamps the caste of Vere de Vere.

"Well, what about it?" she cried. "Can't one write to the young gentleman one's keeping company with, without having to get permission from every——" She paused to marshal her forces for the assault. "Without having to get permission from every great, ugly, red-faced copper with big feet and broken noses in London ?"

Constable Plimmer's wrath faded into a dull unhappiness. Yes, she was right. That was the correct description. That was how an impartial Scotland Yard would be compelled to describe him, if ever he got lost. "Missing. A great, ugly, red-faced copper with big feet and a broken nose." They would never find him otherwise.

"Perhaps you object to my walking out with Alf? Perhaps you've got something against him? I suppose you're jealous!"

She threw in the last suggestion entirely in a sporting spirit. She loved battle, and she had a feeling that this one was going to finish far too quickly. To prolong it, she gave him this opening. There were a dozen ways in which he might answer, each more insulting than the last; and then, when he had finished, she could begin again. These little encounters, she held, sharpened the wits, stimulated the circulation, and kept one out in the open air.

"Yes," said Constable Plimmer.

It was the one reply she was not expecting. For direct abuse, for sarcasm, for dignity, for almost any speech beginning "What! Jealous of *you*. Why——" she was prepared. But this was incredible. It disabled her, as the wild thrust of an unskilled fencer will disable a master of the rapier. She searched in her mind and found that she had nothing to say.

There was a tense moment in which she found him, looking her in the eyes, strangely less ugly than she had supposed; and then he was gone, rolling along on his beat with that air which all policemen must achieve, of having no feelings at all, and—as long as it behaves itself—no interest in the human race.

Ellen posted her letter. She dropped it into the box thoughtfully, and thoughtfully returned to the flat. She looked over her shoulder, but Constable Plimmer was out of sight.

Peaceful Battersea began to vex Constable Plimmer.

To a man crossed in love, action is the one anodyne; and Battersea gave no scope for action. He dreamed now of the old Whitechapel days as a man dreams of the joys of his childhood. He reflected bitterly that a fellow never knows when he is well off in this world. Any one of those myriad drunk and disorderlies would have been as balm to him now. He was like a man who has run through a fortune and in poverty eats the bread of regret. Amazedly he recollected that in those happy days he had grumbled at his lot. He remembered confiding to a friend in the station-house, as he rubbed with liniment the spot on his right shin where the well-shod foot of a joyous costermonger had got home, that this sort of thing—meaning militant costermongers—was "a bit too thick." A bit too thick! Why, he would pay one to kick him now. And as for the three loyal friends of the would-be wife-murderer who had broken his nose, if he saw them coming round the corner he would welcome them as brothers.

And Battersea Park Road dozed on—calm, intellectual, law-abiding.

A friend of his told him that there had once been a murder in one of these flats. He did not believe it. If any of these white-corpuscled clams ever swatted a fly, it was much as they could do. The thing was ridiculous on the face of it. If they were capable of murder, they would have murdered Alf Brooks.

He stood in the road, and looked up at the placid buildings resentfully.

"Grr—rr—rr!" he growled, and kicked the side-walk.

And, even as he spoke, on the balcony of a second-floor flat there appeared a woman, an elderly, sharp-faced woman, who waved her arms and screamed, "Policeman! Officer! Come up here! Come up here at once!"

Up the stone stairs went Constable Plimmer at the run. His mind was alert and questioning. Murder? Hardly murder, perhaps. If it had been that, the woman would have said so. She did not look the sort of woman who would be reticent about a thing like that.

Well, anyway, it was something; and Edward Plimmer had been long enough in Battersea to be thankful for small favours. An intoxicated husband would be better than nothing. At least he would be something that a fellow could get his hands on to and throw about a bit.

The sharp-faced woman was waiting for him at the door. He followed her into the flat.

"What is it, ma'am?"

"Theft! Our cook has been stealing!"

She seemed sufficiently excited about it, but Constable Plimmer felt only depression and disappointment. A stout admirer of the sex, he hated arresting women. Moreover, to a man in the mood to tackle anarchists with bombs, to be confronted with petty theft is galling. But duty was duty. He produced his notebook.

"She is in her room. I locked her in. I know she has taken my brooch. We have missed money. You must search her."

"Can't do that, ma'am. Female searcher at the station."

"Well, you can search her box."

A little, bald, nervous man in spectacles appeared as if out of a trap. As a matter of fact, he had been there all the time, standing by the bookcase; but he was one of those men you do not notice till they move and speak.

"Er—Jane."

"Well, Henry?"

The little man seemed to swallow something.

"I—I think that you may possibly be wronging Ellen. It is just possible, as regards the money——" He smiled in a ghastly manner and turned to the policeman. "Er—officer, I ought to tell you that my wife—ah—holds the purse-strings of our little home; and it is just possible that in an absent-minded moment *I* may have——"

"Do you mean to tell me, Henry, that *you* have been taking my money?"

"My dear, it is just possible that in the abs——"

"How often?"

He wavered perceptibly. Conscience was beginning to lose its grip.

"Oh, not often."

"*How* often? More than once?"

Conscience had shot its bolt. The little man gave up the struggle.

"No, no, not more than once. Certainly not more than once."

"You ought not to have done it at all. We will talk about that later. It doesn't alter the fact that Ellen is a thief. I have missed money half a dozen times. Besides that, there's the brooch. Step this way, officer."

Constable Plimmer stepped that way—his face a mask. He knew who was waiting for them behind the locked door at the end of the passage. But it was his duty to look as if he were stuffed, and he did so.

She was sitting on her bed, dressed for the street. It was her afternoon out, the sharp-faced woman had informed Constable Plimmer, attributing the fact that she had discovered the loss of the brooch in time to stop her a direct interposition of Providence. She was pale, and there was a hunted look in her eyes.

"You wicked girl, where is my brooch?"

She held it out without a word. She had been holding it in her hand.

"You see, officer!"

"I wasn't stealing of it. I 'adn't but borrowed it. I was going to put it back."

"Stuff and nonsense! Borrow it, indeed! What for?"

"I—I wanted to look nice."

The woman gave a short laugh. Constable Plimmer's face was a mere block of wood, expressionless.

"And what about the money I've been missing? I suppose you'll say you only borrowed that?"

"I never took no money."

"Well, it's gone, and money doesn't go by itself. Take her to the police-station, officer."

Constable Plimmer raised heavy eyes.

"You make a charge, ma'am?"

"Bless the man! Of course I make a charge. What did you think I asked you to step in for?"

"Will you come along, miss?" said Constable Plimmer.

Out in the street the sun shone gaily down on peaceful Battersea. It was the hour when children walk abroad with their nurses; and from the green depths of the Park came the sound of happy voices. A cat stretched itself in the sunshine and eyed the two as they passed with lazy content.

They walked in silence. Constable Plimmer was a man with a rigid sense of what was and what was not fitting behaviour in a policeman on duty: he aimed always at a machine-like impersonality. There were times when it came hard, but he did his best. He strode on, his chin up and his eyes averted. And beside him——

Well, she was not crying. That was something.

Round the corner, beautiful in light flannel, gay at both ends with a new straw hat and the yellowest shoes in South-West London, scented, curled, a prince among young men, stood Alf Brooks. He was feeling piqued. When he said three o'clock, he meant three o'clock. It was now three-fifteen, and she had not appeared. Alf Brooks swore an impatient oath, and the thought crossed his mind, as it had sometimes crossed it before, that Ellen Brown was not the only girl in the world.

"Give her another five min——"

Ellen Brown, with escort, at that moment turned the corner.

Rage was the first emotion which the spectacle aroused in Alf Brooks. Girls who kept a fellow waiting about while they fooled around with policemen were no girls for him. They could understand once and for all that he was a man who could pick and choose.

And then an electric shock set the world dancing mistily before his eyes. This policeman was wearing his belt; he was on duty. And Ellen's face was not the face of a girl strolling with the Force for pleasure.

His heart stopped, and then began to race. His

cheeks flushed a dusky crimson. His jaw fell, and a prickly warmth glowed in the parts about his spine.

"Goo'!"

His fingers sought his collar.

"Crumbs!"

He was hot all over.

"Goo' Lor'! She's been pinched!"

He tugged at his collar. It was choking him.

Alf Brooks did not show up well in the first real crisis which life had forced upon him. That must be admitted. Later, when it was over, and he had leisure for self-examination, he admitted it to himself. But even then he excused himself by asking Space in a blustering manner what else he could ha' done. And if the question did not bring much balm to his soul at the first time of asking, it proved wonderfully soothing on constant repetition. He repeated it at intervals for the next two days, and by the end of that time his cure was complete. On the third morning his "Milk—oo—oo" had regained its customary care-free ring, and he was feeling that he had acted in difficult circumstances in the only possible manner.

Consider. He was Alf Brooks, well known and respected in the neighbourhood; a singer in the choir on Sundays; owner of a milk-walk in the most fashionable part of Battersea; to all practical purposes a public man. Was he to recognize, in broad daylight and in open street, a girl who walked with a policeman because she had to, a malefactor, a girl who had been pinched?

Ellen, Constable Plimmer woodenly at her side, came towards him. She was ten yards off—seven—five—three——

Alf Brooks tilted his hat over his eyes and walked past her, unseeing, a stranger.

He hurried on. He was conscious of a curious feeling that somebody was just going to kick him, but he dared not look round.

Constable Plimmer eyed the middle distance with an earnest gaze. His face was redder than ever. Beneath his blue tunic strange emotions were at work. Something seemed to be filling his throat. He tried to swallow it.

He stopped in his stride. The girl glanced up at him in a kind of dull, questioning way. Their eyes met for the first time that afternoon, and it seemed to Constable Plimmer that whatever it was that was interfering with the inside of his throat had grown larger, and more unmanageable.

There was the misery of the stricken animal in her gaze. He had seen women look like that in Whitechapel. The woman to whom, indirectly, he owed his broken nose had looked like that. As his hand had fallen on the collar of the man who was kicking her to death, he had seen her eyes. They were Ellen's eyes, as she stood there now—tortured, crushed, yet uncomplaining.

Constable Plimmer looked at Ellen, and Ellen looked at Constable Plimmer. Down the street some children were playing with a dog. In one of the flats a woman had begun to sing.

"Hop it," said Constable Plimmer.

He spoke gruffly. He found speech difficult.

The girl started.

"What say?"

"Hop it. Get along. Run away."

"What do you mean?"

Constable Plimmer scowled. His face was scarlet. His jaw protruded like a granite break-water.

"Go on," he growled. "Hop it. Tell him it was all a joke. I'll explain at the station."

Understanding seemed to come to her slowly.

"Do you mean I'm to go?"

"Yes."

"What do you mean? You aren't going to take me to the station?"

"No."

She stared at him. Then, suddenly, she broke down.

"He wouldn't look at me. He was ashamed of me. He pretended not to see me."

She leaned against the wall, her back shaking.

"Well, run after him, and tell him it was all——"

"No, no, no."

Constable Plimmer looked morosely at the side-walk. He kicked it.

She turned. Her eyes were red, but she was no longer crying. Her chin had a brave tilt.

"I couldn't—not after what he did. Let's go along. I—I don't care."

She looked at him curiously.

"Were you really going to have let me go?"

Constable Plimmer nodded. He was aware of her eyes searching his face, but he did not meet them.

"Why?"

He did not answer.

"What would have happened to you, if you had have done?"

Constable Plimmer's scowl was of the stuff of which nightmares are made. He kicked the unoffending side-walk with an increased viciousness.

"Dismissed the Force," he said curtly.

"And sent to prison, too, I shouldn't wonder."

"Maybe."

He heard her draw a deep breath, and silence fell upon them again. The dog down the road had stopped barking. The woman in the flat had stopped singing. They were curiously alone.

"Would you have done all that for me?" she said.

"Yes."

"Why?"

"Because I don't think you ever did it. Stole that money, I mean. Nor the brooch, neither."

"Was that all?"

"What do you mean—all?"

"Was that the only reason?"

He swung round on her, almost threateningly.

"No," he said hoarsely. "No, it wasn't, and you know it wasn't. Well, if you want it, you can have it. It was because I love you. There! Now I've said it, and now you can go on and laugh at me as much as you want."

"I'm not laughing," she said soberly.

"You think I'm a fool!"

"No, I don't."

"I'm nothing to you. *He's* the fellow you're stuck on."

She gave a little shudder.

"No."

"What do you mean?"

"I've changed." She paused. "I think I shall have changed more by the time I come out."

"Come out?"

"Come out of prison."

"You're not going to prison."

"Yes, I am."

"I won't take you."

"Yes, you will. Think I'm going to let you get yourself in trouble like that, to get me out of a fix? Not much."

"You hop it, like a good girl."

"Not me."

He stood looking at her like a puzzled bear.

"They can't eat me."

"They'll cut off all of your hair."

"D'you like my hair?"

"Yes."

"Well, it'll grow again."

"Don't stand talking. Hop it."

"I won't. Where's the station?"

"Next street."

"Well, come along, then."

The blue glass lamp of the police-station came into sight, and for an instant she stopped. Then she was walking on again, her chin tilted. But her voice shook a little as she spoke.

"Nearly there. Next stop, Battersea. All change! I say, mister—I don't know your name."

"Plimmer's my name, miss. Edward Plimmer."

"I wonder if—I mean it'll be pretty lonely where I'm going—I wonder if—— What I mean is, it would be rather a lark, when I come out, if I was to find a pal waiting for me to say 'Hallo.'"

Constable Plimmer braced his ample feet against the stones, and turned purple.

"Miss," he said, "I'll be there, if I have to sit up all night. The first thing you'll see when they open the doors is a great, ugly, red-faced copper with big feet and a broken nose. And if you'll just say 'Hallo' to him when he says 'Hallo' to you, he'll be as pleased as Punch and as proud as a duke. And, miss"—he clenched his hands till the nails hurt the leathern flesh—"and, miss, there's just one thing more I'd like to say. You'll be having a good deal of time to yourself for awhile; you'll be able to do a good bit of thinking without anyone to disturb you; and what I'd like you to give your mind to, if you don't object, is just to think whether you can't forget that narrow-chested, God-forsaken blighter who treated you so mean, and get half-way fond of some one who knows jolly well you're the only girl there is."

She looked past him at the lamp which hung, blue and forbidding, over the station door.

"How long'll I get?" she said. "What will they give me? Thirty days?"

He nodded.

"It won't take me as long as that," she said. "I say, what do people call you?—people who are fond of you, I mean?—Eddie or Ted?"

A SEA OF TROUBLES

MR. MEGGS'S mind was made up. He was going to commit suicide.

There had been moments, in the interval which had elapsed between the first inception of the idea and his present state of fixed determination, when he had wavered. In these moments he had debated, with Hamlet, the question whether it was nobler in the mind to suffer, or to take arms against a sea of troubles and by opposing end them. But all that was over now. He was resolved.

Mr. Meggs's point, the main plank, as it were, in his suicidal platform, was that with him it was beside the question whether or not it was nobler to suffer in the mind. The mind hardly entered into it at all. What he had to decide was whether it was worth while putting up any longer with the perfectly infernal pain in his stomach. For Mr. Meggs was a martyr to indigestion. As he was also devoted to the pleasures of the table, life had become for him one long battle, in which, whatever happened, he always got the worst of it.

He was sick of it. He looked back down the vista of the years, and found therein no hope for the future. One after the other all the patent medicines in creation had failed him. Smith's Supreme Digestive Pellets—he had given them a more than fair trial. Blenkinsop's Liquid Life-Giver—he had drunk enough of it to float a ship. Perkins's Premier Pain-Preventer, strongly recommended by the sword-swallowing lady at Barnum and Bailey's—he had wallowed in it. And so on down the list. His interior organism had simply sneered at the lot of them.

"Death, where is thy sting?" thought Mr. Meggs, and forthwith began to make his preparations.

Those who have studied the matter say that the tendency to commit suicide is greatest among those who have passed their fifty-fifth year, and that the rate is twice as great for unoccupied males as for occupied males. Unhappy Mr. Meggs, accordingly, got it, so to speak, with both barrels. He was fifty-six, and he was perhaps the most unoccupied adult to be found in the length and breadth of the United Kingdom. He toiled not, neither did he spin. Twenty years before, an unexpected legacy had placed him in a position to indulge a natural taste for idleness to the utmost. He was at that time, as regards his professional life, a clerk in a rather obscure shipping firm. Out of office hours he had a mild fondness for letters, which took the form of meaning to read right through the hundred best books one day, but actually contenting himself with the daily paper and an occasional magazine.

Such was Mr. Meggs at thirty-six. The necessity for working for a living and a salary too small to permit of self-indulgence among the more expensive and deleterious dishes on the bill of fare had up to that time kept his digestion within reasonable bounds. Sometimes he had twinges; more often he had none.

Then came the legacy, and with it Mr. Meggs let himself go. He left London and retired to his native village, where, with a French cook and a series of secretaries to whom he dictated at long intervals occasional paragraphs of a book on British Butterflies on which he imagined himself to be at work, he passed the next twenty years. He could afford to do himself well, and he did himself extremely well. Nobody urged him to take exercise, so he took no exercise. Nobody warned him of the perils of lobster and welsh rabbits to a man of sedentary habits, for it was nobody's business to warn him. On the contrary, people rather encouraged the lobster side of his character, for he was a hospitable soul and liked to have his friends dine with him. The result was that Nature, as is her wont, laid for him, and got him. It seemed to Mr. Meggs that he woke one morning to find himself a chronic dyspeptic. That was one of the hardships of his position, to his mind. The thing seemed to hit him suddenly out of a blue sky. One moment, all appeared to be peace and joy; the next, a lively and irritable wild-cat with red-hot claws seemed somehow to have introduced itself into his interior.

So Mr. Meggs decided to end it.

In this crisis of his life the old methodical habits of his youth returned to him. A man cannot be a clerk in even an obscure firm of shippers for a great length of time without acquiring system, and Mr. Meggs made his preparations calmly and with a forethought worthy of a better cause.

And so we find him, one glorious June morning, seated at his desk, ready for the end.

Outside, the sun beat down upon the orderly streets of the village. Dogs dozed in the warm dust. Men who had to work went about their toil moistly, their minds far away in shady public-houses.

But Mr. Meggs, in his study, was cool both in mind and body.

Before him, on the desk, lay six little slips of paper. They were bank-notes, and they represented, with the exception of a few pounds, his entire worldly wealth. Beside them were six letters, six envelopes, and six postage-stamps. Mr. Meggs surveyed them calmly.

He would not have admitted it, but he had had a lot of fun writing those letters. The deliberation as to who should be his heirs had occupied him pleasantly for several days, and, indeed, had taken his mind off his internal pains at times so thoroughly that he had frequently surprised himself in an almost cheerful mood. Yes, he would have denied it, but it had been great sport sitting in arm-chair, thinking whom he should pick out from England's teeming millions to make happy with his money. All sorts of schemes had passed through his mind. He had a sense of power which the mere possession of the money had never given him. He began to understand why millionaires make freak wills. At one time he had toyed with the idea of selecting some one at random from the London Directory and bestowing on him all he had to bequeath. He had only abandoned the scheme when it occurred to him that he himself would not be in a position to witness the recipient's stunned delight. And what was the good of starting a thing like that, if you were not to be in at the finish?

Sentiment succeeded whimsicality. His old friends of the office—those were the men to benefit. What good fellows they had been! Some were dead, but he still kept intermittently in touch with half a dozen of them. And—an important point—he knew their present addresses.

This point was important, because Mr. Meggs had decided not to leave a will, but to send the money direct to the beneficiaries. He knew what wills were. Even in quite straightforward circumstances they often made trouble. There had been some slight complication about his own legacy twenty years ago. Somebody had contested the will, and before the thing was satisfactorily settled the lawyers had got away with about twenty per cent. of the whole. No, no wills. If he made one, and then killed himself, it might be upset on a plea of insanity. He knew of no relative who might consider himself entitled to the money, but there was the chance that some remote cousin existed; and then the comrades of his youth might fail to collect after all.

He declined to run the risk. Quietly and by degrees he had sold out the stocks and shares in which his fortune was invested, and deposited the money in his London bank. Six piles of large notes, dividing the total into six equal parts; six letters couched in a strain of reminiscent pathos and manly resignation; six envelopes, legibly addressed; six postage-stamps; and that part of his preparations was complete. He licked the stamps and placed them on the envelopes; took the notes and inserted them in the letters; folded the letters and thrust them into the envelopes; sealed the envelopes; and unlocking the drawer of his desk produced a small, black, ugly-looking bottle.

He opened the bottle and poured the contents into a medicine-glass.

It had not been without considerable thought that

Mr. Meggs had decided upon the method of his suicide. The knife, the pistol, the rope—they had all presented their charms to him. He had further examined the merits of drowning and of leaping to destruction from a height.

There were flaws in each. Either they were painful, or else they were messy. Mr. Meggs had a tidy soul, and he revolted from the thought of spoiling his figure, as he would most certainly do if he drowned himself; or the carpet, as he would if he used the pistol; or the pavement—and possibly some innocent pedestrian, as must infallibly occur should he leap off the Monument. The knife was out of the question. Instinct told him that it would hurt like the very dickens.

No; poison was the thing. Easy to take, quick to work, and on the whole rather agreeable than otherwise.

Mr. Meggs hid the glass behind the inkpot and rang the bell.

"Has Miss Pillenger arrived?" he inquired of the servant.

"She has just come, sir."

"Tell her that I am waiting for her here."

Jane Pillenger was an institution. Her official position was that of private secretary and typist to Mr. Meggs. That is to say, on the rare occasions when Mr. Meggs's conscience overcame his indolence to the extent of forcing him to resume work on his British Butterflies, it was to Miss Pillenger that he addressed the few rambling and incoherent remarks which constituted his idea of a regular hard, slogging spell of literary composition. When he sank back in his chair, speechless and exhausted like a Marathon runner who has started his sprint a mile or two too soon, it was Miss Pillenger's task to unscramble her shorthand notes, type them neatly, and place them in their special drawer in the desk.

Miss Pillenger was a wary spinster of austere views, uncertain age, and a deep-rooted suspicion of men—a suspicion which, to do an abused sex justice, they had done nothing to foster. Men had always been almost coldly correct in their dealings with Miss Pillenger. In her twenty years of experience as a typist and secretary she had never had to refuse with scorn and indignation so much as a box of chocolates from any of her employers. Nevertheless, she continued to be icily on her guard. The clenched fist of her dignity was always drawn back, ready to swing on the first male who dared to step beyond the bounds of professional civility.

Such was Miss Pillenger. She was the last of a long line of unprotected English girlhood which had been compelled by straitened circumstances to listen for hire to the appallingly dreary nonsense which Mr. Meggs had to impart on the subject of British Butterflies. Girls had come, and girls had gone, blondes, ex-blondes, brunettes, ex-brunettes, near-blondes, near-brunettes; they had come buoyant, full of hope and life, tempted by the lavish salary which Mr. Meggs had found himself after a while compelled to pay; and they had dropped off, one after another, like exhausted bivalves, unable to endure the crushing boredom of life in the village which had given Mr. Meggs to the world. For Mr. Meggs's home-town was no City of Pleasure. Remove the Vicar's magic-lantern and the try-your-weight machine opposite the post office, and you practically eliminated the temptations to tread the primrose path. The only young men in the place were silent, gaping youths, at whom lunacy commissioners looked sharply and suspiciously when they met. The tango was unknown, and the one-step. The only form of dance extant—and that only at the rarest intervals—was a sort of polka not unlike the movements of a slightly inebriated boxing kangaroo. Mr. Meggs's secretaries and typists gave the town one startled, horrified glance, and stampeded for London like frightened ponies.

Not so Miss Pillenger. She remained. She was a business woman, and it was enough for her that she received a good salary. For five pounds a week she would have undertaken a post as secretary and typist to a Polar Expedition. For six years she had been with Mr. Meggs, and doubtless she looked forward to being with him at least six years more.

Perhaps it was the pathos of this thought which

touched Mr. Meggs, as she sailed, notebook in hand, through the doorway of the study. Here, he told himself, was a confiding girl, all unconscious of impending doom, relying on him as a daughter relies on her father. He was glad that he had not forgotten Miss Pillenger when he was making his preparations.

He had certainly not forgotten Miss Pillenger. On his desk beside the letters lay a little pile of notes, amounting in all to five hundred pounds—her legacy.

Miss Pillenger was always business-like. She sat down in her chair, opened her notebook, moistened her pencil, and waited expectantly for Mr. Meggs to clear his throat and begin work on the butterflies. She was surprised when, instead of frowning, as was his invariable practice when bracing himself for composition, he bestowed upon her a sweet, slow smile.

All that was maidenly and defensive in Miss Pillenger leaped to arms under that smile. It ran in and out among her nerve-centres. It had been long in arriving, this moment of crisis, but here it undoubtedly was at last. After twenty years an employer was going to court disaster by trying to flirt with her.

Mr. Meggs went on smiling. You cannot classify smiles. Nothing lends itself so much to a variety of interpretations as a smile. Mr. Meggs thought he was smiling the sad, tender smile of a man who, knowing himself to be on the brink of the tomb, bids farewell to a faithful employée. Miss Pillenger's view was that he was smiling like an abandoned old rip who ought to have been ashamed of himself.

"No, Miss Pillenger," said Mr. Meggs, "I shall not work this morning. I shall want you, if you will be so good, to post these six letters for me."

Miss Pillenger took the letters. Mr. Meggs surveyed her tenderly.

"Miss Pillenger, you have been with me a long time now. Six years, is it not? Six years. Well, well. I don't think I have ever made you a little present, have I?"

"You give me a good salary."

"Yes, but I want to give you something more. Six

years is a long time. I have come to regard you with a different feeling from that which the ordinary employer feels for his secretary. You and I have worked together for six long years. Surely I may be permitted to give you some token of my appreciation of your fidelity." He took the pile of notes. "These are for you, Miss Pillenger."

He rose and handed them to her. He eyed her for a moment with all the sentimentality of a man whose digestion has been out of order for over two decades. The pathos of the situation swept him away. He bent over Miss Pillenger, and kissed her on the forehead.

Smiles excepted, there is nothing so hard to classify as a kiss. Mr. Meggs's notion was that he kissed Miss Pillenger much as some great general, wounded unto death, might have kissed his mother, his sister, or some particularly sympathetic aunt; Miss Pillenger's view, differing substantially from this, may be outlined in her own words.

"Ah!" she cried, as, dealing Mr. Meggs's conveniently placed jaw a blow which, had it landed an inch lower down, might have knocked him out, she sprang to her feet. "How dare you! I've been waiting for this, Mr. Meggs. I have seen it in your eye. I have expected it. Let me tell you that I am not at all the sort of girl with whom it is safe to behave like that. I can protect myself. I am only a working-girl——"

Mr. Meggs, who had fallen back against the desk as a stricken pugilist falls on the ropes, pulled himself together to protest.

"Miss Pillenger," he cried, aghast, "you misunderstand me. I had no intention——"

"Misunderstand you? Bah! I am only a working-girl——"

"Nothing was farther from my mind——"

"Indeed! Nothing was farther from your mind! You give me money, you shower your vile kisses on me, but nothing was farther from your mind than the obvious interpretation of such behaviour!" Before coming to Mr. Meggs, Miss Pillenger had been secretary to an Indiana novelist. She had learned style from the master. "Now that you have gone too far, you are frightened at what you have done. You well may be, Mr. Meggs. I am only a working-girl——"

"Miss Pillenger, I implore you——"

"Silence! I am only a working-girl——"

A wave of mad fury swept over Mr. Meggs. The shock of the blow and still more of the frightful ingratitude of this horrible woman nearly made him foam at the mouth.

"Don't keep on saying you're only a working-girl," he bellowed. "You'll drive me mad. Go. Go away from me. Get out. Go anywhere, but leave me alone!"

Miss Pillenger was not entirely sorry to obey the request. Mr. Meggs's sudden fury had startled and frightened her. So long as she could end the scene victorious, she was anxious to withdraw.

"Yes, I will go," she said, with dignity, as she opened the door. "Now that you have revealed yourself in your true colours, Mr. Meggs, this house is no fit place for a wor——"

She caught her employer's eye, and vanished hastily.

Mr. Meggs paced the room in a ferment. He had been shaken to his core by the scene. He boiled with indignation. That his kind thoughts should have been so misinterpreted—it was too much. Of all ungrateful worlds, this world was the most——

He stopped suddenly in his stride, partly because his shin had struck a chair, partly because an idea had struck his mind.

Hopping madly, he added one more parallel between himself and Hamlet by soliloquizing aloud.

"I'll be hanged if I commit suicide," he yelled.

And as he spoke the words a curious peace fell on him, as on a man who has awakened from a nightmare. He sat down at the desk. What an idiot he had been ever to contemplate self-destruction. What could have induced him to do it? By his own hand to remove himself, merely in order that a pack of ungrateful brutes might wallow in his money—it was the scheme of a perfect fool.

He wouldn't commit suicide. Not if he knew it. He would stick on and laugh at them. And if he did have an occasional pain inside, what of that? Napoleon had them, and look at him. He would be blowed if he committed suicide.

With the fire of a new resolve lighting up his eyes, he turned to seize the six letters and rifle them of their contents.

They were gone.

It took Mr. Meggs perhaps thirty seconds to recollect where they had gone to, and then it all came back to him. He had given them to the demon Pillenger, and, if he did not overtake her and get them back, she would mail them.

Of all the mixed thoughts which seethed in Mr. Meggs's mind at that moment, easily the most prominent was the reflexion that from his front door to the post office was a walk of less than five minutes.

Miss Pillenger walked down the sleepy street in the June sunshine, boiling, as Mr. Meggs had done, with indignation. She, too, had been shaken to the core. It was her intention to fulfil her duty by posting the letters which had been entrusted to her, and then to quit for ever the service of one who, for six years a model employer, had at last forgotten himself and showed his true nature.

Her meditations were interrupted by a hoarse shout in her rear; and, turning, she perceived the model employer running rapidly towards her. His face was scarlet, his eyes wild, and he wore no hat.

Miss Pillenger's mind worked swiftly. She took in the situation in a flash. Unrequited, guilty love had sapped Mr. Meggs's reason, and she was to be the victim of his fury. She had read of scores of similar cases in the newspapers. How little she had ever imagined that she would be the heroine of one of these dramas of passion.

She looked for one brief instant up and down the street. Nobody was in sight. With a loud cry she began to run.

" Stop ! "

It was the fierce voice of her pursuer. Miss Pillenger increased to third speed. As she did so, she had a vision of headlines.

" Stop ! " roared Mr. Meggs.

" UNREQUITED PASSION MADE THIS MAN MURDERER," thought Miss Pillenger.

" Stop ! "

" CRAZED WITH LOVE HE SLAYS BEAUTIFUL BLONDE," flashed out in letters of crimson on the back of Miss Pillenger's mind.

" Stop ! "

" SPURNED, HE STABS HER THRICE."

To touch the ground at intervals of twenty yards or so—that was the ideal she strove after. She addressed herself to it with all the strength of her powerful mind.

In London, New York, Paris, and other cities where life is brisk, the spectacle of a hatless gentleman with a purple face pursuing his secretary through the streets at a rapid gallop would, of course, have excited little, if any, remark. But in Mr. Meggs's home-town events were of rarer occurrence. The last milestone in the history of his native place had been the visit, two years before, of Bingley's Stupendous Circus, which had paraded along the main street on its way to the next town, while zealous members of its staff visited the back premises of the houses and removed all the washing from the lines. Since then deep peace had reigned.

Gradually, therefore, as the chase warmed up, citizens of all shapes and sizes began to assemble. Miss Pillenger's screams and the general appearance of Mr. Meggs gave food for thought. Having brooded over the situation, they decided at length to take a hand, with the result that as Mr. Meggs's grasp fell upon Miss Pillenger the grasp of several of his fellow-townsmen fell upon him.

" Save me ! " said Miss Pillenger.

Mr. Meggs pointed speechlessly to the letters, which she still grasped in her right hand. He had taken practically no exercise for twenty years, and the pace had told upon him.

Constable Gooch, guardian of the town's welfare, tightened his hold on Mr. Meggs's arm, and desired explanations.

" He—he was going to murder me," said Miss Pillenger.

" Kill him," advised an autere bystander.

" What do you mean you were going to murder the lady ? " inquired Constable Gooch.

Mr. Meggs found speech.

" I—I—I—I only wanted those letters."

" What for ? "

" They're mine."

" You charge her with stealing 'em ? "

" He gave them me to post with his own hands," cried Miss Pillenger.

" I know I did, but I want them back."

By this time the constable, though age had to some extent dimmed his sight, had recognized beneath the perspiration, features which, though they were distorted, were nevertheless those of one whom he respected as a leading citizen.

" Why, Mr. Meggs ! " he said.

This identification by one in authority calmed, if it a little disappointed, the crowd. What it was they did not know, but it was apparently not a murder, and they began to drift off.

" Why don't you give Mr. Meggs his letters when he asks you, ma'am ? " said the constable.

Miss Pillenger drew herself up haughtily.

" Here are your letters, Mr. Meggs, I hope we shall never meet again."

Mr. Meggs nodded. That was his view, too.

All things work together for good. The following morning Mr. Meggs awoke from a dreamless sleep with a feeling that some curious change had taken place in him. He was abominably stiff, and to move his limbs was pain, but down in the centre of his being there was a novel sensation of lightness. He could have declared that he was happy.

Wincing, he dragged himself out of bed and limped to

the window. He threw it open. It was a perfect morning. A cool breeze smote his face, bringing with it pleasant scents and the soothing sound of God's creatures beginning a new day.

An astounding thought struck him.

"Why, I feel well!"

Then another.

"It must be the exercise I took yesterday. By George, I'll do it regularly."

He drank in the air luxuriously. Inside him, the wildcat gave him a sudden claw, but it was a half-hearted effort, the effort of one who knows that he is beaten. Mr. Meggs was so absorbed in his thoughts that he did not even notice it.

"London," he was saying to himself. "One of these physical culture places. . . . Comparatively young man. . . . Put myself in their hands. . . . Mild, regular exercise. . . ."

He limped to the bathroom.

THE MAN WITH TWO LEFT FEET

STUDENTS of the folk-lore of the United States of America are no doubt familiar with the quaint old story of Clarence MacFadden. Clarence MacFadden, it seems, was "wishful to dance, but his feet wasn't gaited that way. So he sought a professor and asked him his price, and said he was willing to pay. The professor" (the legend goes on) "looked down with alarm at his feet and marked their enormous expanse; and he tacked on a five to his regular price for teaching MacFadden to dance."

I have often been struck by the close similarity between the case of Clarence and that of Henry Wallace Mills. One difference alone presents itself. It would seem to have been mere vanity and ambition that stimulated the former; whereas the motive force which drove Henry Mills to defy Nature and attempt dancing was the purer one of love. He did it to please his wife. Had he never gone to Ye Bonnie Briar-Bush Farm, that popular holiday resort, and there met Minnie Hall, he would doubtless have continued to spend in peaceful reading the hours not given over to work at the New York bank at which he was employed as paying-cashier. For Henry was a voracious reader. His idea of a pleasant evening was to get back to his little flat, take off his coat, put on his slippers, light a pipe, and go on from the point where he had left off the night before in his perusal of the BIS-CAL volume of the "Encyclopædia Britannica"—making notes as he read in a stout notebook. He read the BIS-CAL volume because, after many days, he had finished the A-AND, AND-AUS, and the AUS-BIS. There was something admirable—and yet a little horrible—about Henry's method of study. He went after Learning with the cold and dispassionate relentlessness of a stoat pursuing a rabbit. The ordinary man who is paying instalments on the "Encyclopædia Britannica" is apt to get over-excited and to skip impatiently to Volume XXVIII (VET-ZYM) to see how it all comes out in the end. Not so Henry. His was not a frivolous mind. He intended to read the "Encyclopædia" through, and he was not going to spoil his pleasure by peeping ahead.

It would seem to be an inexorable law of Nature that no man shall shine at both ends. If he has a high forehead and a thirst for wisdom, his fox-trotting (if any) shall be as the staggerings of the drunken; while, if he is a good dancer, he is nearly always petrified from the ears upward. No better examples of this law could have been found than Henry Mills and his fellow-cashier, Sidney Mercer. In New York banks paying-cashiers, like bears, tigers, lions, and other fauna, are always shut up in a cage in pairs, and are consequently dependent on each other for entertainment and social intercourse when business is slack. Henry Mills and Sidney simply could not find a subject in common. Sidney knew absolutely nothing of even such elementary things as Abana, Aberration, Abraham, or Acrogenæ; while Henry, on his side, was scarcely aware that there had been any developments in the dance since the polka. It was a relief to Henry when Sidney threw up his job to join the chorus of a musical comedy, and was succeeded by a man who, though full of limitations, could at least converse intelligently on Bowls.

Such, then, was Henry Wallace Mills. He was in the middle thirties, temperate, studious, a moderate smoker, and—one would have said—a bachelor of the bachelors, armour-plated against Cupid's well-meant but obsolete artillery. Sometimes Sidney Mercer's successor in the teller's cage, a sentimental young man, would broach the topic of Woman and Marriage. He would ask Henry if he ever intended to get married. On such occasions Henry would look at him in a manner which was a blend of scorn, amusement, and indignation; and would reply with a single word:

"Me!"

It was the way he said it that impressed you.

But Henry had yet to experience the unmanning atmosphere of a lonely summer resort. He had only just reached the position in the bank where he was permitted to take his annual vacation in the summer. Hitherto he had always been released from his cage during the winter months, and had spent his ten days of freedom at his flat, with a book in his hand and his feet on the radiator. But the summer after Sidney Mercer's departure they unleashed him in August.

It was meltingly warm in the city. Something in Henry cried out for the country. For a month before the beginning of his vacation he devoted much of the time that should have been given to the "Encyclopædia Britannica" in reading summer-resort literature. He decided at length upon Ye Bonnie Briar-Bush Farm because the advertisements spoke so well of it.

Ye Bonnie Briar-Bush Farm was a rather battered frame building many miles from anywhere. Its attractions included a Lovers' Leap, a Grotto, golf-links—a five-hole course where the enthusiast found unusual hazards in the shape of a number of goats tethered at intervals between the holes—and a silvery lake, only portions of which were used as a dumping-ground for tin cans and wooden boxes. It was all new and strange to Henry and caused him an odd exhilaration. Something of gaiety and reckless abandon began to creep into his veins. He had a curious feeling that in these romantic surroundings some adventure ought to happen to him.

At this juncture Minnie Hill arrived. She was a small, slim girl, thinner and paler than she should have been, with large eyes that seemed to Henry pathetic and stirred his chivalry. He began to think a good deal about Minnie Hill.

And then one evening he met her on the shores of the silvery lake. He was standing there, slapping at things that looked like mosquitoes, but could not have been, for the advertisements expressly stated that none were ever found in the neighbourhood of Ye Bonnie Briar-Bush Farm, when along she came. She walked slowly, as if she were tired. A strange thrill, half of pity, half of something else, ran through Henry. He looked at her. She looked at him.

"Good evening," he said.

They were the first words he had spoken to her. She never contributed to the dialogue of the dining-room, and he had been too shy to seek her out in the open.

She said "Good evening," too, tying the score. And there was silence for a moment.

Commiseration overcame Henry's shyness.

"You're looking tired," he said.

"I feel tired." She paused. "I overdid it in the city."

"It?"

"Dancing."

"Oh, dancing. Did you dance much?"

"Yes; a great deal."

"Ah!"

A promising, even a dashing start. But how to continue? For the first time Henry regretted the steady determination of his methods with the "Encyclopædia." How pleasant if he could have been in a position to talk easily of Dancing. Then memory reminded him that, though he had not yet got up to Dancing, it was only a few weeks before that he had been reading of the Ballet.

"I don't dance myself," he said, "but I am fond of reading about it. Did you know that the word 'ballet' incorporated three distinct modern words, 'ballet,' 'ball,' and 'ballad,' and that ballet-dancing was originally accompanied by singing?"

It hit her. It had her weak. She looked at him with awe in her eyes. One might almost say that she gaped at Henry.

"I hardly know anything," she said.

"The first descriptive ballet seen in London, England," said Henry, quietly, "was 'The Tavern Bilkers,' which was played at Drury Lane in—in seventeen—something."

"Was it?"

"And the earliest modern ballet on record was that

given by—by some one to celebrate the marriage of the Duke of Milan in 1489."

There was no doubt or hesitation about the date this time. It was grappled to his memory by hoops of steel owing to the singular coincidence of it being also his telephone number. He gave it out with a roll, and the girl's eyes widened.

"What an awful lot you know!"

"Oh, no," said Henry, modestly. "I read a great deal."

"It must be splendid to know a lot," she said, wistfully. "I've never had time for reading. I've always wanted to. I think you're wonderful!"

Henry's soul was expanding like a flower and purring like a well-tickled cat. Never in his life had he been admired by a woman. The sensation was intoxicating.

Silence fell upon them. They started to walk back to the farm, warned by the distant ringing of a bell that supper was about to materialize. It was not a musical bell, but distance and the magic of this unusual moment lent it charm. The sun was setting. It threw a crimson carpet across the silvery lake. The air was very still. The creatures, unclassified by science, who might have been mistaken for mosquitoes had their presence been possible at Ye Bonnie Briar-Bush Farm, were biting harder than ever. But Henry heeded them not. He did not even slap at them. They drank their fill of his blood and went away to put their friends on to this good thing; but for Henry they did not exist. Strange things were happening to him. And, lying awake that night in bed, he recognized the truth. He was in love.

After that, for the remainder of his stay, they were always together. They walked in the woods, they sat by the silvery lake. He poured out the treasures of his learning for her, and she looked at him with reverent eyes, uttering from time to time a soft "Yes" or a musical "Gee!"

In due season Henry went back to New York.

"You're dead wrong about love, Mills," said his sentimental fellow-cashier, shortly after his return. "You ought to get married."

"I'm going to," replied Henry, briskly. "Week to-morrow."

Which stunned the other so thoroughly that he gave a customer who entered at that moment fifteen dollars for a ten-dollar cheque, and had to do some excited telephoning after the bank had closed.

Henry's first year as a married man was the happiest of his life. He had always heard this period described as the most perilous of matrimony. He had braced himself for clashings of tastes, painful adjustments of character, sudden and unavoidable quarrels. Nothing of the kind happened. From the very beginning they settled down in perfect harmony. She merged with his life as smoothly as one river joins another. He did not even have to alter his habits. Every morning he had his breakfast at eight, smoked a cigarette, and walked to the Underground. At five he left the bank, and at six he arrived home, for it was his practice to walk the first two miles of the way, breathing deeply and regularly. Then dinner. Then the quiet evening. Sometimes the moving-pictures, but generally the quiet evening, he reading the "Encyclopædia"—aloud now—Minnie darning his socks, but never ceasing to listen.

Each day brought the same sense of grateful amazement that he should be so wonderfully happy, so extraordinarily peaceful. Everything was as perfect as it could be. Minnie was looking a different girl. She had lost her drawn look. She was filling out.

Sometimes he would suspend his reading for a moment, and look across at her. At first he would see only her soft hair, as she bent over her sewing. Then, wondering at the silence, she would look up, and he would meet her big eyes. And then Henry would gurgle with happiness, and demand of himself, silently:

"Can you beat it!"

It was the anniversary of their wedding. They celebrated it in fitting style. They dined at a crowded and exhilarating Italian restaurant on a street off Seventh Avenue, where red wine was included in the bill, and excitable people, probably extremely clever, sat round at small tables and talked all together at the top of their voices. After dinner they saw a musical comedy. And then—the great event of the night—they went on to supper at a glittering restaurant near Times Square.

There was something about supper at an expensive restaurant which had always appealed to Henry's imagination. Ernest devourer as he was of the solids of literature, he had tasted from time to time its lighter fare—those novels which begin with the hero supping in the midst of the glittering throng and having his attention attracted to a distinguished-looking elderly man with a grey imperial who is entering with a girl so strikingly beautiful that the revellers turn, as she passes, to look after her. And then, as he sits and smokes, a waiter comes up to the hero and, with a soft "Pardon, m'sieu!" hands him a note.

The atmosphere of Geisenheimer's suggested all that sort of thing to Henry. They had finished supper, and he was smoking a cigar—his second that day. He leaned back in his chair and surveyed the scene. He felt braced up, adventurous. He had that feeling, which comes to all quiet men who like to sit at home and read, that this was the sort of atmosphere in which he really belonged. The brightness of it all—the dazzling lights, the music, the hubbub, in which the deep-throated gurgle of the wine-agent surprised while drinking soup blended with the shriller note of the chorus-girl calling to her mate—these things got Henry. He was thirty-six next birthday, but he felt a youngish twenty-one.

A voice spoke at his side. Henry looked up, to perceive Sidney Mercer.

The passage of a year, which had turned Henry into a married man, had turned Sidney Mercer into something so magnificent that the spectacle for a moment deprived Henry of speech. Faultless evening dress clung with loving closeness to Sidney's lissom form. Gleaming shoes of perfect patent leather covered his feet. His light hair was brushed back into a smooth sleekness on which the electric lights shone like stars on some beautiful pool. His practically chinless face beamed amiably over a spotless collar.

Henry wore blue serge.

"What are you doing here, Henry, old top?" said the vision. "I didn't know you ever came among the bright lights."

His eyes wandered off to Minnie. There was admiration in them, for Minnie was looking her prettiest.

"Wife," said Henry, recovering speech. And to Minnie: "Mr. Mercer. Old friend."

"So you're married? Wish you luck. How's the bank?"

Henry said the bank was doing as well as could be expected.

"You still on the stage?"

Mr. Mercer shook his head importantly.

"Got better job. Professional dancer at this show. Rolling in money. Why aren't you dancing?"

The words struck a jarring note. The lights and the music until that moment had had a subtle psychological effect on Henry, enabling him to hypnotize himself into a feeling that it was not inability to dance that kept him in his seat, but that he had had so much of that sort of thing that he really preferred to sit quietly and look on for a change. Sidney's question changed all that. It made him face the truth.

"I don't dance."

"For the love of Mike! I bet Mrs. Mills does. Would you care for a turn, Mrs. Mills?"

"No, thank you, really."

But remorse was now at work on Henry. He perceived that he had been standing in the way of Minnie's pleasure. Of course she wanted to dance. All women did. She was only refusing for his sake.

"Nonsense, Min. Go to it."

Minnie looked doubtful.

"Of course you must dance, Min. I shall be all right. I'll sit here and smoke."

The next moment Minnie and Sidney were treading the complicated measure; and simultaneously Henry ceased to be a youngish twenty-one and was even conscious of a fleeting doubt as to whether he was really only thirty-five.

Boil the whole question of old age down, and what it amounts to is that a man is young as long as he can dance without getting lumbago, and, if he cannot dance, he is never young at all. This was the truth that forced itself upon Henry Wallace Mills, as he sat watching his wife moving over the floor in the arms of Sidney Mercer. Even he could see that Minnie danced well. He thrilled at the sight of her gracefulness; and for the first time since his marriage he became introspective. It had never struck him before how much younger Minnie was than himself. When she had signed the paper at the City Hall on the occasion of the purchase of the marriage licence, she had given her age, he remembered now, as twenty-six. It had made no impression on him at the time. Now, however, he perceived clearly that between twenty-six and thirty-five there was a gap of nine years; and a chill sensation came upon him of being old and stodgy. How dull it must be for poor little Minnie to be cooped up night after night with such an old fogy? Other men took their wives out and gave them a good time, dancing half the night with them. All he could do was to sit at home and read Minnie dull stuff from the "Encyclopædia." What a life for the poor child! Suddenly, he felt acutely jealous of the rubber-jointed Sidney Mercer, a man whom hitherto he had always heartily despised.

The music stopped. They came back to the table, Minnie with a pink glow on her face that made her younger than ever; Sidney, the insufferable ass, grinning and smirking and pretending to be eighteen. They looked like a couple of children—Henry, catching sight of himself in a mirror, was surprised to find that his hair was not white.

Half an hour later, in the cab going home, Minnie, half asleep, was aroused by a sudden stiffening of the arm that encircled her waist and a sudden snort close to her ear.

It was Henry Wallace Mills resolving that he would learn to dance.

Being of a literary turn of mind and also economical, Henry's first step towards his new ambition was to buy a fifty-cent book entitled "The A B C of Modern Dancing," by "Tango." It would, he felt—not without reason—be simpler and less expensive if he should learn the steps by the aid of this treatise than by the more customary method of taking lessons. But quite early in the proceedings he was faced by complications. In the first place, it was his intention to keep what he was doing a secret from Minnie, in order to be able to give her a pleasant surprise on her birthday, which would be coming round in a few weeks. In the second place, "The A B C of Modern Dancing" proved on investigation far more complex than its title suggested.

These two facts were the ruin of the literary method, for, while it was possible to study the text and the plates at the bank, the home was the only place in which he could attempt to put the instructions into practice. You cannot move the right foot along dotted line A B and bring the left foot round curve C D in a paying-cashier's cage in a bank, nor, if you are at all sensitive to public opinion, on the pavement going home. And while he was trying to do it in the parlour of the flat one night when he imagined that Minnie was in the kitchen cooking supper, she came in unexpectedly to ask how he wanted the steak cooked. He explained that he had had a sudden touch of cramp, but the incident shook his nerve.

After this he decided that he must have lessons.

Complications did not cease with this resolve. Indeed, they became more acute. It was not that there was any difficulty about finding an instructor. The papers were full of their advertisements. He selected a Mme. Gavarni because she lived in a convenient spot. Her house was in a side street, with a station within easy reach. The real problem was when to find time for the lessons. His life was run on such a regular schedule that he could hardly alter so important a moment in it as the hour of his arrival home without exciting comment. Only deceit could provide a solution.

"Min, dear," he said at breakfast.

"Yes, Henry?"

Henry turned mauve. He had never lied to her before.

"I'm not getting enough exercise."

"Why you look so well."

"I get a kind of heavy feeling sometimes. I think I'll put on another mile or so to my walk on my way home. So—so I'll be back a little later in future."

"Very well, dear."

It made him feel like a particularly low type of criminal, but, by abandoning his walk, he was now in a position to devote an hour a day to the lessons; and Mme. Gavarni had said that that would be ample.

"Sure, Bill," she had said. She was a breezy old lady with a military moustache and an unconventional manner with her clientèle. "You come to me an hour a day, and, if you haven't two left feet, we'll make you the pet of society in a month."

"Is that so?"

"It sure is. I never had a failure yet with a pupe, except one. And that wasn't my fault."

"Had he two left feet?"

"Hadn't any feet at all. Fell off of a roof after the second lesson, and had to have 'em cut off him. At that, I could have learned him to tango with wooden legs, only he got kind of discouraged. Well, see you Monday, Bill. Be good."

And the kindly old soul, retrieving her chewing gum from the panel of the door where she had placed it to facilitate conversation—dismissed him.

And now began what, in later years, Henry unhesitatingly considered the most miserable period of his existence. There may be times when a man who is past his first youth feels more unhappy and ridiculous than when he is taking a course of lessons in the modern dance, but it is not easy to think of them. Physically, his new experience caused Henry acute pain. Muscles whose existence he had never suspected came into being for—apparently—the sole purpose of aching. Mentally he suffered even more.

This was partly due to the peculiar method of instruction in vogue at Mme. Gavarni's, and partly to the fact that, when it came to the actual lessons, a sudden niece was produced from a back room to give them. She was a blonde young lady with laughing blue eyes, and Henry never clasped her trim waist without feeling a black-hearted traitor to his absent Minnie. Conscience racked him. Add to this the sensation of being a strange, jointless creature with abnormally large hands and feet, and the fact that it was Mme. Gavarni's custom to stand in a corner of the room during the hour of tuition, chewing gum and making comments, and it is not surprising that Henry became wan and thin.

Mme. Gavarni had the trying habit of endeavouring to stimulate Henry by frequently comparing his performance and progress with that of a cripple whom she claimed to have taught at some previous time.

She and the niece would have spirited arguments in his presence as to whether or not the cripple had one-stepped better after his third lesson than Henry after his fifth. The niece said no. As well, perhaps, but not better. Mme. Gavarni said that the niece was forgetting the way the cripple had slid his feet. The niece said yes, that was so, maybe she was. Henry said nothing. He merely perspired.

He made progress slowly. This could not be blamed upon his instructress, however. She did all that one woman could to speed him up. Sometimes she would even pursue him into the street in order to show him on the side-walk a means of doing away with some one of his numerous errors of *technique*, the elimination of which would help to make him definitely the cripple's superior. The misery of embracing her indoors was as nothing to the misery of embracing her on the side-walk.

Nevertheless, having paid for his course of lessons in advance, and being a determined man, he did make progress. One day, to his surprise, he found his feet going through the motions without any definite exercise of will-power on his part—almost as if they were endowed with an intelligence of their own. It was the turning-point. It filled him with a singular pride such as he had not felt since his first rise of salary at the bank.

Mme. Gavarni was moved to dignified praise.

"Some speed, kid!" she observed. "Some speed!"

Henry blushed modestly. It was the accolade.

Every day, as his skill at the dance became more manifest, Henry found occasion to bless the moment when he had decided to take lessons. He shuddered sometimes at the narrowness of his escape from disaster. Every day now it became more apparent to him, as he watched Minnie, that she was chafing at the monotony of her life. That fatal supper had wrecked the peace of their little home. Or perhaps it had merely precipitated the wreck. Sooner or later, he told himself, she was bound to have wearied of the dullness of her lot. At any rate, dating from shortly after that disturbing night, a lack of ease and spontaneity seemed to creep into their relations. A blight settled on the home.

Little by little Minnie and he were growing almost formal towards each other. She had lost her taste for being read to in the evenings and had developed a habit of pleading a headache and going early to bed. Sometimes, catching her eye when she was not expecting it, he surprised an enigmatic look in it. It was a look, however, which he was able to read. It meant that she was bored.

It might have been expected that this state of affairs would have distressed Henry. It gave him, on the contrary, a pleasurable thrill. It made him feel that it had been worth it, going through the torments of learning to dance. The more bored she was now the greater her delight when he revealed himself dramatically. If she had been contented with the life which he could offer her as a non-dancer, what was the sense of losing weight and money in order to learn the steps? He enjoyed the silent, uneasy evenings which had supplanted those cheery ones of the first year of their marriage. The more uncomfortable they were now, the more they would appreciate their happiness later on. Henry belonged to the large circle of human beings who consider that there is acuter pleasure in being suddenly cured of toothache than in never having toothache at all.

He merely chuckled inwardly, therefore, when, on the morning of her birthday, having presented her with a purse which he knew she had long coveted, he found himself thanked in a perfunctory and mechanical way.

"I'm glad you like it," he said.

Minnie looked at the purse without enthusiasm.

"It's just what I wanted," she said, listlessly.

"Well, I must be going. I'll get the tickets for the theatre while I'm in town."

Minnie hesitated for a moment.

"I don't believe I want to go to the theatre much to-night, Henry."

"Nonsense. We must have a party on your birthday. We'll go to the theatre and then we'll have supper at Geisenheimer's again. I may be working after hours at the bank to-day, so I guess I won't come home. I'll meet you at that Italian place at six."

"Very well. You'll miss your walk, then?"

"Yes. It doesn't matter for once."

"No. You're still going on with your walks, then?"

"Oh, yes, yes."

"Three miles every day?"

"Never miss it. It keeps me well."

"Yes."

"Good-bye, darling."

"Good-bye."

Yes, there was a distinct chill in the atmosphere. Thank goodness, thought Henry, as he walked to the station, it would be different to-morrow morning. He had rather the feeling of a young knight who has done perilous deeds in secret for his lady, and is about at last to receive credit for them.

Geisenheimer's was as brilliant and noisy as it had been before when Henry reached it that night, escorting a reluctant Minnie. After a silent dinner and a theatrical performance during which neither had exchanged more than a word between the acts, she had wished to abandon the idea of supper and go home. But a squad of police could not have kept Henry from Geisenheimer's. His hour had come. He had thought of this moment for weeks, and he visualized every detail of his big scene. At first they would sit at their table in silent discomfort. Then Sidney Mercer would come up, as before, to ask Minnie to dance. And then—then—Henry would rise and, abandoning all concealment, exclaim grandly: "No! *I* am going to dance with my wife!" Stunned amazement of Minnie, followed by wild joy. Utter rout and discomfiture of that pin-head, Mercer. And then, when they returned to their table, he breathing easily and regularly as a trained dancer in perfect condition should, she tottering a little with the sudden rapture of it all, they would sit with their heads close together and start a new life. That was the scenario which Henry had drafted.

It worked out—up to a certain point—as smoothly as ever it had done in his dreams. The only hitch which he had feared—to wit, the non-appearance of Sidney Mercer, did not occur. It would spoil the scene a little, he had felt, if Sidney Mercer did not present himself to play the rôle of foil; but he need have had no fears on this point. Sidney had the gift, not uncommon in the chinless, smooth-haired type of man, of being able to see a pretty girl come into the restaurant even when his back was towards the door. They had hardly seated themselves when he was beside their table, bleating greetings.

"Why, Henry! Always here!"

"Wife's birthday."

"Many happy returns of the day, Mrs. Mills. We've just time for one turn before the waiter comes with your order. Come along."

The band was staggering into a fresh tune, a tune that Henry knew well. Many a time had Mme. Gavarni hammered it out of an aged and unwilling piano in order that he might dance to it with her blue-eyed niece. He rose.

"No!" he exclaimed grandly. "*I* am going to dance with my wife!"

He had not under-estimated the sensation which he had looked forward to causing. Minnie looked at him with round eyes. Sidney Mercer was obviously startled.

"I thought you couldn't dance."

"You never can tell," said Henry, lightly. "It looks easy enough. Anyway, I'll try."

"Henry!" cried Minnie, as he clasped her.

He had supposed that she would say something like that, but hardly in that kind of voice. There is a way of saying "Henry!" which conveys surprised admiration and remorseful devotion; but she had not said it in that way. There had been a note of horror in her voice. Henry's was a simple mind, and the obvious solution, that Minnie thought that he had drunk too much red wine at the Italian restaurant, did not occur to him.

He was, indeed, at the moment too busy to analyse vocal inflexions. They were on the floor now, and it was beginning to creep upon him like a chill wind that the scenario which he had mapped out was subject to unforeseen alterations.

At first all had been well. They had been almost alone on the floor, and he had begun moving his feet along dotted line A B with the smooth vim which had characterized the last few of his course of lessons. And then, as if by magic, he was in the midst of a crowd—a mad, jigging crowd that seemed to have no sense of direction, no ability whatever to keep out of his way. For a moment the tuition of weeks stood by him. Then, a shock, a stifled cry from Minnie, and the first collision had occurred. And with that all the knowledge which he had so painfully acquired passed from Henry's mind, leaving it an agitated blank. This was a situation for which his slidings round an empty room had not prepared him. Stage-fright at its worst came upon him. Somebody charged him in the back and asked querulously where he thought he was going. As he turned with a half-formed notion of apologizing, somebody else rammed him from the other side. He had a momentary feeling as if he were going down the Niagara Rapids in a barrel, and then he was lying on the floor with Minnie on top of him. Somebody tripped over his head.

He sat up. Somebody helped him to his feet. He was aware of Sidney Mercer at his side.

"Do it again," said Sidney, all grin and sleek immaculateness. "It went big, but lots of them didn't see it."

The place was full of demon laughter.

"Min!" said Henry.

They were in the parlour of their little flat. Her

back was towards him, and he could not see her face. She did not answer. She preserved the silence which she had maintained since they had left the restaurant. Not once during the journey home had she spoken.

The clock on the mantelpiece ticked on. Outside, an Elevated train rumbled by. Voices came from the street.

"Min, I'm sorry."

Silence.

"I thought I could do it. Oh, Lord!" Misery was in every note of Henry's voice. "I've been taking lessons every day since that night we went to that place first. It's no good. I guess it's like the old woman said. I've got two left feet, and it's no use my ever trying to do it. I kept it secret from you, what I was doing. I wanted it to be a wonderful surprise for you on your birthday. I knew how sick and tired you were getting of being married to a man who never took you out, because he couldn't dance. I thought it was up to me to learn, and give you a good time, like other men's wives. I——"

"Henry!"

She had turned, and with a dull amazement he saw that her whole face had altered. Her eyes were shining with a radiant happiness.

"Henry! Was *that* why you went to that house—to take dancing lessons?"

He stared at her without speaking. She came to him, laughing.

"So that was why you pretended you were still doing your walks?"

"You knew!"

"I saw you come out of that house. I was just going to the station at the end of the street, and I saw you. There was a girl with you, a girl with yellow hair. You hugged her!"

Henry licked his dry lips.

"Min," he said huskily. "You won't believe it, but she was trying to teach me the Jelly Roll."

She held him by the lapels of his coat.

"Of course I believe it. I understand it all now.

I thought at the time that you were just saying good-bye to her! Oh, Henry, why ever didn't you tell me what you were doing? Oh, yes, I know you wanted it to be a surprise for me on my birthday, but you must have seen there was something wrong. You must have seen that I thought something. Surely you noticed how I've been these last weeks?"

"I thought it was just that you were finding it dull."

"Dull! Here, with you!"

"It was after you danced that night with Sidney Mercer. I thought the whole thing out. You're so much younger than I, Min. It didn't seem right for you to have to spend your life being read to by a fellow like me."

"But I loved it!"

"You had to dance. Every girl has to. Women can't do without it."

"This one can. Henry, listen! You remember how ill and worn out I was when you met me first at that farm? Do you know why it was? It was because I had been slaving away for years at one of those places where you go in and pay five cents to dance with the lady instructresses. I was a lady instructress. Henry! Just think what I went through! Every day having to drag a million heavy men with large feet round a big room. I tell you, you are a professional compared with some of them! They trod on my feet and leaned their two hundred pounds on me and nearly killed me. Now perhaps you can understand why I'm not crazy about dancing! Believe me, Henry, the kindest thing you can do to me is to tell me I must never dance again."

"You—you——" he gulped. "Do you really mean that you can—can stand the sort of life we're living here? You really don't find it dull?"

"Dull!"

She ran to the bookshelf, and came back with a large volume.

"Read to me, Henry, dear. Read me somet now. It seems ages and ages since you used to. Re me something out of the 'Encyclopædia'!"

Henry was looking at the book in his hand. In the

midst of a joy that almost overwhelmed him, his orderly mind was conscious of something wrong.

"But this is the MED-MUM volume, darling."

"Is it? Well, that'll be all right. Read me all about 'Mum.'"

"But we're only in the CAL-CHA——" He wavered. "Oh, well——!" he went on, recklessly. "I don't care. Do you?"

"No. Sit down here, dear, and I'll sit on the floor."

Henry cleared his throat.

"'Milicz, or Militsch (d. 1374), Bohemian divine, was the most influential among those preachers and writers in Moravia and Bohemia who, during the fourteenth century, in a certain sense paved the way for the reforming activity of Huss.'"

He looked down. Minnie's soft hair was resting against his knee. He put out a hand and stroked it. She turned and looked up, and he met her big eyes.

"Can you beat it?" said Henry, silently, to himself.